SUMMER'S END
A RIVER CAMPS NOVEL

JILL SANDERS

This is a work of fiction. Names, characters, organizations, places, events, and incidents are either products of the author's imagination or are used fictitiously.

Text copyright © 2020 Jill Sanders

Printed in the United States of America

All rights reserved.

No part of this book may be reproduced, stored in a retrieval system, or transmitted in any form or by any means, electronic, mechanical, photocopying, recording, or otherwise, without express written permission of the publisher.

Published by Grayton Press

ISBN-13: 978-1-945100-15-4

Amazon Paperback: 978-8-670003-60-5

IS Paperback: 978-1-945100-26-0

SUMMARY

What do you get when you combine five best friends, a run-down summer camp, a slew of wealthy out-of-control snowbirds, and a dash of romance? Wildflowers Series will be on your must-read list.

Just because she has fiery red hair doesn't mean that Aubrey has the temperament to match it. Actually, it was quite the opposite. Aubrey was the shy one out of the group of friends. Maybe it was the horrors she'd had to endure growing up. Or maybe it was because, until she'd met her four best friends that summer long ago, she'd never felt a connection before. Now, as her best friends all find love, she dreams about the day she could open her own life to something bigger. She's known for a while now who she wanted to share it with.

Aiden was the first employee the five friends had hired on. He'd been there since the first nail was struck and was excited when they had decided to keep him on as head of maintenance around the camps. He couldn't help feeling proud about what his hard work had done for the place. The only thing that made his steps falter was bumping into the very sexy but shy Aubrey.

PROLOGUE

*E*ight-year-old Aubrey stood in the entryway of the massive home and shivered. She held all of her possessions—or at least the ones that the woman who had been sent by her father to come get her would allow her to grab—in the small bag that she clung to her chest.

"Don't dawdle in the hallway." The woman, Miss Ellison, as she had instructed Aubrey to call her, nudged her forward, causing her worn sneakers to slip on the smooth tile floor. "Careful," the woman hissed. "If you break anything in this house, Mr. Smith will have my head." The woman scowled down at her.

Aubrey tried to focus on walking carefully and followed after the woman through the massive house. She got so distracted watching the way Miss Ellison's crisp slacks almost crackled with each step that she forgot to pay attention to where the woman was leading her. The woman's short narrow heels echoed in the large home, lulling Aubrey into a zombie-like state.

Suddenly, she appeared in a narrow hallway after what seemed like a maze of stairs, doors, and wider hallways.

"These are your rooms," Miss Ellison said as she opened double doors and stood back to allow Aubrey to step inside.

The room was white. Very bright white. Everything inside was so stark, it almost blinded Aubrey. Blinking a few times, Aubrey set her bag down on the floor. Miss Ellison scooped it up quickly.

"I'll just put your things away." She moved over towards a dresser.

"No," she shouted, rushing to grab her bag away from the woman. "They're mine." She hugged it once more to her chest.

Miss Ellison leaned down until they were face to face. "There will be no more of that kind of outburst in this house. Do I make myself clear?"

Aubrey held in a sniffle but nodded. "I'm sorry," she said softly.

"Very well, put your own things away. I expect this room to be tidy at all times. Your father has arranged for clothing." She opened two tall mirrored doors. There were more pretty clothes in the massive walk-in closet than Aubrey had seen in any store. Setting her bag down again, she walked over and ran a finger down the soft lace of a pink dress. "Your bathroom is in there." Miss Ellison motioned towards a doorway. The woman's eyes ran up and down Aubrey. "I expect you to clean up and get dressed into something more appropriate. Be downstairs for dinner in"—she glanced at the thin silver watch on her wrist—"an hour sharp."

With that, the woman turned around and left the room. Aubrey heard the sounds of the woman's heels echoing down the hallway as she disappeared into the house.

She was enthralled with all the clothes and spent a long time in the closet. She was a little shocked to see that most of the clothes were pink. Not that she didn't like the color pink, but almost every item was a different shade of the color. Nothing was orange, green, red, or her favorite color, blue.

Leaving the closet, she opened the bathroom door and wasn't surprised to see the white space. A large claw bathtub sat in front of an oval stained-glass window. A glass and tile shower sat in the back corner with two white sinks on white countertops directly across from it. Even the towels were white.

She turned away and sat on the white carpet to open her small bag.

Pulling out a worn picture, she looked down at her mother's beautiful face and cried for her loss.

A little over an hour later, she pushed her unruly red hair away from her eyes and stepped into what she hoped was the dining room. She'd spent too much time trying to find her way around the empty rooms and long hallways. The place scared her but what scared her more was not knowing where she was. She vowed to learn every inch of the place as quickly as possible.

"You're late," Miss Ellison said sternly.

"I'm sorry, I... got lost." She looked around the massive room. She promised herself that it would never happen again. She wanted to be able to escape any room, even in the dark, if necessary.

She'd seen her father only once before, the day of her mother's funeral. Now the older man sat at the end of a very long table surrounded by servants as candlelight danced over his features.

"Well, come on then," Miss Ellison said, taking her shoulders. Then she knelt down beside her and tucked her long hair further behind her ears. She straightened the white dress Aubrey had picked out to wear and frowned down at the sneakers she was still wearing. "Didn't the shoes fit you?" she asked her.

"No." Aubrey frowned. "They were too big."

The woman nodded. "You'll grow into them." She stood up

and straightened her skirt. "Now, go on and have a seat." She motioned to the chair across from her father.

Aubrey walked over, willing herself not to trip, and sat down in the tall chair. Miss Ellison scooted the chair in until Aubrey's stomach was pushed up tight against the table.

There were so many plates and so much silverware in front of her that she tucked her hands in her lap, afraid to touch anything.

"I expect you to be on time." Her father's voice boomed across the space, causing her to jump slightly.

"Yes, sir," she answered quickly.

Her father's eyes narrowed. The fact that they matched her own eyes caused her stomach to flip.

She had her mother's fiery red hair and light pale completion, but everything else about her matched the man sitting across from her.

Her father was old and wrinkled, and she wondered if he'd been that way when her mother and him had made her. She knew all about how babies were made, thanks to Marcy Moore, a girl in her class. Marcy's mother was expecting a baby and had told Marcy all about it. Of course, Marcy had told her everything, since they were best friends.

The thought of her mother loving the man sitting across from her had Aubrey's stomach rolling again.

"Well," her father called out, "the girl is here." He waved towards a thin bald man, who snapped his fingers. Several staff members rushed around the table, removing empty plates and bringing a bowl of orange liquid.

She wondered quickly why the plates were there in the first place if they were going to just be removed.

Aubrey frowned down at the orange liquid in the bowl that had been set in front of her. "What is it?" she asked.

"Squash soup," Miss Ellison answered. She hadn't realized that the woman was still standing behind her.

"I don't like—"

"You'll eat what I provide for you," her father said loudly. "Every drop." His eyes narrowed.

Swallowing the determination to fight, she picked up one of the three spoons and scooped some into her mouth. After the first bite, she'd shut down everything, even the will to live.

Was this going to be her new life? Stuck in a new world, in a new house? Belonging to this old man? She was his property now, that was made very obvious.

He wouldn't deny that she was his child, as long as she obeyed his every rule. He would feed her, clothe her, and send her to the best schools, as long as she obeyed.

She hated it, but since there wasn't anyone else in her life that could or would watch out for her, she figured it was better than being stuck in an orphanage.

Maybe her father would grow to love her. She had seen the movie *Annie*. Twice. Maybe, just maybe, dreams could come true for her as well.

CHAPTER 1

Eleven-year-old Aubrey stood and watched the black limo disappear down the dusty drive. Once it was out of sight, she darted her eyes around and held in a sob. It had been three years since her father had taken over her entire existence.

Now, standing alone in a strange place, she realized that she'd never felt so abandoned in her entire life. Even after her mother's death, she'd had Miss Ellison to snatch her up and show her where to go, what to wear, and how to eat. Her father had dictated every aspect of her life. This was the first time she'd been left unattended in all that time.

Three long years of learning how to be a lady had almost squashed her spirit. But this, this just might do it.

She didn't know what she'd done to deserve being dumped at an all-girls summer camp. She'd never been to such a place before. What did they even do here? How was she supposed to make friends? Especially dressed like she was.

She looked down at the starched dress Miss Ellison had forced her to wear.

Tears blinded her eyes as she started following a group of girls towards a large building.

She was so busy holding back the tears and keeping anyone from noticing them that she bumped into a dark-haired girl roughly her own age.

"Sorry," she said softly after the girl turned around.

"It's okay," the girl said with a slight frown. Aubrey knew that she was running her eyes over her. For the past three years, it seemed that all anyone had done was look at her with calculation in their eyes.

She was in one of the outfits that had been picked out for her. It was uncomfortable to begin with, but Miss Ellison had starched it until it was so stiff, she felt like she was wearing a straitjacket instead of a sundress.

Then a blond girl stepped forward and asked, "Are you okay?"

"Yes," Aubrey answered as she looked down at her feet while her eyes burned even more. She would not cry in front of these girls. They'd probably burst out laughing and make fun of her.

"I'm Elle. This is Hannah, Zoey, and Scarlett." The blond girl motioned to each of them as she talked.

"Aubrey," she answered quickly as her eyes returned to her tennis shoes. She was at least thankful that Miss Ellison hadn't been in the car ride from the airport, where she'd slipped out of the stupid sandals that she'd forced her to wear.

Her eyes were so blurry from the tears that she didn't get a good look at any of them. Not really.

"We were going to bunk together," Elle said softly. "Would you like to join us? There's room for one more."

Aubrey's head jerked up, and she took a second to search each of their eyes. It only took a moment for her to realize that they weren't being mean or making fun of her. Instead, what she found in each of them was just as much sadness and loneliness as she felt herself. "Sure." She nodded quickly and fell in step with them. "Thank you."

Over that first summer, the five friends, known as the Wildflowers, grew inseparable. To be honest, she doubted she would have made it through the first day without any of them, let alone that whole first summer.

For the next five years, even when the friends were separated by distance, they were her line of defense against her father and all the horrors of the life he forced on her.

She was shipped out in the winters to a boarding school in upper New York where she attended classes on everything from ballet to baking and was molded into a perfect socialite. Still, her father's reach was long, and she didn't have many freedoms even there. The only place she felt like she could breathe was during her time at River Camps with her Wildflowers.

However, during her high school years, without her father's knowledge, she'd managed to enroll in a couple of off-campus classes. Taking tai chi and judo was the only thing she had ever done in direct defiance of his wishes.

Both classes were a great place to channel her pent-up anger, and she excelled in each area. She easily gained her black belts long before graduation.

When she wasn't attending classes, she trained herself in other ways. She would walk the hallways of her home or school at night, in the dark, to strengthen her ability to escape any situation. This helped her feel less trapped in life.

The classes and the summers spent at the camp got her through some of the darkest years of her life. When the five friends had grown too old to attend camp themselves, they'd returned as counselors. She'd lied to her father about the summer job and instead told him that the camp now allowed older girls. She would find out years later that Elle's grandfather Joe had convinced him of that story at Elle's request.

Shortly after their last summer at River Camps and a week

after she'd graduated school, the Wildflowers took a trip together. Since then, they'd tried to get together every summer and head somewhere tropical for a week or at least a weekend. Their last trip had been to Cabo, last year.

She'd been working for one of her father's businesses, the third one to date. She'd flown through jobs at Harold Smith's many ventures more than most people changed hairstyles.

She tried to fit in anywhere, but the fact was, she just didn't.

Over the years, she'd tried everything to grow closer to her father. Even Miss Ellison had disappeared a few months after Aubrey's sixteenth birthday.

At first, Aubrey had tried to look for the woman, believing she'd been fired by her father. Then she'd overheard several of the staff talking about how Pricilla Ellison had retired and moved to Italy to be closer to her ailing sister.

Her father had made her life hell. He'd controlled every aspect of her day-to-day life when she was in New York. Looking back at her youth, she realized that her time at school and the campgrounds had been the only chance she'd had at freedom.

Shortly after her eighteenth birthday, she'd come home to find a small suitcase in the front entry. At first, she'd believed they had a guest, even if that had never happened once over the ten years she'd lived there. She had been excited at the prospect.

Then she'd read the note on the table and her heart had sunk.

Aubrey,

This fulfills my financial obligation to you. I will expect you to remove your items, which I have had packed up, and be out of my home before I return from work at 6:00 p.m. sharp. As previously discussed, there is a job waiting for you at my offices downtown. I've given them your name and they will expect a call from you today.

Harold

It stung, at first, that she'd only been an obligation. Over the next few years, she'd realized that's all she had ever been to him. She should have never expected anything more.

She went to great lengths to keep her connection to Harold a secret. She was thankful that no one in the office where she had been hired as an entry-level filing clerk knew she was the boss's daughter.

She'd slowly worked her way up the corporate ladder at the office and was close to becoming a team lead. Then one day, she'd walked in to find Terry Osborn reclining at her desk with his feet up on her paperwork.

"Terry." She pushed his feet off her paperwork and glared at him. "What can I help you with this morning?" She tossed her bag and umbrella down on the floor. Since it usually took her half an hour to warm up after the brisk walk and subway ride into work, she kept her thick heavy jacket on.

"I'm here to help you," Terry answered with a smile as he slowly stood up. "I hear you have family in... high places." His eyes ran over her, and she felt her entire body shiver with disgust. The man was easily a hundred pounds overweight and at least twice her age. Not to mention that she knew he was married. She'd heard rumors that he'd had several affairs while working there but had yet to find anyone in the office who liked him, let alone would sleep with him.

"I don't know what you mean." She moved past him, but he caged her in.

"Oh, I think you do. It's come to my attention that you've been keeping a secret from us. A pretty big one." His eyes narrowed. "Harold Smith"—he wiggled his eyebrows— "is your father."

She felt her back teeth grind as she pushed past him. "I am not keeping it a secret." She sat down in her chair and logged into her computer. "Anyone with a brain could have figured it out." She glanced up at him, hoping he didn't see her hands shake or her temper grow. "Was there something else?"

Terry was frowning down at her, and his face was growing red like it did every time he was agitated. "No one else knows." He moved closer to her and reached out. He would have placed his hand on her shoulder had she not scooted her chair back a few steps. Arching her eyebrows, she chuckled.

"I will happily head out right now"—she nodded towards the door— "with a bullhorn and let everyone in on my secret." She air quoted the last word.

His face grew even redder. His eyes moved around as if gauging his next move. "Then I'm sure you won't mind if I let your father in on your last client."

She laughed. "Why don't you regroup?" She pushed herself back towards her desk and turned her attention towards her screen. "When you come up with something else you deem worth blackmailing me for to get to my father's money, let me know." She glanced up and smiled and then dismissed him and returned to her work.

Shortly after the man left her office, she felt the tension in her body relax. God! She hated her job. She hated being associated with one of the richest men in the world.

It took Terry a week to come up with a new angle. He barged in while she was finishing up with an email.

"Kasey, I'm going to have to call you back." She hung up. "Yes?"

Terry had moved over and sat across from her and had gone as far as to prop his feet up on the edge of her desk again.

"I was thinking," Terry started slowly. She bit the edges of her tongue.

"Yes?" She glanced at the clock and realized she only had a few minutes before she could technically clock out.

"I've gone about this the wrong way." His smile grew. "I think we should have drinks."

She laughed. A burst of it escaped her before she could control herself.

"That is not going to happen." She hit send on the email. The email instantly popped back at her that her account was locked, and she frowned.

"I think you'll reconsider." He motioned to her computer.

"What did you do?" she asked, hitting send again. She sighed and leaned back. "Paid off the IT guys?"

His eyes narrowed. "It's amazing what you can find going through someone else's email. I think your father would find a few of these very interesting." He set down two papers he'd been holding.

She didn't even spare them a glance. Instead, she stood up and smiled at him. "Thank you, Terry," she began as she leaned on the desk. "You've made this decision easier for me."

The man's bushy eyebrows rose slightly as he removed his feet from her desk. "We can discuss this over—"

She laughed again. "When hell freezes over." She pulled her purse and jacket from the bottom drawer and took her time slipping on her jacket. "You've just made it easier for me to walk out." She smiled and started out of her office.

He followed her until she stopped by Barb's desk. Her supervisor glanced up at her with annoyance.

"Terry here has seen fit to have my email account locked, which has finally given me the spine to quit," she said with a smile. Then she leaned down closer to her boss. "In the last two years that I've worked under you, not once did I see you stick up for what was right. You treated your employees like tools to better your own career." The woman looked put off and annoyed. "Terry has also informed me that it may not be common knowledge who my father is." She smiled when Barb glared up at her. "The name Harold Smith might ring a bell."

She waited until she could see in Barb's eyes that she'd made the connection before turning around and leaving.

It was the best feeling in the world, until she stepped out on the snow-covered curb and shivered. How the hell was she going to pay her rent next month?

That night, sitting in her small one-room studio apartment listening to sirens outside her window while she sipped the cup of noodles, she realized the magnitude of her actions.

She had been paying for night classes at the closest community college in hopes that her art career would take off. But now that she couldn't even afford a meal beyond what she was currently eating, she knew her entire life would have to be put on hold.

She had some money in her savings account that she could live off if she had to, but she preferred not to touch it. At least not yet.

She was job hunting on the small secondhand laptop she'd purchased a few years back when her phone rang.

Seeing the unmarked number, she almost didn't answer it, but then she remembered she'd put her number on a few online applications.

"Hello?"

"Tell me it's not true you quit today?" Her father's voice boomed in her ears. She hadn't seen him since the day before her eighteenth birthday and she wondered if he was older and frailer looking now.

"Yes," she answered. "My hand was forced—"

"You'll go back tomorrow." It was a demand not a request or question.

"No, I won't," she said quickly. No matter what happened to her, she would no longer be indebted to anyone.

"Yes, you will. I've arranged everything with your supervisor."

"I don't care. I won't go back."

"Then you leave me no choice to see to it that you will have no references. I'll make sure that it's noted that you were officially fired. I can even arrange to make sure that it's difficult for you to be hired anywhere else in the city."

"I don't care." She shut her eyes and tried to hold firm. "I don't need anyone's handouts."

"How will you pay for the room you call an apartment?" he asked, causing her eyebrows to rise. Did he know where she lived? If so, why? Why was he keeping track of her? His exact words from a few years ago were that his obligations as far as she went was over. Why would he care where she lived? Or even worked?

"I'm no longer your obligation." She threw his own words back at him.

He was silent for a while and she almost believed that he had hung up. Then he said. "A job isn't an obligation."

She was in complete shock and almost missed his next statement.

"Think about coming back to the office. I've secured a leadership position for you. Your supervisor had nothing but great things to say about your work ethics. She's the one that suggested I move you to the eleventh floor."

She held her breath. How long had she been trying to reach that goal? From the moment she'd learned about the leadership team positions almost two years ago, she'd worked on moving up in the company.

"I'll think about it," she said softly.

"Don't take too long."

"I'll let you know by Friday," she added before hanging up.

She was torn. Part of her wanted to tell her father where he could take his new job offer while the other part of her liked the thought of eating more than noodles and broth for dinner.

That night she had little sleep as she made a mental list of the pros and cons of going back to work for her father's company.

The following day, Aubrey had gotten the call that Elle's

grandfather Joe had died. During her trip back down to the camp to console her friends, Elle had proposed that the friends all chip in and rebuild the defunct campground. She'd been the first one to jump at the chance. After all, there hadn't really been anything for her back in New York. Her friends needed her. So, without a second thought, she'd pulled most of her money from her savings account to be with the only people she deemed family. And, in the process, she'd found her new life.

CHAPTER 2

*T*hree months later...

Aiden stood with his back to the sun and felt his breath hitch in his lungs when the pretty redhead came bouncing down the pathway. Who the hell was she? he thought to himself quickly.

His cousin Elle rushed after her and called out the woman's name.

"Aubrey, wait up," Elle said.

He'd known Elle Saunders his entire life. The fact that they were second cousin had helped him secure the job fixing up the summer camp she'd inherited. It had been owned by her grandfather Joe, his great-uncle.

Shortly after Joe's death, Elle had called him with a crazy idea, one that he jumped at.

Not only was he going to refurbish the entire campgrounds, but he was in charge of overseeing the remodeling of each of the twenty small cabins. He was going to take the old cabins, which used to house a dozen preteen girls, and turn them into exclusive private cabins that could be enjoyed by wealthy adults. It was just the project he needed at the moment.

Having Danelle break things off with him a few months ago had left him raw. He'd known better than to invest his heart into a woman who was damaged and unwilling to commit. Still, he'd hoped, and had a broken heart to show for it.

He figured the new camp project would help get his mind off his heartbreak and financial issues. Danelle had taken off with almost everything he owned after maxing out his credit cards.

She'd even moved out most of his furniture when he'd been at work, leaving him with only an air mattress, a worn leather chair, a single dish, and a spoon that she had probably forgotten in the bottom of the dishwasher. She'd even taken his refrigerator, washer, and dryer.

"Hey," Aiden said to Elle when the two women stopped in front of him.

"Hey," she said a little breathless. "Aiden, this is Aubrey." She motioned to her friend. "Aub, this is my second cousin Aiden."

Elle had mentioned her friend Aubrey tons of times over the years, along with Zoey, Scarlett, and Hannah, the other Wildflowers, as they called themselves.

"Hey," he said, removing his sunglasses to get a better look at the sexy redhead.

Aiden had a type. Or so he'd thought. Every single girl he'd dated before had been tall, brunette, and built.

So he was slightly confused as to why he felt an instant sexual pull for the short, curvy redhead with porcelain skin and eyes the color of the sky on a clear day.

"Hi," Aubrey said as she glanced beyond him. "Gosh, you've gotten so much done already." She walked past him into the cabin.

He and his crew had pulled out the built-in bunkbeds and the old flooring and had cleared out the connected bathrooms, leaving only electric wires and exposed plumbing.

"I can't believe how big this cabin is after everything's been removed," Elle said, walking in circles.

"There's plenty of room," he agreed, walking over to unroll the plans he'd drawn up for this particular cabin. "There'll be a small sitting area and a kitchenette, a larger bedroom area, and the bathroom..." He motioned to the plans as both the ladies looked on. When he leaned closer, he was rewarded with the soft scent of Aubrey's perfume. She smelled like flowers and sex.

He straightened and took a step back. He'd gone several months now without sex and knew that the pull was probably due to that.

As he talked to them both about the other cabins, his eyes kept darting towards Aubrey.

When she asked him about permitting and contractor licenses, he was a little shocked that she knew so much about the business. He talked to her about the city's permitting schedule and how he was a licensed state engineer, which cut down on the time frame for work to start.

"Besides, Marg and I go way back." He chuckled.

"Oh?" Aubrey asked.

He shrugged. "She used to babysit me." He smiled. "She has a soft spot for me still."

"Most women do." Elle chuckled and nudged Aubrey, who blushed slightly. Her pale skin turned a soft shade of pink, causing his blood to heat. Elle didn't notice it since she was too busy walking around the cabin again.

He watched as the two friends chatted about furniture, decorations, and the camp's future. He watched Aubrey closely and wondered if she was single. Okay, a lot of other thoughts rushed through his head as well, but the first and foremost was if she was free.

He'd made the mistake of not checking to see if someone he was interested in was unattached before and it had burned him.

Elle's phone rang and, after glancing down at it, she held up her finger and took the call. Shortly after answering, she stepped outside the cabin.

"So." Aubrey turned to him. "You're Elle's cousin?"

"My grandmother Nancy and Elle's grandfather Joe were brother and sister. My grandmother died a long time ago."

"We all loved Grandpa Joe." Aubrey's smile brightened. "It's funny, Elle had never mentioned you, at least not until we started planning this all out. Then you're all she could talk about. How you'd just come back from college. Architect?" she asked as she tilted her head.

"Bachelor of Design in Architecture." He nodded. "FSU."

"I was going to school." Her eyes turned towards the large windows his crew had ripped out earlier that morning. A few bugs buzzed in and out of the empty spaces.

"For?" he asked when she didn't continue.

Her blue eyes moved back to him. "Art," she said with a sigh.

"Sounds like you miss it?" He tucked his hands in his jean pockets.

She shrugged and walked over to the fireplace and ran a finger over the worn wood. He had plans to refurbish the old thing with oak. The fireplaces in all of the cabins would be modernized into gas fireplaces, but he planned on keeping the hearths classic and rustic looking. It would be part of the charm of each cabin.

"I do sometimes. I suppose when there is more work around here for us to do, I won't be so..."

His eyebrows drew up. "Bored?"

She chuckled softly. "I guess living in a city has turned me into a time snob." She glanced over at him.

"We could always use some extra help," he suggested. "If you were an art major, I'm sure you'll have no issues picking up a paintbrush." He nodded to the walls. "We start painting in here in about a week. Course, we'll tape it all off and spray, but..."

"Oh, that sounds wonderful. I know how to use a sprayer." She clasped her hands together as if excited.

"I'm sure I can find other things for you to do around here." He glanced around just as Elle stepped back inside.

"I've got to go meet the cleaning crew for the main building." She glanced at her watch. "Aub..."

"I think I'm going to help out around here. Aiden says he could use the extra help," Aubrey jumped in.

Elle's eyebrows shot up as she glanced his way.

He nodded quickly, confirming. "If you can spare her today."

"She's all yours," Elle said with a smile as she turned to go.

"Well?" Aubrey asked with a smile. "Where do you want me?"

The question right then was where didn't he want her? His mind played over kissing her and taking her everywhere he could. Against the wall with her legs wrapped around him. She bent over his workbench as he pounded into her soft flesh. Taking her in a soft bed somewhere.

When she shifted, he cleared his mind and motioned towards the bathroom area.

"How are you with swinging a sledgehammer?" he asked.

She smiled. "I have some pent-up issues I could release on a wall."

He chuckled and she followed him back to the bathroom.

"How about knocking out all this old pink tile?" He motioned to the wall of showers that had been tiled in a soft pink square tile so many years ago.

"You're going to let me do all this?" she asked as her eyes grew big.

He ran his eyes up and down her and then smiled. "You look strong enough to handle it."

She chuckled. "Oh, I am. I'm just happily surprised you aren't treating me like a wilting wildflower."

He smiled at this. "As I said, you look strong enough. When it really comes down to it though, it's not strength, it's how much pent-up frustration you have to keep you hitting the crap out of the tile."

Her eyes move over towards the wall and grew a little unfocused and sad. She shivered once and then nodded. "How many bathrooms like this need to be done?"

"All twenty cabins."

She frowned. "I could easily do twice that." She picked up the hammer.

"Here." He handed her a pair of leather gloves and some eye protection. "There's a hard hat." He motioned to the workbench. "Rule number one, safety at all times on the job site."

She slipped on the gloves and glasses. "What's rule number two?" she asked, picking up the hard hat.

"Have fun." He motioned towards the wall.

He stood back for a few moments and watched her swing the hammer at the tile.

"You won't be there the entire time, will you? It's very intimidating. I'm sure you're a pro at swinging this thing by now."

He chuckled. "No, I think you've got it. If you need anything, I'll be in the other room."

She waved him off and returned to swinging the large hammer. Pink tiles flew off the wall, and she kicked them aside as she kept moving.

An hour later, he stepped in to check on her progress. She had knocked all the tiles off the shower area and was shoveling the broken bits into a wheelbarrow.

"Wow, you work fast." He nodded to her progress.

She smiled up at him, and he could tell she wasn't even really winded.

"I'll haul all these to the dumpster and start on the next cabin tomorrow," she said with a smile.

"Take a break." He held up a bottle of water.

She set the shovel down, removed the leather gloves, and

took the water from him. He watched as she took a slow drink from it.

Leaning against the wall, he asked, "So, are you seeing someone?"

Her eyes moved to his. "No," she said softly. "You?"

He shook his head slowly. "Interested in going out sometime?"

He could tell she was thinking for a moment. He watched her smile slip slightly.

"I... don't do relationships in the normal sense," she warned. "And, if we did anything... together"—her eyes moved to the door—"I wouldn't want them to know about it."

His eyebrows shot up. "Embarrassed of me?"

She chuckled. "No, it's just... my friends can be a little..."

"Overprotective?"

"God no, I was going to say pushy." She laughed. "Very much so when it comes to everyone needing to find someone to be with."

"Don't you think you have a someone out there?" he asked.

She shrugged. "There is no such thing as true love," she said with conviction.

He thought about how Danelle had left him raw and hurting and nodded in agreement. "So, casual then?"

Her smile returned. "Mutual pleasure is just fine with me." He watched her bite that sexy bottom lip of hers and decided to test the waters to see if there was any spark between them. Placing his hands on the small of her back, he nudged her forward until their bodies bumped up against each other. He heard her breath hitch as he moved even closer.

"We might as well see if there's anything here," he suggested. Her eyes moved to his lips and then back to his eyes before she nodded her agreement.

When he brushed his mouth over hers, it was his breath that

caught. Her body seemed to melt against his as her hands moved up to his shoulders. He slanted his mouth over hers, pressing, enjoying, tasting.

He lost track of time as he enjoyed the feel and taste of her.

Hearing a vehicle approach, he pulled back quickly. She swayed slightly. He glanced towards the windows and saw a golf cart zip by the cabin driven by Zoey. Moments later another one drove by, this one driven by her sister Scarlett.

"They race on those things all the time," Aubrey said as she rolled her eyes.

He turned back towards her and realized he had yet to let her go. Dropping his hands, he took a step back. If he didn't step away now, he might not want to and could end up taking her there in the middle of all the rubble.

"I guess we can confirm that there's definitely something there," he said with a chuckle.

She smiled. "Yes, definitely something."

"I've got a trailer I'm staying at near the construction entrance. If you find yourself bored again this evening…" He smiled and ran a hand up her back slowly. He felt himself grow hard when she arched into his touch and made a soft sound. His smile grew.

This time when he kissed her, he felt his excitement grow at the knowledge that there was a bigger possibility of seeing her, enjoying her, later.

"After dinner." She sighed. "I can probably sneak away." She rested her forehead against his chest.

His phone rang suddenly, stopping him from replying.

"Aiden," he answered as his eyes locked with hers. Moments later he hung up and groaned. "I have to head over to the next cabin. If you want, leave the cleanup for my guys."

"No." She shook her head quickly. "I made the mess. Besides, I still have plenty of pent-up energy left over."

He left her hauling the rubble out and headed down to oversee the next cabin's work. His steps were light, and he felt like he was walking on air for the first time in months. After all, he had something to look forward to. Sex. With a hot redhead who kissed like sin and had eyes that he could get lost in.

CHAPTER 3

What had she been thinking? Setting up a sex date with Elle's second cousin had been a spur of the moment deal. Okay, she had to admit that her loins had done all the thinking when he'd been in the same room as her.

She's been watching him from afar since seeing the man meet with Elle almost two weeks ago and had been jonesing to taste the guy.

She'd been honest with him. There was no way she was looking for the same things as her friends. Each member of the Wildflowers had dreamed of finding their own Prince Charming since the first summer they'd met so many years ago. With the exception of Aubrey.

Aubrey had never really believed in happy-ever-afters. Not after being raised how she had and knowing that there was no such thing as Prince Charmings who lived in massive castles.

She thought of her father and the last phone call she'd had with him as she finished hauling and cleaning up the busted tile.

After moving down there, she'd waited almost two weeks before calling him and telling him where she was and what her plans were.

"You're what?" His voice had echoed, causing her ear to ring.

She'd been so nervous to tell him that she was staying in Florida and putting all her savings into rebuilding an old summer camp for girls with her four best friends.

As far as business plans go, it wasn't a terrible one. They'd pooled enough money to hire Aiden and, with his estimates on repairs and updates, they figured they had just enough money to make it work.

That was until that fateful phone call with her father.

"I'm staying in Florida," she repeated. "We've decided—"

"Who is we?" her father broke in.

"My friends. The four other girls I met at River Camps that first summer you sent me here," she reminded him. It wasn't as if she and her father talked a lot. But she knew for a fact that she'd mentioned the Wildflowers to him more than a dozen times over the years. "Elle has inherited the camp, and well, we're all pitching in—"

"So, it's finally come down to money with that gang?" Her father's chuckle caused goosebumps to race down her spine. "How much do they want from you?"

She could just hear her father gloating and mentally preparing to write a check.

"Nothing," she said between clenched teeth. "As I said, we're all business partners. We're all putting in equal amounts to reopen the camp."

Her father had been quiet. "I won't allow it."

She rolled her eyes. "Well, since your... responsibilities for me ended on my eighteenth birthday, I'd wager you have no control of what I do. I was just calling to let you know where I was. You know, a courtesy call."

"I thought you were going back to work. What's her name has been calling about you. She's anxious to get you back in the office."

What's her name? She rolled her eyes again. Why did it seem

like every time she talked to her father over the phone, her eyes turned into marbles rolling all over the place? One day she would roll them one too many times and they'd fall right out of their sockets.

"I'm sorry to disappoint," she'd said and had added a quick goodbye. Since that day, she'd been avoiding her father's phone calls.

"Wow, did you just do all this yourself?" Zoey Rowlett asked as she stepped into the now clean space.

"Yes." She smiled as she leaned against the shovel. There was sweat rolling down her face, her back ached, and she was pretty sure she had a blister on the inside of her thumb. "It was so much fun. I've requested to help out on the next cabin tomorrow." She tossed the last of the trash and then removed the gloves and tucked them in her jean pockets.

"It's your back." Zoey shrugged.

"Who won the race?" she asked as Scarlett's golf cart stopped out front.

Zoey's smile grew. "Who always wins?"

"That's because you know that cart number eight has some… modifications to it." She lowered her voice since Scarlett was out front talking with someone.

Zoey glanced over her shoulder and then narrowed her eyes at Aubrey. "If she finds out, I'll know who tattled on me."

Aubrey laughed and then motioned as if she was sealing her lips and locking them.

Zoey reached up and took the invisible key from her fingers and made a show of swallowing it, a move the friends had done since that first year together.

Aubrey laughed again. "So, what are you two up to now?"

"We were heading back for a swim," Zoey answered. "Floating in the water helps the knee." She wiggled her left leg a couple times. Zoey had hurt her knee a few months back when she'd attended the Olympics in Rio. Her softball team had gone on to win without her.

Aubrey knew that if Zoey hadn't hurt herself, she wouldn't have been in a position to drop everything and join them in opening the camp back up.

"Count me in." She set the gloves and shovel down. "I need to cool off."

She thought about a quick dip before dinner and then, after eating with her friends, taking a long walk out to Aiden's trailer. She knew he'd moved the trailer onto the land a couple weeks ago but, since she'd been basically stalking him and hadn't officially been introduced to him, she'd steered clear of the area during her evening walks.

She thought about her upcoming night with Aiden as she held on to the golf cart while Zoey raced Scarlett back to the main building. Gravel spit up as they skidded to a halt moments before Scarlett.

Laughing, they rushed up to the third-floor apartment they shared and changed into their swimsuits.

There'd been a time when the five friends hadn't bothered with swimsuits. But now the place was swarming with crew members working on every part of the grounds, including their own apartment. Aiden had worked on the other bathroom the first week they'd lived there, but she'd been busy setting up their new computers down in the offices on the main floor.

Since she was the one with the most experience with computers, having taken a class in college, she'd been tasked with setting everything up, including their new printers.

They had each picked a room on the main floor for their offices. Elle had the biggest one, Zoey and Scarlett shared a smaller one, Hannah had one across the hallway, and Aubrey had a medium-sized one since it had been decided she would hire and oversee all the counselors.

Still, at the rate they were moving, they had estimated it

would be close to a year before they opened the gates to their first guests.

The moment she dove into the pool, her mind cleared. Finally, a moment of peace from all the worry and anxiety that had been building in her head for the past month.

Floating on the water, listening to her friends chat as they splashed around her, she took several deep breaths and felt every muscle in her body relax.

Then she was gasping for air as she was shoved under the water by one of her friends.

"You're not paying attention," Hannah said when she surfaced and spit out the water.

"I was trying to relax." She swiped her soaking-wet red hair out of her eyes.

"Relax later, we have decisions to make," Elle said, swimming over to them.

"Okay, like what?" she asked, treading water.

"Should we turn those back rooms in the pool house into massage rooms and hire a masseuse?" Elle asked.

"Duh," she replied. "Yes. I could use a massage now." She rolled her shoulders. "What else?"

Elle tilted her head as if she were trying to think of items on her list.

"Kitchen staff," she finally said.

"I've got an idea there," Hannah broke in. "Let me look into some things, and I'll let you know soon."

Everyone just looked at Hannah until she added,

"I know people."

"Okay," Elle said slowly. "Next on the list is whether we should add a zip line. There's plenty of room, and a lot of adults can zipline with minimal skills and health restraints."

"Yes," Aubrey said quickly and laid back in the water while everyone else agreed.

"Now we just need to come up with a list of classes we're

going to offer. I think we all agreed on yoga. What else?" Elle asked.

She thought quickly of the classes she'd taken and how she wouldn't mind teaching tai chi and judo. Feeling her heart skip, she jumped in.

"I can teach basic tai chi or judo." She thought about it for a moment. "Or something like self-defense classes. I mean, women pay a ton of money to attend classes like that all the time in the city."

"That's a wonderful idea," Scarlett replied. "We're going to have so many wonderful activities. Of course, we'll need a sand volleyball court."

"We can put it in by the pool. That way when everyone gets overheated, they can just jump in."

"What about adding an outdoor bar and dining area near there? We can have Aiden design an opening on the side of the pool house," Elle added. "I need my phone." She glanced around and swam over to the edge of the pool and made several notes while they continued to brainstorm.

"I've got the local shelter keeping their eye open for horses that would fit our needs," Scarlett said. "The barn needs some work, but we should have enough room for at least half a dozen horses, if not more, for guests to ride. Maybe even offer romantic sunset rides?"

"What about all the boats? Are we going to have someone look at them?" Zoey asked. "Sunset sails are key. Along with kayaks, paddleboards, and canoes for daytime fun."

"Of course. I have a local kid looking at all that stuff. Grandpa Joe hired him a few summers back to fix up the old fishing boat of his."

"Kid?" Hannah asked.

"Well, Joe always called him that. Damion is a few years younger than us." Elle chuckled. "I've already called him. He said he'll stop by later this week to start looking over what is left in the boathouse."

"I can't believe this is all coming together. When will Aiden start on the new cabins?" Hannah asked.

"After his crew finishes the work on the old ones," Elle answered and then turned towards her. "I heard you had fun breaking out all those pink tiles in cabin one today."

Aubrey smiled, remembering how wonderful it felt to smash things and destroy the pretty wall that reminded her so much of all those stupid pink dresses she'd been forced to wear for years.

"It was highly therapeutic," she responded. "I'll start on cabin two tomorrow."

"We need new names," Hannah broke in.

Zoey laughed. "Okay, dibs on Tawanda."

"No." Hannah rolled her eyes. "For the cabins. I mean, Cabin One isn't sexy at all."

Everyone was quiet for a moment. "Our cabin's name was River Cabin," Scarlett said. "Why not call all the other cabins by unique names as well?"

"The first twenty cabins are basically all the same," Elle pointed out.

"Right, but we could have unique designs and decorations inside. You know, decorate each cabin with a different theme," Aubrey suggested. "Then give them names to match. Of course, we'll have to wait and see what Aiden does with each cabin's interior before choosing names."

"He has started working on the designs for the new cabins. I could suggest this idea to him and maybe he could add some unique features that will help separate each of them?" Elle offered.

"This is coming together so quickly." Scarlett sighed as she floated back. "Enough talk." She splashed them. "I want to relax before we eat. Look, the sun's going down."

Everyone turned and watched the last rays of the sun slip behind the trees.

"I'm starving," Zoey said once they were shadowed in the pool lights.

"Is it bad that I can't wait until we have a working kitchen so that we don't have to cook or eat cold sandwiches anymore?"

"Oh, to have a chef at your beck and call..." Zoey moaned as someone's stomach let out a loud growl.

When everyone turned to her, she realized it was her own stomach. "I forgot to eat lunch." She shrugged.

"Okay, food then sleep," Zoey suggested as everyone started making their way to the edge of the water.

"Hey," a deep voice sounded from somewhere in the darkness. "I was just coming in to join you."

Aubrey watched as Aiden moved to the edge of the pool. He was still wearing his work clothes, only they were now covered in a white powder and sweat.

"We were just heading in for dinner," Elle told him as she wrapped a towel around her.

"I'm starving," Zoey added, taking up her own towel.

Aiden sat down and untied his work boots and then toed them off. "Well, I'm still going to enjoy a dip," he said with a shrug.

Aubrey remained where she was in the water. She was suddenly more interested in seeing him in swim trunks than she was about eating a cold turkey sandwich.

"Coming, Aub?" Scarlett asked as everyone disappeared down the pathway that led back to the main building.

"I'm going to stick around for a few more minutes then maybe go for a walk. Don't wait up."

"Don't blame me if I eat your sandwich," Zoey called back and rushed to catch up with everyone else.

"Guess you earned a few extra minutes in there today, huh?" Aiden asked, tossing his work shirt onto the chair.

Aubrey's breath caught in her lungs as the pool lights danced over his toned chest.

"Yes, I sure did." She ducked her mouth under the water so he wouldn't see the huge smile on her lips. How did the man get such a perfect six-pack? Did he know just how sexy his little striptease was? He stood up and started unbuckling his jeans, and she watched as they slid down his narrow hips and lower over his muscular thighs until they pooled at his feet.

Now he stood in front of her in nothing but a pair of blue boxer briefs and smiled at her from across the pool.

"Like what you see?" he asked her.

Since her mouth was still under the water, she simply nodded slowly.

Then she laughed as he ran to the edge of the pool and did a cannonball into the water. She was wiping the water from her eyes when warm hands circled her waist and pulled her under.

When they surfaced, his mouth covered hers as his hands roamed over her skin. She hadn't realized the water had cooled off until her skin started to heat under his touch.

"I'm glad I decided to come up here for a swim," he said against her skin.

"Me too." She sighed and held onto those muscular arms of his. Feeling his pecs against her own chest had her body reacting and heating. Then her legs brushed up against his and lit even more fires in her. Wrapping her legs around him, she held on while he treaded water, keeping their heads above the surface.

"You know, I have some of my mom's leftover lasagna at my place. You could always have dinner at my place?" he suggested.

"Deal," she said with a laugh. "I've had cold turkey sandwiches for the past week. Anything is better than one more night of it."

He chuckled, the sound reverberating.

"God, I want to kiss you again," he said, pulling her closer.

"Me too." She sighed and covered his lips with her own. "Aiden, take me back to your place," she said when they surfaced from the kiss again.

"I thought you'd never ask." He kicked off, sending them towards the stairs.

After drying off, under the very watchful gaze of Aiden, she pulled on the shorts and sweatshirt that she'd worn to the pool earlier. She followed him down the path towards the parking area and got in his truck when he opened the passenger side door for her.

It was a standard work truck and, when she glanced in the back seat, she noticed the box of tools on the floor.

"Sorry, work truck smell." He shrugged.

"It smells good, like you." She smiled. "Like tools and wood shavings."

He chuckled. "Then you'll love my place. When I left this morning, I didn't know I was going to have company later." He started driving.

"You should see my room. I share it with Hannah. She's a typical type A personality and, well, I'm not." She shrugged.

He chuckled. "Elle has talked about the five of you for years. I can't remember a time she didn't brag about her Wildflower friends." He glanced at her.

"Elle saved all of us," she admitted.

"Oh?" he asked as he parked in front of the trailer and shut off the truck.

"We were all lost and broken in our own ways."

"That's not how she tells it." He turned to her and brushed his thumb down the side of her face. "The way she tells it, her friends are the ones who saved her. She'd been in a dark place. You know what happened to her mother?"

Aubrey nodded slightly. "Her father murdered her mother. We didn't know about it for a few years after we met her."

"She'd been bullied, that first year she moved in with Joe." He shook his head and looked off into the darkness. "Kids can be so mean. I tried to stop most of it, but her self-esteem took a major hit. Then she met you four." He smiled. "And she seemed to blossom."

She thought of her own past and the horrors she'd come from. Still, everything she'd been through paled in comparison to what Elle had lived through. Knowing that your father had killed your mother out of rage must have been way worse than having a father who didn't feel anything at all.

"Hungry?" Aiden asked, breaking into her thoughts.

"Starved."

CHAPTER 4

Sitting across his kitchen table eating leftovers with Aubrey made the trailer feel more like a home. He'd moved into the place almost two weeks ago and had yet to have a single person over. Not even his best friend Brett had stopped by yet.

Then again, he'd been so busy working, he hadn't had time to come up for air. Nor had he wanted to. Until he'd spotted Aubrey, that is.

Then it was all he could think of. Taking time with her. Being with her. His libido had kicked into full gear the moment she'd flirted back with him.

They talked about the plans for the camp as they ate. She mentioned school and the subject turned to what classes they'd taken.

He was interested in seeing some of the art that she mentioned she had done.

"I'd like to see some of the plans you've made up for the cabins. Elle mentioned you had a few already done?"

He nodded. "They're over here." He stood up, taking his beer with him, and moved over to his work area, which was basically the entire living room. He had a sofa and a flat-screen, but he also had a large desk and the computer system he worked on nightly.

She followed him over, taking her glass of wine with her.

He pulled out the printed plans that he'd submitted to the city just yesterday.

"These will be the first two we build. Of course, we won't start until after we've finished with the old remodels."

She glanced over the drawings, and he could see that she grew excited about them. "These are amazing. You designed them yourself?"

"Yeah." He set his beer down and then took her glass of wine from her and set it down. She stepped easily into his arms. He allowed her to reach up and place her soft lips over his. Something told him that she wanted to drive and, the way she was making him feel, he figured he'd lean back and enjoy the ride.

When she pressed her body against his, a soft moan escaped her lips. A deeper one emanated from her when his hands reached under her shirt and played with her soft skin just above her jean shorts.

"I want to see you naked," she said as she nibbled on his ear.

"God, yes," he growled out, and he started backing her towards the bedroom.

He met her urgency, her passion, her fire with his own. His skin burned for her; his fingers itched to roam over that porcelain skin of hers.

She peeled off his shirt then tugged on the pants he'd pulled on after their swim.

"Here." He pulled back from her and quickly removed his boots and jeans and tossed them over the chair in the corner of his bedroom. Thankfully, he'd taken a moment to tidy up that morning before heading into work.

Of course, he'd never imagined he'd invite someone back to

his place that evening. Especially a sexy redhead that made his blood boil when she touched him.

Reaching out, he used a finger to nudge the shoulder of her sweatshirt down, exposing the soft skin. He unzipped the front and smiled when the sexy red bikini she'd been wearing in the pool was exposed.

"Sexy," he said with a smile.

"Oh god," she moaned and rolled her head slightly back as he removed the sweatshirt and reached for her shorts.

His hands brushed against her skin as he pulled the shorts from her hips. Standing back, he let his eyes roam over her slowly.

"How is it we haven't met before this?" he asked her as she stepped back into his arms.

"Bad timing, I guess." She smiled up at him.

"Lucky for me you showed up today." He kissed her again and backed her to the edge of his bed.

"It wasn't luck. I wanted to meet you. Wanted this." She surprised him by tugging on his shorts and then quickly gripping him in her hands. "I don't know about you, but it's been far too long for me. I don't think I want to go slow." She practically purred against him.

For a split second he thought about Danelle, then Aubrey reached up and in one quick move sent her bikini top falling to the floor, and his mind quite literally went blank of anything but her.

She had to be the most perfect woman on the planet. With shaky hands, he reached up and cupped her. Her eyes turned an even lighter shade of blue, and his body responded to how soft she felt under his fingertips.

"No, I doubt I could go slow now," he said just before crushing her lips under his.

They fell backwards, their mouths never leaving one another as her swim bottoms were tugged from her legs.

He grabbed a small foil package from his nightstand and slid the protection on moments before she gripped his hips and wrapped her legs around him.

They moved together like they'd done it a million times before, as if being together was second nature.

"More," he growled against her skin. He hoisted her hips as he pounded into her.

"Aiden," she cried out as he felt her tense under him. Moments later, he followed her and felt his entire body release. He hadn't realized how much of a need he'd built up since Danelle had left him. Not until he'd seen Aubrey walking towards him.

"I needed that." Aubrey sighed as she ran her hands over his back.

"Ditto," he said into her hair. "Thanks."

He felt and heard her chuckle. "Any time."

He leaned up and looked down at her. "You mean that?"

She smiled slowly. "Sure, why not? I mean, we both seemed to enjoy ourselves. I've got some free time and god knows I could use the release."

He thought about it and then nodded. "Okay, I'll take you up on that."

Her smile slipped slightly. "The only request I have is that we keep things lighthearted and"—she bit her bottom lip— "keep this a secret. My friends… would try to make something more out of this than there should be."

"Is that your way of telling me your heart is off the menu?" he asked.

She smiled. "Now you're getting it."

He thought for a moment. He still hadn't healed from Danelle, so he figured that he had nothing to lose in a mutual physical relationship.

"So?" she asked after a moment. "How about it?"

"As I said, count me in." He leaned down to an inch from her lips and waited. "But while you're making demands, I've got my own."

"Shoot," she said, her eyes glued to his as her hands stilled on his cooled skin.

"We don't see other people. If you get bored or want to move on, you tell me first. It makes things easier if it's just between you and I."

She smiled quickly. "I don't see a string of men lining up—"

He kissed her before she could finish. "Deal?" he asked.

"Yes." She sighed and pulled him back down to her.

This time, they slowed down and enjoyed exploring one another.

He wasn't surprised that, after, she pulled on her clothes and requested he take her back to the main building. He knew that, if this was going to remain a secret, she had roommates to contend with.

"Drop me off here," she said less than a quarter of a mile from the building. "I'll walk from here."

"Are you sure?"

She nodded. "I don't want them to see you drop me off. They're probably looking out for me already. I'll have to tell them I went for a walk."

He pulled over and spent a few moments kissing her again.

"When can I see you again?" she asked as she pulled away.

"I'm free most evenings," he admitted. "Work in the cabins can't go on after dark. At least until the electric gets fixed and turned back on. So I have to stop when the sun goes down."

She cocked her head as if thinking it through. "I'll see what I can do to get out to your place tomorrow night."

He kissed her again. "Looking forward to it. You still plan on working on the second cabin tomorrow?"

Her smile grew. "Yes, I'm looking forward to it and to you again tomorrow night." She jumped out of his truck.

He watched her disappear down the driveway until he knew

she was in the building that housed the apartment the five friends shared on the top floor.

He didn't think life could get any better. He had a dream job, his own place, and now he had a soft, gorgeous woman to look forward to enjoying, no strings attached.

SOMEHOW, because he knew he was keeping his heart from her, he didn't think twice about his life over the next year. Sure, there were times he wished they could share their relationship with their friends. Even if it was only during the times when the gang was all hanging out together, and he itched to hold her hand or kiss her in front of everyone. Like at the New Year's party. Instead, he'd kept his word and his distance when the others were around.

To his knowledge, no one else in the group knew they were enjoying one another's company every moment they could sneak away. Everything was going perfectly. Or so he thought.

Eleven months later, shortly before the camp opened its doors, he'd made the mistake of blurting out three words that had Aubrey pulling back.

It had been a rainy night about a month before the camp was set to open.

She and her friends had an interview that day with a local paper. He'd stood back and watched the five friends pose for pictures at the main gate of the campgrounds.

He'd painted the gates himself only a few weeks earlier. There were only a handful of things left to do around the grounds before they would be ready for guests. He and his team had started working on a couple of the new cabins and those wouldn't be ready for a few more months. But they had finished ten new cabins in addition to refurbishing the twenty original ones.

He'd been in one of the new cabins when the downpour had

started that day. He hadn't expected Aubrey to come rushing in, soaking wet, a few minutes later.

She'd laughed about being soaked and had started slowly removing her clothes as he watched, and his mouth watered. How had he not realized sooner how perfect she was for him?

His heart jumped in his chest each time she laughed and looked at him with desire. He knew at that moment he'd never felt that way about someone before. Nor did he think he could ever feel that way about someone else.

"I thought I could make it out here to you before the rain started," she said, moving slowly across the room towards him.

In the past twelve months that they'd been enjoying one another's company, she had yet to stay one single night in his arms. He'd desperately wished she'd fall asleep with him, but so far, he hadn't gotten that lucky.

She'd been so concerned about her friends finding out about them that he'd begun to wonder if there were other reasons that she wanted to keep their relationship a secret. It was strange, but he'd grown to trust her more than anyone else he'd ever dated. Not that he could call what was between them dating. After all, they only ate meals together when it was a group of people and, even then, they never sat together.

"I'm glad you made it." He smiled as she pulled her wet camp T-shirt over her head. Then his mind went blank when he noticed the see-through cream-colored bra she was wearing. Her pink nipples poked out towards him, begging for his attention.

"My god," he groaned as she reached for her jean shorts.

When she stood in front of him in nothing but the matching underwear set, he felt his entire body start to shake. At that moment, he knew he would never get enough of her and part of the locks he'd placed over his heart slipped away.

He should have pulled back then, but his dick was in control and, instead, he moved towards her as his hands itched to touch her soft perfect skin.

Bending his head down, he covered the material with his mouth and sucked her as her fingers dug into his hair, gripping him to her.

Pulling the silk aside, he took her in his mouth and enjoyed the moans and soft sounds he'd come to love over the past year. She tasted as fresh as she looked.

He and Danelle had never been this good together.

There wasn't anything Aubrey didn't allow him to try or do to her. At least anything he'd asked of her thus far. She'd been there, willing and eager and even at times with her own demands.

"Aiden," she begged as his hands moved lower over her hips.

"Tell me what you want," he said, trailing his mouth over her as he removed the last barriers she wore.

"Lick me, kiss me, all over." She arched against the kitchen countertop he'd been installing a small microwave under. There was a layer of dust on the surface but that didn't stop him from hoisting her hips up and setting her on the edge so that he could kneel between her legs and lap at her soft skin.

Her taste was something that he would never forget, nor tire of. Shortly after they'd started their little game, he'd made sure to never leave the house without a pocketful of condoms.

Aubrey was more demanding than anyone he'd ever been with before, thankfully. He'd never imagined being with a woman who matched his own desires beat for beat.

When he felt and tasted her convulse against his mouth, he stood up, pulled himself free of his work jeans, and slid on the condom before returning to her. Her legs wrapped around his hips, and he moaned when his mouth found her nipple again as he slipped slowly into her.

"God, I love this," he said against her skin. He hadn't registered her stiffening at first, but after a moment, he realized she'd frozen completely.

Glancing up at her, he frowned when he noticed her go white.

"What?" He stilled. "What's wrong?"

She nudged him back and jumped quickly down from the counter.

"I…" She shook her head. "I need to go."

He watched in complete shock as she quickly dressed and rushed through the rain from the cabin and away from him.

It took him a few moments to realize his mistake. He thought about going after her, but then figured he'd give her some time to come to terms with how he felt.

He knew he'd promised her their feelings were off limits, but it had been over a full year. What was he supposed to do? Not have feelings for the woman he thought about more often than he thought about food or sleep?

The following week she avoided him and was damn good at it too. No matter where he went looking for her, she was always somewhere else. By the time the camp opened, he had still been unable to get her alone. Of course, his own schedule kept him busy enough that he didn't have a moment to think, let alone much time to hunt her down.

It had been one of the first nights after guests flooded the grounds that he'd gotten a knock on his door just past ten o'clock.

He'd opened his front door and frowned down at a very drunk Aubrey, who stood swaying in his doorway.

"Hi," he said with a smile as his heart and his dick both jumped with joy.

"Hi." She giggled.

He leaned against the doorframe, crossed his arms over his chest, and watched her, taking in the sexy hiking boots, the tight khaki shorts, and the tight-fitting camp shirt, which had his smile growing. How was it that even in that outfit she was sexy as sin?

"Looking for something?" he asked, feeling a little cocky.

She giggled again and then flung her body towards him. Thankfully, he reached out and caught her before they both toppled over.

Her mouth plastered to his as she pushed him back into the room and slammed his door shut behind them.

"Aub?" he said between kisses, wanting to clear a few things up before they returned to normal.

"No." She shook her head. "Don't," she warned. "I need..." She was pulling at the buttons on his shirt. When her nails scraped against his skin, he moaned. She reached for the button of his jeans and, after freeing him, she wrapped her hand around him. "I just need..." She leaned over and ran her teeth over his shoulder.

All the arguments he'd thought of over the past week and a half left him. All he could think about now was being with her again and how he was going to persuade her to take a chance on him. For good.

No matter what happened now, he knew Aubrey was the woman he wanted. And if he had to wait forever, he was prepared to wait forever.

CHAPTER 5

Over a year later...

Aubrey knew something was changing. She could feel it in the air.

For over two and a half years, she'd enjoyed her time with Aiden and enjoyed knowing it was still a secret from her friends even more.

Every single one of her friends, the Wildflowers, were now fully in love and engaged to be married, except for her. But it was for the best. She knew she didn't belong in that elite group. She didn't deserve love.

It was difficult to explain, but she had promised herself long ago to never marry. Not that she didn't think others should, it just wasn't right for her.

Every single time she felt Aiden growing too close to her, she'd pull back. What was between them was just supposed to be fun. Just sex. That's all she wanted from him. That's all she could afford to give him. It was what they had arranged when they'd first started being together.

Besides, the man was very good at the physical stuff. Okay,

the best she'd ever experienced. He helped her take her mind off... well, everything dark from her past.

Over the past few years, she estimated that he probably knew as much about her as her sisters did. And the reverse could be said about him. She knew everything there was to know about Aiden Stark.

Besides knowing all the intimate details about him, like his favorite sex position and how he liked to snuggle afterwards, she knew that he was twenty-five and had a Bachelor of Design in Architecture from FSU. He was an only child of Robin and Carl Stark, whom she had met on a few occasions when they visited the camp. Aiden's grandmother Nancy had been the sister of Elle's grandfather Joe and had passed away long before Aiden had come along.

He'd been in only one long-term relationship with a woman named Danelle. She gathered that he'd been broken after that relationship had ended but hadn't asked who had ended it or why.

It had been almost six months since she'd broken things off with him for the last time. He'd spooked her that first time he'd mentioned the L word. Sure, he'd convinced her that he was only talking about their time together, but she'd bolted just the same.

She'd kicked herself more than a dozen times after that. Each time she'd needed a release, she'd gone crawling back to him. This last time, however, she'd been left sexually frustrated and hornier than, well... ever. Aiden had been there to scratch that itch for so long that she'd grown accustomed to being liberated from her pent-up frustration.

Now, almost six months to the day since she'd called it off with him for the last time, she walked around the campgrounds agitated enough that she was surprised she didn't bite anyone's head off. Sure, her classes helped relieve some of the physical tension, and she had her friends to talk to. But still, the secret she'd kept from them weighed heavily on her, and she knew that if they ever found out about it, she'd have some explaining to do.

Seeing how happy her four friends were with their fiancés had her even more agitated. Not that she didn't like the four men. Levi was one of her favorite people on the campgrounds, and he and Scarlett were perfect together. Dylan, Liam, and Owen Costas had grown on her over the past year as well.

Even Scarlett and Zoey's mother, Kimberly, was now happily and openly seeing Reed Cooper, a local who lived in a massive mansion across the water from the camp.

Now that it was just her living alone in the three-bedroom apartment on the third floor of the main camp building, she tried to convince herself she deserved to be alone.

Still, part of her heart ached for something more. Someone to share the rest of her life with. But then reality would come crashing back down to her in the form of a call from her father.

Since she'd stepped out of his grasp, he'd tried everything to get her back under his control, short of suing the camp business itself.

She hadn't confided in her friends all the methods he'd used, but they knew of some of them. He'd tried to blackmail her into working for his company by telling her that some of her clients' money had gone missing and that the company was looking at her. If she didn't return, she could be sued and possibly jailed. When she'd laughed that threat off and informed him that she hadn't dealt with any of the money accounts and had only set up their accounts and then handed everything to the next person up the chain, he'd backed off.

Her father hadn't even really known what she'd done for his business, which made her feel relieved and pissed at the same time. She'd expected that he'd at least followed her career a little. Now she knew he hadn't and, more importantly, he hadn't cared enough after she'd left to investigate the allegations someone had made against her.

With all the frustrations building, she knew it was only a matter of time before something gave. Something was coming, and she was bracing for it.

To top everything off, they had less than a week before Zoey and Dylan's wedding. Not to mention that Zoey was almost two months pregnant now.

A baby changed everything. Which might be the weight Aubrey felt, causing the slight drift between her and the rest of her Wildflowers.

Her four friends were about to have husbands and start their own families. They had different things in their future than she did. What did she even really have besides the camp?

Not that the camp wasn't enough for her. It was the only thing, besides Aiden and her friends, that had kept her grounded over the past few years.

Making her way up to her apartment to change for the dinner party, she realized just how lonely the rooms on the third floor were now that all her friends had moved out.

Upstairs, she slid on the rose-colored dress and matching heels, then glanced at herself in the full-length mirror and realized just how lonely she'd become. She'd pushed everyone away from her lately. Her friends had been too busy with their own lives to notice, but the fact was, she'd distanced herself from them beforehand.

Now, loneliness was the price. She was surrounded by strangers on a daily basis and filled some of her free time with her friends, but she had done this to herself. Pushing people away—including Aiden—was the defense mechanism she'd put in place long ago to protect her heart.

Her phone buzzed, reminding her that she had only a few minutes to get down to the dining hall. Shaking off the foul mood, she straightened her shoulders and rushed to work.

This would be the last group of visitors before Zoey and Dylan's wedding the following weekend. The camp wouldn't officially be closed down, but they had blocked out more than fourteen cabins for family and friends to fill for the event instead of guests. The wedding would be held on the small strip of private beach, with the reception filling the dining hall.

They had hosted a few weddings at the campgrounds, but the friends were thinking of making it a bigger part of what they offered. After all, their place was perfect for hosting the events. Their only problem was ensuring the wedding guests didn't interfere with their normal guests.

The main issue would be families wanting to bring children into an all-adult environment. Just the thought of families had her thinking about Zoey and the baby again.

She was very excited for her friend and couldn't help getting caught up in all the baby excitement. She'd even purchased some blankets and outfits for the baby.

But her mind kept throwing her for a loop by wondering what her own children would look like. She kept telling herself that she didn't want kids. Ever. But her subconscious wasn't listening and returned to daydreaming about what they would look like.

"There you are." Hannah took her arm and forced her to walk faster across the room. "You're up." She motioned to the stage.

Aubrey groaned. "Why do I have to do this tonight?"

"Your turn," Hannah said, shoving her on the stage.

Aubrey pasted on a smile and walked over to tap on the microphone to get everyone's attention. "Ladies and gentlemen." She waited until the voices died down and every eye was turned on her. "Tonight's talent show will start in five minutes. Remember, if you want to take part, you have to fill out the entry forms and have them up to us before the show starts." She motioned to the small table in front of the stage. "Thank you." She walked off the stage.

"That was... dry," Hannah said with a chuckle.

"Hey, if you wanted perky, you should've had Scarlett do it," she joked as she grabbed a bottle of water from the bar area.

"You're in a mood." Hannah leaned on the bar and ran her eyes over her. "Tired?"

"No," she said after taking a sip of the water. What she wanted was a glass of wine and a bubble bath. What she needed was... sex. Hard, fast sex that left her too exhausted to think about anything else. Just then something caught her eye, and she glanced up to see Aiden stroll across the room towards her. He was wearing a suit. Why was he wearing a suit? "Why is he wearing a suit?" she asked Hannah.

Hannah frowned and followed Aubrey's gaze.

"I asked him to fill in for Dylan," Hannah answered with a shrug. "Dylan had some... things to tend to tonight."

God, the man looked good in a suit, she thought as he stopped in front of her.

"So," he said, after his eyes had run over Aubrey. "Where do you want me?" he asked.

Aubrey's mind flashed to the last time they'd been together. How they'd practically ripped each other's clothes off.

She could just imagine removing that tie from around his neck and using it to keep his hands above his head while she took her time running her mouth over every inch of...

"Earth to Aubrey." Hannah snapped her fingers in front of her face. "You're up." Her friend shoved her towards the stage again.

Damn. She'd been so focused on her sex daydream that five whole minutes had fled by.

As she introduced each talent, her eyes and mind kept returning to Aiden. She watched him help set up each talent show participant, even escorting people up and down the narrow stage stairs.

Over an hour later, Aubrey's head was splitting, and she'd changed from water to a soda for the extra energy.

"Tired?" Aiden asked her as she leaned on the bar and sipped her drink.

She turned slightly towards him. "So, now you're working dinners?" she asked. "Is there anything you can't do around here?"

His smile slipped. "Apparently I can't keep a relationship."

She tensed just as Elle stopped by. "Thanks for your help tonight," she said to Aiden. "Getting everything together for the wedding next week has us stretched thin. Dylan and Zoey still have so much they have to do to get ready for their big day. They'll have two whole weeks off." She glanced around the emptying dining hall. "I guess it's time we finally hired more help around here," she said with a sigh.

"Just say the word and I'm on it," Aubrey supplied. She'd already hired a few new counselors, as they called them—employees to help out with the events and their guests' needs during their stay.

"No, Brent will get on it, since we need more staff here than we do around the grounds. Opening up the dining to non-guests two nights a week has brought in a lot of money and demand for more workers." Elle leaned against the bar. "But it was a great idea." She smiled. "And guests don't seem to mind having dinner a little earlier on Fridays and Saturdays."

Aubrey shrugged and turned back to her drink. "Tired?" Elle asked her.

"Long day." She glanced towards Aiden who was still watching her.

"You look tired. Go on. We can handle it from here. Get some rest." Elle laid a hand on her arm, then turned to Aiden. "Why don't you walk her back? We're done with you too." Elle left without waiting for an answer. "Thanks for your help tonight, cuz," she called over her shoulder as she made her way up to the stage area.

"Think she knows something?" Aiden asked her, causing her to stiffen.

"What?" Her eyes moved to the back of her friend.

"Relax, I meant it as a joke." He sighed and took her arm. "Would it be so bad? I mean, we aren't even seeing one another anymore." He frowned down at her. "Technically, we were never really seeing each other." He shrugged.

"No," she said as they stepped out into the warm night air. "The only thing I miss about New York is the fall," she said, changing the topic. "Cool fall nights, the leaves turning colors."

"What leaves?" he joked. "You lived in the city."

She chuckled. "I used to run in the park all the time." She shrugged. "Still, I wouldn't trade this life for anything," she admitted.

"You seem off lately," he told her. He tugged on her arm until she stopped to look at him. "What has you down?"

She shook her head. "I'm not..." She stopped when his eyebrows shot up. Sighing, she rolled her eyes. He obviously knew her too well for her to get away with lying to him. "I guess it's the wedding. I feel like I'm losing a friend."

She walked over towards a railing area that overlooked the bay and leaned on it, looking out over the dark water. He moved to stand next to her.

"You know, I still don't have a date for the big event." He nudged her shoulder. "We could always go as friends?"

She glanced up at him and frowned. She'd thought about asking him several times but had put it off for fear of him getting the wrong impression.

"Friends?" she asked.

"Sure. Whatever else there is between us, I still think of you as my friend." He turned so that his back was facing the water and leaned his elbows on the railing as his eyes ran over her slowly. "We may have our differences as far as what we want, but we will always have a great past between us." He smiled, then leaned closer to her. "Nothing can take that away from us." His eyes moved to her lips. "Even if you no longer want it, it will always be there."

She felt her heart skip and sink at the same time. She was about to respond to him when he leaned back and smiled. "So? What do you say? Is it a date between friends?" He held out his hand for hers.

Taking a deep breath, she nodded and shook his hand. "Fine, it's a date."

CHAPTER 6

When the big day of Zoey and Dylan's wedding finally arrived, Aiden was stuffed into another uncomfortable suit. He was standing at the base of the stairs, waiting for Aubrey and her friends to meet him in the lobby area. He'd volunteered to pick up the group and drive them out to the beach area in one of the golf carts that had been decorated especially for the wedding.

He'd heard through the grapevine that the five friends had enjoyed a bachelorette party two nights ago when he'd been out with the guys in Destin at a local bar for Dylan's bachelor party. It hadn't been a wild party, mainly filled with food and beer, but he'd enjoyed getting to know the Costa men a little more.

He'd helped set up the folding chairs on the beach earlier that morning as well as a small arch Liam had made for the bride and groom to stand under during the ceremony.

It had been a few years since he'd attended a wedding. It had been the wedding of one of Danelle's friends, and the event had been full of people he didn't know. The entire day had been uncomfortable and strained. Shortly after, Danelle had left him, claiming she'd wanted to go a different direction.

He was better off for it. He could now say that, thanks to Aubrey.

He glanced up just as the five friends made their way down the stairs. He glanced quickly at Zoey's soft white off-the-shoulder wedding dress. They were carefully descending the stairs while Zoey's long wedding train was carried for her by the four friends.

"Easy," Elle said, shifting slightly.

"We're too early," Hannah broke in.

Just then, everyone noticed him standing at the base of the stairs.

"Oh god." Zoey glanced around nervously. "Where is Dylan?"

He chuckled. "I made sure he and his brothers were already out on the beach before coming to get you five." His eyes moved to Aubrey. She looked amazing in the flowing sky-blue dress. Material draped over her right shoulder, leaving her left one exposed.

Each of the bridesmaid dresses were unique in style and a different soft blue color, creating a rainbow of blue surrounding their friend.

"Ready?" he asked when they'd reached the bottom.

"Hang on." Zoey stopped them all, then tugged on her friends' hands until they made a circle. "I just wanted to take a moment to breathe." She took a deep breath then smiled. "No matter what path each of us takes in the next few months"—her eyes moved around to each of her friends as he stood outside the circle, watching— "we will always be sisters. We came to this camp alone and broken, each of us. But we left stronger because of this." She held up their joined hands. "Something that time couldn't take away from us nor could anyone else who tried to pull us apart."

His eyes moved to Aubrey, and he noticed her blue eyes tearing up.

"Don't make us cry," Elle warned.

"Shut up." Zoey smiled. "No crying on my wedding day. I'll finish up with this... We are and will always be Wildflowers through and through."

"Wildflowers," the rest of them said softly before hugging each other.

"Are you ready now?" he asked dryly, chuckling softly to show he was joking.

"Men." Aubrey rolled her eyes as she wiped a tear from her eyes.

"Yes." Zoey smiled up at him, then reached out and took his arm.

"Who's giving you away?" he asked as he helped her into the golf cart. Zoey and Scar's dad had passed away the year before, and he hadn't heard who would be walking her down the aisle. Only that he was to deliver the group to the entrance of the beach at exactly six o'clock.

He glanced at his watch and figured they had just enough time.

"I'll be walking myself down." Zoey smiled. "It's a modern age." She shifted and touched his arm. "Thanks for driving us."

He chuckled as they started down the path. "Hey, no skin off my back. Besides..." He glanced back at Aubrey and winked. "I get a sneak peek at you lovely flowers."

Zoey chuckled. "If I hadn't fallen head over heels for Dylan." She sighed and nudged him.

"Why don't you have a girlfriend?" Scarlett asked as he slowed down to turn on the correct pathway.

"Who says I don't?" he responded.

"Do you?" she retorted.

"That's for me to know and you to find out," he joked back.

"Did you at least bring a date?" Zoey asked.

"He's my date today," Aubrey spoke up. "What?" she said when all of her friend's eyes turned to her. "He mentioned to me the other night that he didn't have one, and we suggested going as friends." She shrugged and glanced off towards the beach as he stopped the cart.

"We're here," he said, turning to Zoey. "Go get 'em." He smiled at her.

He'd grown to like Zoey and the rest of the Wildflowers over the past few years. Even though Elle was his only cousin, he thought of the others, except for Aubrey, as family.

He helped Zoey out of the cart and stood back as her friends fixed her train. Then he rushed ahead of them through the clearing and nodded to Liam, who was waiting for his signal.

Watching the wedding procession from the sidelines, his eyes kept returning to Aubrey. What had it meant that she'd been the one to mention to her friends they were a date for the event?

For almost three years, she'd kept everything about them, about their relationship, a secret. He couldn't count how many times he'd wanted to tell someone, or better yet, show them, by pulling Aubrey into his arms and kissing her in front of her friends, but he'd promised her he'd keep it a secret. It had almost killed him doing so. Especially when she'd pulled away. So many times he'd wished he could talk to his cousin about her friend and ask her how he could win Aubrey back.

Now, she was the one breaking that barrier. He hoped it meant that she was ready and willing to open up to her friends about them and possibly take the next step in a real relationship with him. But something told him he would have to force her hand and take drastic measures himself to get her to take those steps.

When the ceremony was over, he helped shuttle the guests towards the dining hall. After everyone had shuffled into the main hall, he found Aubrey sitting in the front with her friends. He took the spot next to her, and she smiled over at him and offered him a glass of champagne.

"So?" he asked after a sip. "What's next?"

"Now we sit back and enjoy some food, then cake and dancing." She smiled over at him.

Her eyes told him that she understood he hadn't been talking about the wedding, but about them.

Setting down his glass, he took her hand in his. "You know what I mean," he said softly as he felt her stiffen slightly.

Her eyes moved away from his as she glanced around, no doubt to see who was watching them. "Now, we enjoy being friends," she said between sips.

"I think you know that's not possible." He leaned closer to her as his thumb played over her palm. He heard her breath catch and knew he'd made his point. There was too much between them to stop now, no matter how hard she tried to pull back. Just knowing that she felt the heat as well had him smiling and moving closer, emboldened by the desire flooding her eyes. "Why the games? Why can't we just..." His eyes moved to her gloss-covered lips and a slight groan escaped him when her tongue darted out to lick them. "Why can't we see what new things we can explore together?"

She didn't answer him at first. Her breathing labored as she thought, and he knew she was trying to come up with an excuse or a reason. When fear started to replace the desire in her eyes, he sighed and leaned back.

"Soon you'll confide in me why intimacy causes you to panic." He took up his glass and drank again, wishing for a beer instead of the sweet champagne.

"I would think that our past proves that I'm not afraid of intimacy," she said softly.

Chuckling, he glanced over at her. "I wasn't talking about sex."

She hissed and nudged him.

"Lower your voice," she said as she glanced around.

He chuckled again. "Afraid someone will find out about us?" He made a show of glancing around. The fact was, everyone around them was so enthralled in chatting that he doubted that a single person was paying attention to them. He knew he was pushing her too far, but he was tired of the games. He missed her and from the looks she had been giving him, she missed him as much.

"Aiden." Her voice was a warning.

"There you are." Hannah rushed over and grabbed up Aubrey. "Sorry, I need to borrow her for pictures," she said to him as she rushed her friend away.

"Saved you," Owen said to him as he sat beside him.

"Oh?" He pushed his champagne away and then smiled when Owen handed him a beer. "Yeah." He motioned with his beer toward the guy and then took a sip. "You did."

"Hannah saved Aubrey," Owen said, nodding to the two friends, who had disappeared out the back doors, no doubt to take pictures with their friends on the patio area.

"Yeah." He sighed.

"I didn't know you and Aubrey were..." Owen dropped off when Aiden glanced over at him. "Umm..." He cleared his throat.

Sinking back in the chair, he shrugged. "No one does. Aubrey's orders." He rolled his eyes.

"Shit." Owen sat up a little straighter. "You're serious? I was just shooting in the dark with that one. Do any of the other friends know?"

Aiden shook his head. He knew Owen Costa could keep secrets but figured that since Aubrey had made the first confession that he was free to let a few things slip out.

"Crap." Owen ran his hands through his longer hair. He shook his head. "You mean, I know something that the Wildflowers don't?"

Aiden chuckled. "What will you do with all that power?"

Owen frowned over at him. "No, you don't understand. I could be in serious trouble here." He glanced over at him.

"You're messing with me, right? I mean, you and Aubrey aren't really an item."

"We aren't anymore." He sighed and sipped his beer. "But if I had my way..." He dropped off and figured a change of topic would be beneficial. He glanced over at Owen. "So, have you and Hannah set a date yet for your big day?"

Owen's smile grew. "Yeah, we figured we'd do this ourselves in the spring. Liam and Elle have a December wedding planned."

"Spacing them out?" he joked.

"Not my idea. If it were up to me, we'd be right there today." He nodded to his brother and his new sister-in-law. "All three of us." He shrugged.

"Not a bad idea." Aiden thought about it.

"Course, that would be too practical." Owen shrugged.

"Could have saved a lot of money too," he added, causing Owen to chuckle.

"See, I knew there was a reason I liked you." He slapped him on the back. "You have a head for business." He sighed. "Speaking of which, how's the swimming pool and club house at Hammock Cove coming along?"

For a few minutes, he filled his boss in on their joint project before Aubrey and Hannah returned to get them for pictures.

He didn't know why he was dragged into the large group, but he stood beside Aubrey and itched to grab her as the photographer snapped pictures of the smiling bunch.

He sat and enjoyed the dinner that the famous chef Isaac Andrew and his team had prepared for the crowd. He chatted with friends while keeping as close to Aubrey as he could.

When the band started to play, he pulled Aubrey out on to the crowded dance floor. The moment her body glided across his, he hoped that the night would never end.

"Enjoying yourself?" he asked and, by the way she sighed as an answer, he knew she was more than a little drunk.

He'd enjoyed a few beers himself and knew that if he'd allow himself, he would be right there with her. Still, he knew she was drunk enough to not care who saw her rubbing her body up against his.

The music slowed and she plastered herself to his body, and he was thankful the lights had dimmed some time ago.

"Aiden." She sighed, "Why is it I can't stop thinking of you?" she said against his chest as she rested her cheek against his shoulder.

"The same reason I can't stop thinking of you either." He closed his eyes for a brief moment, wishing to hold onto the memory of how she felt against him, how her perfume filled his senses and had his loins aching for her.

"I told myself I wasn't going to do this." She glanced up at him briefly, then looked around. "I love my friends, but so help me, if they start getting ideas…"

"Why don't you believe you are due happiness?" he asked, then silently cursed himself when the music stopped, and the band explained that they were taking a fifteen-minute break.

Taking her hand, he pulled her towards the glass French doors and didn't stop walking until they stood on the narrow strip of secluded beach.

"Why?" he asked her after they stopped. "I've avoided asking you and you've avoided telling me. I think after everything we've been through together that I'm due a few answers."

CHAPTER 7

How could Aubrey explain her pain in such a powerful setting? The sun had gone down a few hours ago when Zoey and Dylan had been exchanging their vows. But with the soft sand between her toes, and the gentle sound of the water lapping at the shoreline, she had only to close her eyes to remember the beauty of the place.

She knew she owed Aiden an explanation. After all, over the past three years she'd grown closer to him than she had ever allowed herself to be to a man, even though she still thought of what they had as just physical.

She'd locked away her heart so long ago, she didn't think she knew what it felt like to love anyone other than her friends. And that was a different kind of love than she could ever feel towards a man.

"You know about my father?" she said, pulling her heels off and tossing them into the sand before moving over to sit on one of the swings that Liam had hung from a thick oak branch.

Aiden followed her into the underbrush of the trees and sat beside her on the swing.

"These are nice," he said to her. "I haven't gotten to enjoy them yet." He pushed off, sending them swaying in the breeze. "Go on. I know a little about your father. What you've told me, or I've heard over the years." He motioned to her.

It was officially the last day of summer, which in Florida meant very little, except that it would be cooling down in the evenings soon.

"Not even my sisters know everything." She sighed and rested her head back. He'd wrapped his arm behind her, so her head rested on his bicep. She remembered how wonderful it felt to be held by those strong arms.

Maybe it was all the champagne she'd had over the last few hours, but she no longer cared if anyone saw them together. She knew she could fend off her friends nagging if she had to. After all, the five of them were like sisters. It wasn't as if she hadn't been nagged before this. She had just hoped to keep this part of her life a secret.

"I was eight when I went to live with my father. My mother had... died a day before I was uprooted." She closed her eyes on the pain that always came when she thought about the woman who loved her so much that she would have given anything to be with her.

"How did she die?" he asked.

In the past, she'd skirted around this question. Even her friends didn't know. She'd told them that Nora Murphy had died of a broken heart. She knew they'd assumed she'd died of heart failure or something close to that.

"When she found out that the courts were about to award full custody of me to Harold"—she glanced over at him and held her breath for a split second—"she slit her own wrists." She sighed. This was the first time in Aubrey's entire life that she'd said it out loud. Tears burned behind her eyes, and she had to shut them quickly.

"I'm so sorry." Aiden moved closer and wrapped his arms

around her. She held onto him for a moment, enjoying the safety and warmth he provided.

"Less than a year earlier, my mother had hunted Harold down. She'd claimed that she'd fallen for him when she'd worked for a private airline company. She'd been hired to steward one of his private jet flights and, well, she had always told me that she'd fallen in love with him the moment he walked onto the plane." She sighed, then shook her head. "I was eight. Everything was so… romanticized back then. So, when she got fired from another job, she decided to find him and ask him for help with his child." She glanced over at him. "There were blood tests, court appearances, and social service meetings for several months before it was agreed that I would move in with Harold."

"You must have been crushed," he said softly.

"I was leaving behind everything I'd ever known. Moving out of the love-filled one-room apartment above a gas station to a ten-thousand-square-foot mansion with a father who couldn't be bothered to see his daughter but once or twice a week."

"I'm so sorry," he repeated.

"The worse of it was, shortly after I arrived, I realized just how cruel Harold Smith could be. He started controlling every detail of my life. My clothes, my activities, school, my diet, exercise, every detail was planned out and charted." She stood up suddenly, wrapping her arms around herself as she moved closer to the water's edge. Knowing Aiden would follow her, she didn't even glance back.

"There was punishment when I didn't fall into line." She hugged herself tighter.

"Did he…"

She glanced over and stopped him. "Harold Smith would never stoop as low as to hit anyone," she said stiffly. "His punishments were more… mental." She glanced out at the water. "Things I enjoyed were taken from me. People I grew close to… disappeared."

"Disappeared?"

"I had stumbled into the kitchens one night. After I'd disappointed him with a B in social studies, I'd been sent up to bed without dinner. No biggie, except I'd also had five hours of dance class that day and had only eaten an apple for lunch. Naturally, by midnight, I was starved. I tiptoed down to the kitchen and ran into Luis, my father's private chef. Instead of tattling on me, Luis consoled me and made me a sandwich." She smiled. "Over the next year, he became my first friend in the house. I often snuck down to the kitchen after dark to spend time watching television or enjoying snacks with him." She sighed.

"What happened?" he asked.

She shrugged. "Harold found out. Luis's work visa was cancelled, and he was shipped back to a country he hadn't been to in over fifteen years." She closed her eyes on the new rush of pain. "Less than a month later, a newspaper was left on my breakfast plate." She turned to Aiden as tears rolled down her checks. "The article talked about a chef that had been kidnapped and forced to mule drugs for the cartel. When he'd refused, they'd beheaded him and hung him from a bridge."

"That's terrible." He moved closer to her.

"I was ten." She shook her head as she dashed the tears away. "Suddenly, I knew what kind of man my father was. I knew I couldn't cross him. So I fell into line. For the next few years, I did everything he wanted. I became his perfect protégé. Until one summer, when I was dropped off... here." She glanced around. "I felt so abandoned, so alone, until I bumped into Zoey, Elle, Hannah, and Scarlett." She smiled and her tears dried in the evening breeze. "From that summer on, I made sure to never let on how much this place meant to me, how much my sisters meant to me, for fear that Harold would take them away as well. I complained about having to go to the camp. I even had Joe call and tell Miss Ellison about a new program for older girls, when I had officially outgrown being a camper the summer before, so that I could come here and be a counselor instead." She smiled, then it slipped slightly. "Harold never knew how much this place meant to me until I came back here." She turned back to him. "For the past three years, he's been trying different methods to tear this place down."

"He has?" Aiden tensed. "Why haven't you—"

"He's failed. Of course. Still, I fear that one day he'll find the right buttons to push to close this place for good and take my Wildflowers, my sisters, away from me."

He walked over and wrapped his arms around her. "Is that why you won't allow us, what we have, to move beyond sex?"

She shook her head. "No. Part of it, maybe, but... no." She nudged him back. The champagne buzz had worn off slightly, and she was back to having a level head. "This"—she motioned between them—"can't happen because of so much more. If you knew everything, really, you'd understand."

"Then tell me everything." He reached for her hands, but she pulled them away.

"No." She shook her head and locked her heart away again. "Sex is all I have to give," she said softly. "Nothing more." She turned away from him and walked over to pick up her shoes. "The band has started playing again," she said into the darkness. "We'd better head back before we're missed."

"Aub," he said when they reached the pathway and she'd bent over to slip on her heels again. "You may not want to hear it, but I don't plan on going anywhere. I'm here, waiting, until you're ready to open up to me all the way. You can't scare me off." He turned her until they were eye to eye. "Harold Smith can't scare me away." When he bent down and placed his lips over hers, she felt a shiver race through her. How many times had he kissed her before? So many she couldn't keep count. This kiss, however, was different. It was new. Somehow, the soft kiss seared her soul, made her heart ache for something she knew was impossible.

When her eyes stung again, she turned away from him and started walking towards the music again.

He easily caught up with her and took her hand in his. "See," he said cheerfully, "this is nice too."

She tried to avoid him for the rest of the night, but Aiden was stubborn and kept finding her and dragging her to the dance floor to sway with him. Since she'd been given more champagne, she went along with it and couldn't stop herself from melting or vibrating in his arms.

He even walked her back to the apartment like a real date would have. She kept telling herself not to let him in, since she knew how it went. The moment she let down her guard, her protection surrounding her emotions, he would win her over again and she'd find herself falling head over heels for the man, something she'd told herself she would never do for anyone.

Which is why she'd pulled back from him months ago. When he'd mentioned the word love, fear had consumed her, and she'd run as if the devil himself was on her heels.

Just remembering that had her blocking him from entering her apartment.

They had sent off Dylan and Zoey in the white limo less than half an hour ago. Dylan had surprised Zoey with a trip to Bora Bora for their honeymoon. An entire week in a private cabana on the water sounded so romantic that Aubrey almost wished she could find happiness herself.

"You aren't going to at least let your date kiss you goodnight?" he asked with a smile. Damn him. Why did he have to have a sexy Rhett Butler kind of smile? All those pearly white teeth, that firm jaw line, that mouth that she knew all too well what he could do with.

"No," she said suddenly as she shook her head, blocking those thoughts. Everything spun with the slight motion, and she held onto the door. Damn all that champagne. "Thank you," she managed to say with a smile. She was so relaxed now that she hoped she would be able to make it to her bedroom and change out of the dress and heels before falling on her bed.

"Aubrey." Aiden's deep voice stopped her. "It's just a kiss," he said with another smile that had her knees going weak.

"Fine." She waved her hands. She expected a quick peck on the lips, but his hand slid slowly around her waist. Then he pulled her closer until their bodies bumped together. Her breath hitched at the feeling of his hard body as more memories of what it felt like to explore, to enjoy, that same body had hers reacting.

When his lips finally brushed across hers, she was thankful he was almost holding her upright. Somehow, her fingers had tangled in his hair as she kept him captive.

"More?" he asked against her lips.

"Hm," was her only response as she ran her tongue over his lips.

"My god." The exclamation caused them to jump apart.

She'd removed her heels hours ago and had, before the kiss, been holding them. Now they were at her feet and she tripped over them as she tried to move away from Aiden. Thankfully, Aiden's hands remained on her hips, keeping her upright.

"I can explain," Aubrey said to Elle, who was standing at the base of the stairs, smiling up at them.

"Something tells me that's not the first time the two of you have done that," Elle said as she started up the stairs towards them.

"I can explain," Aubrey said again, causing Aiden to chuckle.

Elle stopped in front of them. "Hey, cousin." Aubrey watched her friend wiggle her perfectly manicured eyebrows at Aiden.

"Hey." Aiden chuckled.

"So?" Elle asked him. "Am I right?"

"Don't," Aubrey warned, but it was too late.

"It's not," Aiden replied.

"So, how long has this been going on?" Again, Elle asked her cousin instead of Aubrey.

"Elle," Aubrey started, but her friend's narrow gaze flew to her and Aubrey shut her mouth.

Aiden glanced over at her before shrugging. "A while."

Elle turned to Aubrey. "Confession time?"

Aubrey wanted nothing more than to slink away and pass out, but she knew her friend all too well. There would be no rest until she had the full story.

"What are you doing here anyway?" Aubrey asked, changing the subject.

Elle laughed. "It won't work. I forgot my bag of things when I changed up here earlier. Now..." She motioned to the pair of them. "How long?"

"Three years," Aubrey mumbled.

"Excuse me?" Elle gasped. "Did you just say..."

Aubrey grabbed her friend's arm and rushed her into the apartment. Aiden followed them inside.

Elle had changed out of her bridesmaid dress and was wearing cotton pants and a flowing tank top. How had she changed so fast? Had Aubrey and Aiden been some of the last to leave the party?

"Three years?" Elle repeated.

"Close to it." Aiden shrugged, then pointed towards Aubrey. "Her idea, not mine."

"Thanks for that," Aubrey hissed.

"What?" Aiden chuckled. "It's true."

"Why?" Elle moved over and sat on the sofa. "Why did you hide it from us? We're your family."

"Not that I don't love you four, but let's face facts. If you'd known about"—she waved between her and Aiden, unable to put a title to what they had other than sex-friends—"you would have assumed there was more than there is."

"Three years," Elle repeated slowly. "There has to be something more after three years..."

"No," Aubrey answered quickly, then glared at Aiden, challenging him to defy her.

Thankfully, he remained quiet. Still, the look in his eyes told her it was killing him to not say anything.

"Three years," Elle repeated as she shook her head. "I'm not buying it."

"See." Aubrey threw her hands in the air as she started pacing the floor, now fully sober and wide awake. "This is what I was afraid of." She sighed and turned back to Elle. "Honest, we're just..." She cringed inwardly, but held her ground. "Sex-friends. A means to mutual release."

Elle glanced over at Aiden and frowned back at her when he didn't even so much as blink in response.

"Fine." Elle sighed. "I'll leave whatever this is between the two of you." She stood up and then walked over to grab up her bag. Throwing it over her shoulder, she walked over and hugged Aubrey. Instantly, Aubrey relaxed.

"It's your secret. I'll keep it if you want," she said softly into her ear. "You'll always be my sister, but..." She pulled back and noticed Elle's slight frown. "Please don't break my cousin."

"I won't. It's just sex," she added quickly. "I think after tonight, the others already know."

Elle sighed again then left the apartment.

"So," Aiden said from behind her, "if this is just sex, why haven't we had any for more than six months?"

CHAPTER 8

Aiden could no longer hide the hurt. Now that they were alone again, he watched Aubrey closely. He'd hidden his pain and feelings from his cousin since he didn't want her pity. Nor did he want the entire story to get back to the rest of her friends or the camp.

"That's because you were trying to turn it into something else," Aubrey said, crossing her arms over her chest.

"Was I?" he asked softly, suddenly feeling too tired to debate the facts.

"You know you were." She started pacing again.

"I remember just saying I loved the feeling of being inside you." He moved closer. "Which I do. Along with loving the way your body fits against mine, the taste of your lips, the smell of your sex when you come for me." He moved even closer to her. She'd made him so hard earlier that he'd spent the entire evening readjusting his suit pants.

"Aiden." Her voice was just shy of a moan.

"I think it's the word love"—she winced when he said it—"that you have an aversion to." He reached out and brushed a finger down her arm and watched her eyes go foggy again.

"Don't you love the feeling of me touching you?" he asked as his fingers continued to slide over her soft skin.

"Hm," she said then shook her head quickly and tried to pull away.

"I can stop if you want," he said, trying a new tactic as he pulled his hand all the way away from her. When she swayed slightly towards him, he smiled and lifted his hand once more. This time, he brushed it over her dress, across her nipples, and watched as they puckered through the thin material for him. "Parts of you love my touch," he said with a smile. "I bet there are lots of ways your body loves to respond to mine."

She sighed and swayed again as his hand moved lower until he brushed a hand over her thigh. When she slid her legs apart slightly so that he could cup her through her dress, he chuckled. "Don't you love being touched?" He continued to use the word that she hated so much, hoping, knowing, she would someday get used to it. "What if I did this." He slid up the material until his palm ran over her bare skin. She arched and grabbed hold of his shoulders to steady herself. "Don't you love the feeling of skin on skin?" He traced her neck with his mouth. "Love me kissing you?" His hands moved up to cup her outside of her underwear. "Love being touched?" He shifted slightly so he could pull the slight material away from her. "I bet you're going to love me sliding my fingers into you." He nudged the material further away from the goal. But instead of touching her, instead of doing what he'd just told her he would, he pulled back completely, leaving Aubrey standing in the middle of the room swaying as she looked at him with confusion.

"When you decide that we can use whatever word we want to describe what's between us, you know where to find me." He desperately wanted to kiss her, to sweep her up into his arms and haul her to her bed and do what he'd been dreaming of to her for the past six months, but he knew he had to make this stand if they were going to go anywhere beyond just sex-friends.

Walking out of her apartment was the hardest thing he'd had to do in his entire life. He knew it was the right thing. If he was going to prove to her that there was more between them, then he had to remove sex from the focus. He needed to prove to her that she wanted him in all the other ways. Which meant sex was going to have to be off the table altogether.

He believed that was the only course he could take to convince Aubrey to take a chance with him on a more personal level.

He'd expected her to suffer, but the following week, he was the one who had grown more frustrated. Aubrey had kept busy with her friends, filling in for Zoey while she was off for her honeymoon.

He had only bumped into her a handful of times, but each time, he'd grown more sexually frustrated. He'd teased her, flirted with her, and didn't give a shit who had watched or known about it.

He could tell she was pissed about it, but then again, he was pretty sure the rest of the Wildflowers knew already. Especially since, the morning after the wedding, Scarlett had saved him a spot next to Aubrey at breakfast and lunch.

Even Liam had mentioned his excitement about him and Aubrey. His assumptions were confirmed almost a full week after the wedding when Owen stopped him at the jobsite over at Hammock Cove. The crew was just finishing up pouring the pool deck when Owen drove up in his new truck.

"Hey, I was just about to call you," Aiden told Owen.

"Saved you a call then." Owen shut the door of his truck. "I was coming out here to see how things are going. Looks like they'll be done early?"

Aiden sighed. "If we can get the rest of the permits on time, we should be on time. Yeah."

"So." Owen glanced around, looking slightly uncomfortable. "Hannah and I were talking wedding and, well, she mentioned something about you and Aubrey being an item. Honest, she didn't hear it from me. Anyway, Hannah wanted to know if you two would be a joint invitation."

He chuckled. "If I can swing it, yes."

Owen's eyebrows shot up. "Problems? I thought you two had just gotten started." He moved aside for a group of contractors.

Aiden leaned against his own truck and crossed his arms over his chest. "Going on three years."

"What?" Owen glanced over at him. "Seriously?"

"It started shortly after we began rebuilding the camp. Aubrey only wanted it to be… physical."

"Now?" Owen asked.

"I've never met a woman more afraid of the L word in my life." He sighed.

"Isn't that usually the man's problem?" Owen joked.

"Oh? You have that problem?" he asked him.

Owen laughed. "For a while, yeah. But then I realized how stupid I was being and… well, you know the rest."

"As far as I can tell, the two of you are stupid happy together," he added with a chuckle.

"We are." Owen's smile grew. "Wedding fever has struck, especially after last week." He motioned to the clubhouse, which was almost finished. "Now we're thinking of adding our own new place to the grounds."

"The nice thing about Hammock Cove is its location," Aiden added with a shrug. "I've been debating snagging a lot for myself. Building a home of my own as well."

Owen slapped him on the shoulder. "Say the word and any lot is yours." He leaned closer to him. "I have an in with the developer."

That evening, he ran into Aubrey and knew that the rest of

her friends were starting to be an issue with her. When he tried to wrap his arms around her, she pushed him away.

"Do you have to keep doing that?" she asked him. "Now everyone knows about us. And we aren't even an item anymore."

"Aren't we?" he said, pulling her even closer. He smiled when she relaxed into his arms. "Normal couples date before… moving on. Just because we're moving backward doesn't mean this isn't still us together."

"We are not moving backward." She tensed again. "Away. We're moving away."

He chuckled and nodded to her hand on his arm. The fact that she was holding him close and not pushing him away made his point.

She dropped her hand instantly. "I'm beginning to let my guard down around you." She groaned and stepped back. He let her go, since they were once again heading in the same direction.

The fact that he still had a tool belt strapped to his hips and worn work boots on while she was draped in silk and wore heels was just another barrier he knew had to be broken.

He'd come a long way in the past three years, from starting his own business with just three crew under him to working with more than two dozen crewmen on two major projects. He'd been excited knowing that he could financially afford a place in Hammock Cove. It made it more possible to have a future with Aubrey, if she'd have him.

"Our little secret is out in the open now." He changed tactics.

"It was bound to get out sooner or later." She sighed. "I should've prepared for this. I guess you could say I've always hated being a planner." She shrugged.

He'd known that she was a fly-by-the-seat person from the moment he'd met her. She could easily be convinced to drop everything at the drop of a hat. That was one of the things he liked so much about her.

Even though she looked and acted high society, she could easily have an impromptu swim at the beach or a hike through the woods before stepping into a ballroom dressed in expensive silk and hobnobbing with the rich and famous.

"Does it bother you?" he asked her. "That your friends know?"

She shifted slightly as if thinking and then shook her head. "I guess I've gotten over it. I mean, for the past three years or so I've been living in fear. I guess you can say it's like a weight that's been lifted."

He nodded. "Okay, so we're out in the open. What next?"

"Does there have to be anything?" she asked. "I mean, we've agreed that—"

"We never agreed. You broke things off. I had no choice in the matter." Now he was pacing. He was still hot and sticky from crawling under one of the older cabins where the plumbing had busted. He needed a shower and his bed. Instead, he was looking at least another hour thanks to the sink in the guest bathroom of the main building.

The buildings around the campground were old. Very old. He'd done what he could to get them up and running three years ago, but now a lot of the old pipes needed work. He hated to bring the troubles to Elle and her gang since they were busy planning weddings.

"No, I supposed you never agreed." She sighed and glanced off towards the dining hall when music started playing in the distance. "I have..." She motioned towards the building.

"Yeah, me too." He nodded and felt defeated once more. What would it take to get through to her? "How about we meet up later to finish this?"

She instantly started to shake her head, but then stopped.

"The beach? Eleven o'clock." She moved back towards the building.

He thought about how tired he was but then realized he didn't care about sleep and nodded quickly. "See you there."

While he worked on the sink, he heard the roaring party going on next door. When he was done replacing the faulty faucet, he poked his head in the door and watched for a few minutes as Aubrey and her friends moved around the guests as if they were born for their jobs.

Did she know that even though she was trying to avoid the L word, it filled every part of her day?

She loved her friends, the camp, and her job, and he knew it was only a matter of time before she owned up to the fact that she loved him.

Why else would she have kept him around all this time? He'd known for a while now that he'd fallen hard for her. It was obvious months after they'd started their strange relationship.

Of course, he'd tried to deny it since he'd been burned before. But shortly after the camp had opened its doors, he'd owned up to his feelings. At least to himself, since he knew how Aubrey would react. Which is why he'd made a point to keep the L word out of his life as much as possible.

He headed back to his place, showered, and changed into some fresh clothes. He cooked himself dinner for once and watched a few minutes of the game before falling fast asleep on the sofa.

His phone ringing woke him hours later. He was so groggy he didn't know where he was for a moment.

"Yeah?" he answered, then cursed himself as realization dawned on him. It was a quarter past eleven. Jumping up, he tripped over his shoes and cursed.

"Forget something?" Aubrey's sexy chuckle stopped him.

"I fell asleep." He sighed. "I guess it was a longer day than I thought."

"No problem. Why don't you open the door and let me in. We can have that talk inside."

He rushed to the door and yanked it open. Aubrey stood outside, holding an umbrella. "It wouldn't have worked anyway. The rain started about half an hour ago." She shook the umbrella off and laughed as she stepped inside.

She'd changed clothes as well. Now she wore jeans and a blue T-shirt. Her long red hair was twisted in an intricate braid and was still wet from either the rain or a shower.

She looked just as lovely as she had in silk and lace.

"You got a new sofa," she said, moving into the living area.

"Yeah, finally." He switched off the television, tossing the remote down and turning back towards her. "Hungry?"

She shook her head and watched him. "I'm not afraid, you know."

"Oh?" he asked, rubbing his hands over his face. "Drink?" He moved into the kitchen and grabbed a beer.

"Sure, I'll have one of those." She motioned to him and sat on his new sofa. He handed her the beer and sat beside her to take a sip of his own.

"You aren't?" he asked her, picking up the conversation. It was something they did, something he'd missed about her being around all the time.

"No." She sighed after taking a sip of the beer. "It's not fear that keeps me backing away."

"If it's not fear…" He left the question hang in the air.

"I'm not afraid. I'm avoiding it on purpose," she admitted.

"Okay. Because of your past?" he asked. "Your father?"

"Yes, it's not for me." She leaned back.

"What isn't?"

She glanced sideways at him. "Love."

He surprised her by laughing.

CHAPTER 9

She felt her frustration levels spike hearing his laughter.

"What?" she asked, but he was still laughing at her. Setting down the beer, she crossed her arms over her chest and frowned and waited for his laughter to die down.

"That has to be the funniest thing you've ever said to me." He smiled over at her.

"You think it's funny?"

"Yes," he answered with a grin. "Love is for everyone."

He'd started using the word in almost every sentence, which of course was annoying the hell out of her even further.

"No, it isn't," she said between gritted teeth.

"Yes." He reached up and touched her arm softly. "It is. There isn't a magical pattern to stop a person from obtaining it. You love your friends, right?"

"Of course," she almost gasped.

"Then, love is for you." He motioned with his beer before taking another sip.

"That's different." She stood up and started walking around his small living space. She'd been in the two-bedroom trailer in the past three years almost as much as she'd been in her own room in the apartment. "Friendship is not romantic."

"So, it is actually romance that you're afraid of then?" His eyes narrowed slightly.

"No. Yes." She threw her hands up. "The forever-after kind of stuff is not for me." She waved towards him. "I've never wanted it. I've never searched for it. I don't deserve it."

He frowned and set his beer bottle down slowly before standing up and walking over to take her shoulders in his hands. "What makes you say that?"

"It can only bring problems." She kept her eyes focused on the middle of his chest. Just being this close to him did things to her. Still. Even after being with him for the past three years, he still had the ability to turn her knees to jelly. One more reason for her to push him away.

She couldn't chance letting any man have that much control over her.

"Because you fear your father?" he asked softly.

Closing her eyes, she nodded. He lifted her chin up until she opened her eyes and met his. They were filled with worry and kindness. In all of her years, she had never met another man like Aiden. He'd given her everything she'd wanted and had met each of her demands, both physical and emotional. But then he'd started pushing her further, needing something she knew that she wouldn't give him. Couldn't give him.

"I told you, I'm not afraid of him." He smiled down at her.

"You should be," she said with a sigh. "I'd better…" She glanced towards the door. "I have an early morning class."

He dropped his hands, and she missed his touch instantly. God, she was a fool.

"I'll drive you back. It's still raining," he said quickly when she opened her mouth to argue with him.

"Fine," she said after thinking about walking back to the main building in the rain and the darkness.

She rode in his truck in silence, watching the rain hit the windshield.

"When are your next days off?" he asked her as he turned into the main parking lot.

She thought about it. "We're all working double until Zoey and Dylan come back. Normally I'd have tomorrow off, but now..."

"Are you working dinners?"

"Yes, until Thursday night. I have that one off."

"Dinner then?" he asked her as he put the truck into park. "As in a date," he clarified.

"No—"

He stopped her by putting his hand on her arm again. "You wanted to know what was next. For me, it's going out on a real date with you. I think I'm owed it," he said softly.

She sighed and tried to find any excuse, any reason to deny him. Then it hit her. In the three years they'd been together, he hadn't denied her once. Not when she'd wanted to keep their relationship a secret from her friends. Not when she'd come to him after breaking things off and needed one more romp.

"Okay," she finally answered him. "Thursday." She reached for the door handle, but he stopped her by pulling her closer.

"Good, now that that is settled." His eyes moved to her lips, and she had a temporary lapse in her strength to deny him as his mouth covered hers in a soft kiss.

She melted against him. God, she'd missed this. Missed being in his arms. Missed feeling his mouth move over hers. When she felt her entire body shake with want, she placed her hand on his chest and nudged him back. He leaned back easily and dropped his hold of her.

Yet another thing he willingly gave her.

"I'll see you on Thursday." She jumped out of the truck before she had second thoughts. She'd forgotten her umbrella at his place, which left her rushing through the drizzle towards the building.

Rushing into the front lobby, she hugged herself as she walked up the stairs and let herself into her apartment. The place was empty and dark, making her miss the times when it had been filled with the five best friends. Sure, it had been crowded, noisy, and there had been no privacy, but it had felt like home. Now, it just felt... lonely.

She peeled off her wet jacket and hung it by the door. Then she toed off her hiking boots and placed them in the shoe rack Liam had built.

Making her way back to her room, she decided that a hot bath would help ward off the chill and loneliness. She was soaking in the tub, totally relaxed, when her phone buzzed, shaking her from her thoughts. Seeing her father's number on the screen, she thought about ignoring his call, but then sighed and answered. After all, it was past midnight. Maybe something was wrong?

"Hello?" She shifted in the water so she wouldn't drop the phone.

"I'm throwing a party on the tenth and require your attendance," her father said.

Her father had never been one for pleasantries. Or for kind words.

"I'm sorry." She held in a sigh. "I won't be going back to New York then."

She'd made herself clear several times now, each time he'd called to request her presence or demand she stop the foolishness of not giving him what he demanded.

"It's not negotiable. This party means a lot—"

"Harold, why can't you understand it? It wasn't just *your* obligation that ended on my eighteenth birthday," she interrupted. "I won't be coming back. There is nothing left in the city for me. I have my life here. My business, which needs me. I can't simply take off every time you demand it."

"This is your final answer?" he asked her.

"It is." She relaxed slightly. It had taken her years to learn how to deal with the man. Pushing him away and keeping him always at least an arm's length away was the only way to handle him.

"Fine." When he hung up, she tossed her phone down and dunked her head under the water and screamed in frustration.

She tried to forget her father's call over the next few days. Staying busy was easy since she had more classes to fill her time. Each day started well before sunup and ended close to midnight. She ached in places she'd never ached before.

She was actually looking forward to having an evening off. The fact that she'd be spending it with Aiden was the only issue she could foresee.

So much of her life had been kept from her friends. It wasn't as if in the past few months, she'd tried to hide anything further from them. It was more like they'd each been so busy with their own private lives during their off hours.

The camp was doing better than the five friends had ever expected. They were booked solid for the next six or so months. With each new cabin finished, more guests signed up until they had to push reservations back. If they had a dozen more cabins, they could fill them.

River Camps was now more successful than any of them could have ever imagined. They had opened up the dining hall for dinners two nights a week so that even the locals could enjoy Isaac's meals. They usually packed out on those evenings and were thinking about starting to take reservations.

Which had her wondering where Aiden was going to take her on their date. It wasn't as if there were a lot of choices in town, but Destin was only fifteen minutes away and had many restaurant choices.

How long had it been since she'd been out on a date? She'd tried dating a few times in school, but each time Harold had interfered, and she'd been left to pick up the pieces of her young heart. How could she explain to Aiden any of that? He wouldn't be able to understand her pain or her fears.

Since she'd met him, he hadn't feared anything really. She knew that his business could be fragile, just as hers was. All it took was the wrong sort of people speaking out and the phones would stop ringing and the money would stop coming in. Could he survive that? Would he want to?

She didn't want to give him a chance to decide. She couldn't afford to.

"What are the chances of you helping out tonight?" Elle asked her during lunch. "I know it's your night off…"

"Can't," she said between bites. Looking around the room of friends, she swallowed and figured there was no use hiding it any longer since it was common knowledge that they'd been together. Even if the relationship didn't go any further, she at least wanted a chance to explore it. For his sake. Who knew, maybe once they started dating, they'd figure out they didn't have anything really in common. "I've got a date."

Everyone sitting around the table stopped and stared at her. "A date?" Elle asked.

"Aiden?" Scarlett asked.

"Of course." Aubrey rolled her eyes. "Who else would it be with?"

"I can't believe you kept that from us all this time," Hannah said.

"I can't believe you didn't tell everyone you were a virgin before Owen," Aubrey countered.

Hannah sighed. "Fine, I guess we're all entitled to our own little secrets."

Aubrey smiled. "I promise, this is one of the last I've been keeping from you."

"One of the last?" Elle asked. "Meaning there are others."

Aubrey laughed. "That's for me to know." She finished her sandwich and stood up. "But not now. Now I have to show a bunch of people how to kick butt." She tossed her trash into the can and left her friends.

Being a black belt in both tai chi and judo had its perks. The movements were like second nature to her now. She didn't even have to think as she moved around the mats. Today there were only four others in her class, which meant she got plenty of time to show them the basics firsthand. She helped them get into each position correctly and even showed them a few fun theatrical flips and tosses for show. Actually, she'd gotten the hint that most of the people who signed up for her classes did so just to see what she could do. Word of mouth had passed around the camp about her skills. She'd even created a few online videos for fun one night and had more than a hundred thousand views. Thankfully, she'd remembered to mention the campgrounds in it. She'd like to think that she had done her part to bring more customers to River Camps.

After her last class of the day, she decided she had time for a quick swim before heading back to shower and dress for her date. Stripping off her sweaty clothes, she showered off quickly at the outdoor shower area before jumping into the cool water. On her fourth lap, she noticed Aiden standing along the edge of the pool.

Damn, he looked so sexy in his work clothes, which entailed worn jeans, work boots, and a T-shirt that stretched over his muscles.

When she stopped at the edge of the water and looked up at him, he knelt closer and smiled down at her.

"Cooling off?" he asked her, his eyes running over her and causing her to heat again.

"Working here does have its perks." She laughed and moved over to sit on the long underwater bench less than a foot away.

"I was on my way to talk to Elle about the new cabins." He glanced up towards the main building.

"I'm sure she's in her office." She relaxed back.

"Now all I want to do is join you in there." He sighed.

She glanced up at him again and noticed that he was sweaty and covered in a layer of sawdust.

"Why don't you? You can meet with Elle later." She motioned towards the water.

He glanced back down at her and shook his head. "Work first, play later," he said with almost a groan.

"Okay, go meet Elle, then come back. We have time." She glanced at the clock that hung over the bar area.

"That I could do." He nodded. "Half an hour. Tops," he promised and stood up. She watched him disappear.

"You're one lucky woman," an older guest said from a few feet away from her in the water.

Aubrey glanced to where Aiden had just disappeared. "Yes, I sure am." She thought about their relationship for the next half hour while she waited for him. She watched guests come and go and ordered a cocktail for herself to enjoy by the pool.

She had just jumped in the water again when Aiden rushed back, tossed his backpack down by her things, and jumped in beside her.

"Awwww," he sighed just before he sank below the water. "God, I needed just a few minutes of downtime," he said after surfacing and pulling her close. She tensed slightly and glanced around. It was a hard habit to break, being concerned about who saw them together. Instantly, she convinced her body to relax into his arms. After all, everyone who mattered already knew about them. "I've got one more meeting before I can head home, shower, then come back and get you tonight."

"I could—"

"No." He shook his head. "Don't reschedule on me," he warned.

She shook her head. "No, I was going to suggest that I meet you at your place to save time."

"No." He smiled at her. "I'll pick you up. Let's do things the proper way. I'll pick you up, drive, pay for the meal"—he leaned closer and lowered his voice— "and kiss you goodnight on your doorstep."

She chuckled but held onto him as he kicked them towards the deeper end of the pool.

"Ten minutes," he warned before kissing her.

Almost exactly ten minutes later, his phone rang, causing him to jump from the water and answer it. His eyes moved over her while he talked on the phone as she walked out of the pool and sat in a lounge chair.

"I've got to go." He stood over her, pulling on his shirt.

"Go." She waved him away playfully. "I'm going to nap for half an hour then head up myself."

Instead of going, Aiden sat beside her and reached out to run a finger up the outside of her thigh. "I'm looking forward to tonight," he said softly. Just the sound of his voice had her melting.

"I am as well," she agreed. She melted further when he leaned in and laid his lips gently over hers.

"Until then," he said softly before leaving her to relax in the sun. The only problem was, that kiss had done so much to her that she no longer was tired or relaxed. She was too wound up to lie back.

Pulling out her phone, she figured she would entertain herself with social media and the news for a while. It had been so long since she'd had time to just browse online. Half the time, she forgot her phone could even do anything other than remind her which classes she was supposed to be teaching or what events were coming up.

She had spent less than five minutes scrolling through her emails before seeing one from Terry. Over the years she'd heard from him a handful of times. Each time she'd block his email, but he always seemed to surface. She knew that after that day, long ago, Terry had been fired from the company. It was a little shocking to see his name in her inbox again, but she figured she'd laugh at his next attempt. Instead, the simple image of an old article shocked her to the core.

It was image of her, back when she was eight-year-old. She was clutching the small bag with nothing more than a pair of Cinderella pajamas and a stuffed dog that was missing one of its eyes, which her mother had given her on her first birthday.

"Billionaire Harold Smith wins custody of his daughter, shortly after the girl's mother, Nora Murphy, committed suicide. Murphy, an exotic dancer at the time, was found dead from suicide with ten pounds of cocaine on her person. The suspected drug use had sparked the legal battle over the child in the first place."

Aubrey sat up and shielded her eyes. Ten pounds of coke? She frowned down at the screen. That wasn't right.

CHAPTER 10

*A*iden knocked on Aubrey's door at exactly seven o'clock that evening. He was sore, tired, and starving. But most importantly, he couldn't wait to see Aubrey again.

When she opened the door, he frowned down at her red eyes and the fact that she was still wearing shorts and a tank top over the swimsuit she'd been wearing hours before at the pool.

"Is everything okay?" he asked, rushing to her side.

"I think my father had my mother killed," she said and threw herself into his arms.

"What?" He tensed but held onto her.

She leaned back and motioned to a laptop sitting on the coffee table. "He killed her," she said, wiping her eyes.

He dropped his hold on her and moved over to the computer. There on the screen was an old article about a woman named Nora Murphy.

"My mother," she supplied as he sat down at the laptop. He glanced down at the grainy black-and-white photo of a woman. Instantly, he was shocked at the similarity between mother and daughter. All except the eyes. He could tell instantly that her mother had brown eyes instead of Aubrey's haunting crystal blue ones.

He scanned the article quickly, which stated that her mother had committed suicide. It went on to claim that, because of all the drugs the police had found with her, they had assumed she was the leader of a local drug ring that had been haunting the area for over a year. They didn't suspect foul play.

"What makes you think your father had your mother killed? The article—"

"We'd only just moved into that apartment," she broke in. "Before that, we'd lived across the state at my grandmother's place. After she died, we had to move. My mother didn't know anyone in town yet. She was out looking for jobs each day, sometimes taking me along..." She shook her head. "I'd have to wait in the car, since she was trying to get jobs at bars, but... she didn't do drugs, let alone sell them. We barely had enough money to buy lunch, let alone all that coke." She took a deep breath. "How would she have gotten it?" She closed her eyes and a tear slipped down her cheek.

He picked up her hand and then pulled her into his arms and held onto her.

"We'll figure this out," he promised her, his eyes going to the screen again. "Why don't you head in and change while I do a little research?"

She sniffled and shook her head. "I don't think..."

"Hey." He pulled back and smiled down at her. "You still need to eat."

"Right." She sighed. "I just don't think I'm up for much."

"Then we won't do much." He smiled. "Go put on something besides your camp clothes."

She glanced down at the T-shirt with the camp logo and her shorts. "Okay." She stood up, her eyes returning to the screen. "I never believed my mother killed herself." Her eyes moved to lock with his. "Never. But until now, I've never looked into her death. I should have," she said softly and turned to walk down the hallway.

For the next half hour, he ignored his hunger and aches and searched the internet. He emailed himself a couple links to articles about the incident and about Harold Smith.

The man had enough resources to hire someone to take care of the woman he'd been in a nasty custody battle with for Aubrey. It did seem strange that it wasn't until just before Nora's death that he had gained custody of Aubrey.

Of course, the man had repeated in several interviews that he would have won custody anyway since Nora had been jobless, penniless, and a druggy. But Aiden hadn't found any evidence of the last part. What he needed was someone who could research the woman's criminal record. If she had one.

He shot an email off to Brett Jewel, a local officer and Aiden's best friend since grade school, asking him if he could find anything on Aubrey's mother. He'd just hit send when Aubrey walked out of the back room dressed in cream-colored capris and a soft blue flowing tank top.

She'd showered and had left her long red hair down, flowing around her face, which she'd left clear of product. She'd never looked as lovely as she did now.

"Are you doing okay?" he asked, standing up and walking over to her.

She nodded. "Did you find anything?"

"Come on, let's head into town and grab some burgers. I'm starving. I'll fill you in on the way." He grabbed one of her rain jackets as they headed out.

By the time they parked at the burger joint, he'd told her everything, including the email he'd sent off to Brett.

"Do you think it's wise including him?" Aubrey asked. "I mean, he seemed nice and all when he dealt with the whole Ryan fiasco, but..."

He shut off the truck engine and turned to her. "He's been my best friend since grade school," he informed her.

"He has?"

He chuckled. "Yeah, something you might have learned if we'd agreed to be... more." His eyes moved to her lips and he sighed. "Not that I didn't like our arrangement, but..."

He watched her eyes turn weary and knew that he'd pushed his luck.

"Come on, I skipped lunch. I'm starved." He rushed out in the light rain and reached her door just as she opened it. He helped her out of the truck and pulled her close as they walked through the front door of Bubba's. The place had been around long before Aiden had been eating solid food. The old building had at one point been remodeled to be filled with decorations from the fifties. Walking inside the double doors was like stepping into the past.

"This place is why we have fifties nights at the camp." Aubrey smiled as she glanced around. "Come on, there's a booth near the back." She started to tug him towards the dark corner, but he pulled her to the bright booth right out front.

"Let's sit here," he suggested, challenging her as he motioned to the table. "We are, after all, done hiding."

He almost chuckled, seeing the spark of fire behind her eyes, but then she sighed and nodded. She tried to sit opposite him, but he easily glided into the booth next to her instead.

"Isn't this cozy?" he asked as he wrapped his arm around her shoulders.

She may be preoccupied with her mother's death and the new information she'd come across, but he had plans for that night and wasn't going to be detoured.

He'd invited her out in hopes of getting her comfortable being seen with him. He wanted to prove to her that there was a huge difference between what they'd been over the past three years and what they could be. Being seen together, eating dinner together, going out in public wasn't the big step, but it was at least forward motion.

"Comfortable?" she asked, glaring over at him.

"Yes." He smiled and pulled her into the crook of his arm as Carrie, a girl he'd gone to school with, strolled up to the booth with a smile on.

"Hey, Aiden." Carrie's eyes moved to Aubrey and her smile grew. "Hi, Aubrey. Gosh, I didn't know you two were an item."

"We aren't," Aubrey said as Aiden answered, "Going on three years now." He chuckled when Aubrey's elbow connected with his ribs. "How about you grab us a bottle of wine?" he said easily to Carrie.

"Sure thing." She turned to Aubrey. "Your favorite?"

"Yes, thanks," Aubrey answered with a smile.

When Carrie had disappeared, Aubrey turned to him. "You did this on purpose," she hissed.

His eyebrows shot up and his smile grew. "I tend to do everything on purpose."

He chuckled when she elbowed him again.

"You know what I mean." She sighed. "I was hoping for a quiet evening."

"And we'll have one," he assured her. He leaned over and used his fingertips to pull her face towards his. "Together," he said softly just before he kissed her.

He kept the kiss light but didn't pull away until he felt her entire body relax against his.

"I hate you," she said with a sigh as she rested her head against his shoulder.

He chuckled. "That's the opposite of what I'd hope to hear from you, but I'll take it. Just as long as you let me continue holding you like this."

"I don't think I could pull away at this point," she admitted. "You've sunk me with my friends."

He frowned as he held onto her. "What does that mean?"

She glanced up at him. "It's like I feared. Now that my sisters know about us, they're constantly asking about us."

"And that's a bad thing?"

She shrugged and watched as Carrie delivered their wine and poured them each a glass.

"Have you two decided what you want to order?" she asked them.

He'd felt Aubrey tense when he wouldn't release her, but then she reached for her wine and took a drink.

"Burgers." He glanced at Aubrey and when she nodded, he held up his fingers. "Two of them, both with fries. Medium well done." He added, "Oh, mine with cheese, hers without, and no onions."

"Okay," Aubrey said with a sigh. "I suppose we've eaten together enough that you know how I like things."

He pulled her close again as he sipped his wine. "And the same could be said in reverse." He tapped his glass to hers. "Three years."

Her eyes narrowed. "Three years?"

He laughed. "Tonight. I even brought you something." He snapped his fingers. "I almost forgot." He set down his glass and pulled the small box from his jacket pocket.

"Tonight?" She frowned then her eyes grew huge when he set the small box in front of her.

"Relax," he said softly. "It's not a ring."

He saw her visibly relax. She turned to him, ignoring the box. "You're saying it's been three years... today?"

"Yes, three years ago, today, I watched you and Elle walk into cabin one. I showed you how to remove the old pink tiles, then kissed you for the first time, and later"—his eyes moved to her lips—"we enjoyed a swim under the stars, and you came back with me to my place." He sighed. "Three years." He lifted the box towards her. "Open this. Please," he added softly.

She swallowed, then reached for the box with shaky hands.

When she opened it and exposed the simple diamond heart dangling from the silver chain, her eyes turned soft.

Reaching in, he removed the necklace and helped her place it around her neck. The heart landed where he'd known it would. Just over her own heart.

She was looking down at it, and he could see happiness in her eyes.

"It's perfect." She smiled up at him.

"Since you won't let me give you my heart..." He ran a fingertip over the diamond. "You'll have to settle for carrying this around instead."

CHAPTER 11

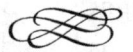

She couldn't breathe. Feeling the cool stone against her skin reminded her of what Aiden had told her. What he'd meant by giving her a diamond in the shape of a heart.

Whether she wanted it or not, she had his heart. One way or another, he'd found a way to get past her defenses.

It was almost impossible to defend herself against his attacks. What was she supposed to do with a man who, in the past three years, had filled her every sexual desire, then in the past few weeks shown her nothing but kindness and patience while she tried to run in the opposite direction?

Watching Aiden leave her at her apartment door the other night had been pure torture. Not only had she not been sexually fulfilled in the past six months, but now he was messing with her, making her even more frustrated than before.

She was about to burst and could only imagine he was feeling the same. But then how had he easily walked away from her after kissing her blind at her door?

She was growing more agitated with work. It wasn't as if she didn't love her job; but having so much pent-up sexual desire was making her daily life hell. Especially since she ran into

Aiden almost every other hour. It was as if he was going out of his way to bump into her.

It was three nights after their three-year anniversary dinner, the date of which she'd marked down in her phone so he wouldn't be able to surprise her again with it. And once again, she was running late to dinner and had yet to change into her fancy costume for that evening's festivities. Tonight's theme was carnival, which meant she had a skimpy outfit with loads of feathers she needed to put on. Thankfully, she could pull her long hair up into a tight bun since the headpiece covered most of her hair. Still, she had her makeup, which would take her some time to pile on.

She was so preoccupied with what she needed to do that she didn't see the dark figure on the pathway until it was too late. She bumped into him and almost toppled the man over.

"Woah." Someone gripped her shoulders to steady them both.

She realized she'd been rushing down the dark pathway from the docks to the main building without so much as watching where she was going.

"Sorry," she immediately apologized.

"It's okay." The tall thin man smiled down at her.

She narrowed her eyes, trying to remember if she knew the man or what the man's name was but came up with a blank. Was he even a guest?

"Are you running from someone?" he asked, glancing behind her as if someone had been chasing her.

"No, I'm just late." She motioned towards the dining hall where even now guests were gathering for dinner.

She'd had a group of kayakers out on the bay and had lost track of time, making them all late for dinner. The guests that had just finished with the tour had opted for private dinners in their cabins, while she raced to change before she was due to help out in the dining hall.

"Aubrey Smith?" the man asked as he ran his eyes up and down her. Her entire body went on guard. After all, they were alone on a dimly lit pathway and he was, even though very skinny, taller and probably stronger than she was. Even with all her years of training, she knew better than to misjudge a person by their appearance.

"Yes," she tensed. Knowing that most men didn't see someone like her as a threat, she readied her body for a fight, just in case. "And you are?" she asked.

The man chuckled, then shook his head. "Not a guest."

"Oh?" She shifted her feet slightly and prepared as she reached for her walkie-talkie.

"No," he sighed. "I'm here because of your father." He held out a folder. It was then that she noticed the man wasn't wearing the normal guest's attire. Instead, he wore a very rich dark suit and tie, which she should have recognized right off since it was middle of the fall season in Florida. The evenings had cooled off, but still, tonight was muggy. The man looked uncomfortable enough that she relaxed and took the folder from his hand.

"This is?" she asked not wanting to open it since she figured it would prolong the disaster her father was trying to inflict. She thought she knew what awaited her inside the pages. Another attempt for him to control her.

"Legal papers." The man shook his head. "I've known your father my entire life. Imagine my surprise when he told me about you. Hell, if I had known he had a daughter..." He shook his head, then stopped and looked her square in the eyes. "You look so much like him that I recognize the fight in you." He sighed as he turned around to go, but then he threw over his shoulder. "You would've kicked my ass, by the way." He chuckled and walked away.

She closed her eyes and took several deep breaths as she calmed herself down. Her body almost vibrated with the need for release at this point. She either needed to kick someone's butt or screw them senseless. And, at this point, she knew the only person she was thinking of doing either to was Aiden.

"If you hadn't, I would have," a deep voice said from the darkness behind her, causing her to squeal and almost drop the folder.

Aiden stepped into the soft glow of the pathway light.

"Sorry," he said as his eyes followed the man in the suit before turning towards her. "So, do you want to see what your dad's goon delivered this time?"

Aiden knew all about the other two times her father's lawyers had shown up at the camp. The first time was three months after she'd moved there to inform her that she was being sued by his company for breach of contract. That was quickly squashed when her lawyers had provided proof that she'd been officially fired from the company. The second time was early last year to let her know that she'd been removed from her father's will.

She'd been grateful to know that she was no longer obligated to the older man she'd deemed as nothing more than a sperm donor and a nuisance for most of her life.

"No." She shook her head and tucked the envelope closer to her.

"Come on," Aiden said, reaching for it.

Even though they hadn't been officially intimate for more than half a year, she still felt desire every time he grew close to her. The cool stone that lay over her heart almost burned when he was around her. Maybe it was because somewhere in the back of her subconscious, she knew the meaning of the heart.

"No," she said again. "I don't care what tricks he's trying now." She tried to jerk the folder away, but he was too quick and, besides, he knew all her moves and easily side-stepped around her blocks.

When he opened the folder and frowned at the papers, she held her breath.

"Shit," he said softly and ran his free hand through his hair. Seeing the concern and worry in his eyes, she tensed again.

"What?" She groaned. "What is he trying now?" She moved closer to look over his shoulder. "Something he hasn't tried before, no doubt."

"Yeah." He handed the papers to her. "I guess you could say that." He watched her closely while she read the top line: Last Will and Testament of Harold Alfred Smith.

She felt her entire body tense once more as the meaning of the papers sunk in. Her father was dead.

Strong arms nudged her towards a bench a few feet away. She didn't know how long she sat there, under the light of the lamps, holding her father's will while Aiden sat beside her, but what finally woke her from the stupor was her walkie-talkie going off.

Aiden reached over and quickly answered it.

"Aubrey's indisposed at the moment," Aiden replied to Elle, who was humorously telling Aubrey she was late, and she'd better get her butt to the dining hall soon.

"Is she okay?" Elle replied with concern.

"No," Aiden said. "She's going to need to skip out on dinner," he said, causing her to jerk out of the funk and reach for the walkie-talkie.

"I'm fine," she started, but Aiden grabbed it back.

"No, she's not. She just found out that her father passed away," he barked out, causing her to punch him in the arm. He winced but continued talking as he rubbed his arm. "I'm taking her up to the apartment. She needs the rest of the night off."

"We'll be there..." Elle said quickly. "Stay with her."

"Will do." He nodded and tucked the walkie-talkie into his jean pocket. "Come on." He lifted her easily so that she stood next to him.

She blinked a few times and looked up into his eyes. "I hate you," she said softly.

"Good." He smiled down at her. "Focus on that instead." He started pulling her down the path towards the main building.

She tried to jerk her arm free, but he held onto her arm, and she fell into step with him.

"I was going this way anyway," she said, trying to pass him.

He chuckled and easily matched her fast pace. Damn, his legs were too long. She couldn't outrace him. She noticed that he had tucked the folder containing her father's will under his arm as they walked through the front door of the building.

When they stepped into the lobby area, Elle and Hannah rushed across the floor towards her. Both of them were dressed in beads and feathers for the dinner.

She found the sight almost pathetic and held in a laugh until she noticed the worry and sadness in her friends' eyes and remembered the papers in Aiden's hands.

Aubrey held up her hands to stop them. "Don't," she warned them, feeling her throat close up, but they didn't stop until their arms were wrapped around their friend.

Then she was being pulled towards the stairs. Aubrey glanced back and noticed that Aiden followed them up the stairs and into the apartment.

Elle push Aubrey down on the sofa while Hannah rushed around and grabbed a bottle of wine and poured each of them a glass. Her friend stopped to remove the silly headdress she'd been wearing.

She noticed that a beer was shoved into Aiden's hand just as Zoey and Scarlett rushed into the room and demanded to know what had happened. They too were wearing silly carnival costumes, making the room seem like a Las Vegas dressing room instead of the apartment the friends had shared the first year they'd lived at the campgrounds.

This was Zoey's first night back at work after her honeymoon. Her friend was practically glowing from her vacation. Not to mention the fact that she was pregnant and married now.

When Elle filled the other two in on what was going on, and the will was mentioned, Aiden handed it over and moved to sit beside Aubrey. Just feeling his leg brush against hers had her stiffening. God, how was it she wanted him now more than she'd wanted him before? Why couldn't she convince herself that she was better off pushing everyone away from her?

She should have never accepted the necklace he'd given her. She should have denied him this next game that he was playing. One in which he was trying to win her heart, something she could never give him.

Why couldn't she get him out of her system? It was as if the more she had him, the more she wanted him. Even now, after cleansing him from her system for the past seven months, the desire for him still grew within her.

Maybe she would never break free from Aiden. Was she doomed to want him for the rest of her life? She knew in her mind and heart that she couldn't let him in. Not really. Not ever. She couldn't afford to let anyone in like her mother had. After all, isn't that what had killed her?

CHAPTER 12

There was only so much Aiden could take. Watching Aubrey hide her feelings about her father's death was pure torture. What he wanted to do was hold her until he felt her relax and let go of the years of pent-up emotions that she'd hidden away most of her life.

Instead, he sat beside her, sipping a beer and listening to her friends try to console her about her father's death. Of course, he knew how much she'd hated the man.

The will had been discarded on the coffee table as the friends chatted amongst each other, so he picked it up and started looking over it. He'd signed enough contracts in his line of business, he figured he could make sense of it.

Then a thought crossed his mind, and he set the paperwork back down and turned to the room.

"Are we sure he's dead?" Aiden broke in to the conversation about whether Aubrey was going to go back to New York for the services or not.

Everyone turned to him as if they'd forgotten he was even there.

"Why else would a lawyer be delivering those?" Elle asked, motioning to the stack of papers.

"Are you saying this could be a ruse?" Zoey suggested.

The four friends were dressed in full-on Vegas-style carnival outfits. He knew they held theme dinners but had yet to see these outfits. He wondered if Aubrey had such an outfit, which led him down the rabbit hole of thinking about her dressed in nothing but feathers and beads.

Shaking that thought from his mind, he said, "From what I've heard about Harold Smith"—his eyes locked with Aubrey's and he watched realization dawn on her as he shrugged—"this could be a trick to get her back to New York."

"Google it," Hannah jumped in. "The death of a man as powerful as your father would be talked about," she said to Aubrey.

Someone grabbed up an iPad and searched while he pulled out his own phone and checked himself.

"Anything?" Aubrey asked a few moments later. Someone had filled her wine glass again, and she was nervously waiting.

"Nothing," he answered.

"Me either," Zoey said.

"So, it's settled. This is a trick." Aubrey sighed and leaned back. "That bastard."

"It could be, or it could've been kept quiet," Hannah supplied.

"No." Aubrey shook her head. "Harold would have made sure that his people knew he wanted a big affair. There is no way it would be kept a secret. He loved the attention too much. So long as it was about him," she added, her eyes locking with his own.

"So, what are we going to do about it?" Scarlett asked.

The five friends huddled over more wine and threw options back and forth.

He enjoyed watching how they interacted and plotted. It gave him a little more insight into the mindset of each of them. He hadn't thought it possible, but after hearing them come up with a plot to help Aubrey end her father's hold over her once and for all, he realized that each of them had a dark side.

"So, its settled." Elle turned to him. "And you're okay with this?"

"What?" He realized he hadn't been paying close enough attention. It had been a long day and the beer on his empty stomach had caused him to be a little more relaxed than he'd counted on.

Elle rolled her eyes. "You, Aubrey, New York?"

"Me?" He balked as he looked around the room.

"Sure, you're the only one we trust with our sister," Zoey offered up. Everyone turned towards Zoey, who beamed and ran a hand over her flat stomach. "Married, baby, home." She smiled. "It's been a crazy year. We trust you with this."

He opened his mouth to list off his own crazy schedule, but then thought of spending some time alone with Aubrey away from the camp.

Sure, for the past seven months they'd been on a sexual hiatus, but it wasn't as if she hadn't pulled away before. Over the last year they'd taken plenty of breaks, though this was their longest one. He'd been itching to touch her again, to hold her as long as he could.

He'd been getting closer to her, now that their secret was out. The way he figured it, the more he worked on getting her to accept that there was more between them, the sooner they could move back into the physical side of their relationship.

But he knew better than to push her. She would only pull back farther. The trip to New York might just be what he needed to get her back all the way and nudge her in the direction he'd been hoping for.

"When do we leave?" he asked, mentally trying to move a few things on his schedule around. He'd have to confirm that his foreman had everything he needed for the work around the campgrounds.

There was work being done on three new cabins, as well as fixing a few minor things on Zoey and Dylan's home, which they'd already moved into since returning home from their honeymoon. Not to mention that he was overseeing the construction of the new housing subdivision he was working on with Owen.

When Owen had come to him about starting up the development of over fifteen hundred homes, he'd jumped at the chance. Hammock Cove was going to draw a lot of opportunity to his small hometown of Pelican Point.

Besides, he couldn't pass up the chance to work with the Costas. His part of the new subdivision was almost complete. He'd designed and overseen the construction of the club house, pools, and sports complex attached to the property. The homes were the next phase and construction would begin on those in the spring.

"We'll leave tomorrow," Aubrey supplied, shaking him from mentally moving his schedule around.

"I'll get you a flight," Hannah broke in. "And find a place for the two of you to stay." She typed something on her phone.

He felt bad now that he hadn't paid more attention to the plans they had been brewing up. What exactly was he being dragged into?

He figured they had plenty of time to discuss everything during their trip.

"Done." Hannah glanced up at them with a smile.

"You booked us tickets and found us a place to stay that quickly?" Aubrey asked with a frown.

Hannah chuckled. "It's easy when you have a fiancé that owns his own private jet and you know someone who owns a home in the city that's empty for the next month. Owen's going to text the both of you the details of your trip." She shrugged and set down the iPad. "He's arranging your flight right now." She leaned back. "Now, since dinner is cancelled for us, can we talk weddings?"

Aiden set his empty beer down and stood up. "This is where I exit. I need food." He glanced down at Aubrey. "I guess I'll see you tomorrow," he said before leaving the friends and making his way to the kitchen to see if there was anything left over after the dinner hour.

He enjoyed living on the campgrounds. Even though his trailer was technically on the edge of the property, he still had access to all the amenities, including the world-renowned chef Isaac Andrews. If it weren't for being on his feet all day and working so hard, he'd probably be a hundred pounds overweight thanks to the great meals he had access to each day.

"Hey." He stepped into the kitchen and glanced around. "Isaac around?"

"Nope," Betty answered him with a smile. "But he did leave you a plate." She motioned to the covered container under the heater. "Told me if you didn't stop by, I'd better send out a search party for you." She laughed and went back to cleaning.

"Thanks." He smiled. Okay, so he was making it a habit to swing by the kitchen for dinner a little too often. Then again, at this rate, he hardly ever left the two sites he was working on.

He couldn't remember the last time he'd taken a few days off. Maybe heading to New York was going to be a well-deserved break.

Taking the meal with him, he made his way towards his truck and was slightly surprised to see Aubrey leaning against it.

"Hey," he said, shifting the food.

"Hey," she sighed. "You don't have to go with me. I don't know why Elle suggested you tag along."

"No, they're right. It would be better if I went." He set the food inside his truck and then turned to her. "Unless you don't want me to go?"

She remained quiet for a moment. "It's just... we don't have to pretend we're an item. I don't even know why that should be a thing with my father."

He noticed she was playing with the diamond heart he'd given her when she said that. He smiled as his eyebrows shot up at her last words.

"I guess I'd zoned out on that part." He smiled slightly as her eyes narrowed.

"Seriously? That was the entire plan." She shook her head. "So, you don't even know..." He waited and after a moment, she rolled her eyes and leaned against his truck again. "Is there enough food for the two of us?" she asked, motioning to the tray.

"Not sure. Isaac always gives me a lot. I'm sure we can work something out," he said with a smile.

"Fine." She waved her hands. "Let's head to the pool. I could use a dip after... everything that's happened in the last hour."

He shrugged and picked up the food container again and followed her to the smaller pool. It was closest to the private beach area and was empty at this time of night after the light rain they'd had earlier.

Setting the tray down, he lifted the lid and smiled when he noticed two chicken breasts lying on homemade noodles covered in a creamy sauce.

"Perfect." He sat across from her and held up a fork for her.

They shared the meal in silence while the pool lights danced, casting shadows around them.

"I'm glad your dad isn't really dead," he said, breaking the silence.

"Thanks," she said softly. "I suppose I should have known he would try something like this," she said between bites. "After all, he's tried so many other things over the years to control me." She set the fork down and frowned at the water. "Makes me wonder why." She sighed and shook her head.

"We haven't really talked a lot about..." He thought about it for a moment. "Well, about our private lives." He chuckled. "I guess we've been focused on the physical side of things, until recently. But over the years I've picked up a few tidbits about your life from your friends."

"It's not like I've hidden where I come from, but there are things I've kept even from my friends." She glanced off over the water and he saw sadness cause her shoulders to sag slightly.

"Like us?" he suggested. Her head snapped back to him, then she nodded slowly.

"Yes, like us."

"Now that that cat is out of the bag, feel free to share any more secrets you want to get off your chest," he said with a smile.

In the years he'd known her, he had never seen her look as defeated as she did now.

"Hey." He reached out and touched her shoulder. "There's something more. What is it?"

Her eyes turned to him. "I don't want you to go with me."

He stiffened with the sting of her admission.

"No, not because of..." She waved between them. "Because of him. He's going to try and destroy you. Because of association. Especially, if we play the relationship card."

He relaxed slightly. "Let him try."

"Oh, he'll do more than try. If we go through with the plans of pretending like we're an item, then he won't stop until he sees everything you've worked hard for ruined."

"My life is pretty secure." He reached for her hand. "I doubt you and your friends are going to fire me here, and Owen... well, things there are going great as well. Besides, I think we can give him a heads-up before your dad makes any moves against my career." He shrugged.

"It won't just be your career he goes after," she warned as she

JILL SANDERS

looked down at her fingers. "He doesn't think twice about hitting below the belt."

He chuckled and lifted her hand to his lips, then brushed a kiss across her knuckles. "Let him try. I have no loans, not even for my truck." He smiled. "I paid her off last year." He shrugged. "There's not much he could use to ruin me. There's not much more to me. I'm not seeing anyone." His eyes met hers. "Not officially, anyway, and my personal life pretty much has been on hold since I started working two full-time jobs."

"I guess you have been stretched pretty thin. We should've given you more time…"

"Aubrey." He waited until she met his gaze again. "I'll be fine. Really. Besides, I'm looking forward to telling your father off." He smiled and enjoyed when her lips turned upwards as well. "Now, how about that swim?" He stood up and pulled off his shirt and shoes. When he reached for his jeans, her eyes ran over him, and he knew instantly that she wanted him.

He'd made a point not to make the moves, since this was her game and not his, but as she pulled off her shorts and tank top to expose the sexy cream-colored bikini, he realized not making a move was one of the hardest things he'd done in a long time.

He jumped into the warm water and turned just in time to see her head disappear under the water with a large splash.

When she surfaced, she was laughing and pushing her red hair out of her eyes.

"So," he said, swimming closer to her, "tell me again this great plan you and your friends came up with."

Their bodies bumped against each other before she moved away. "It's not that complicated. My friends didn't want me to go alone and since you were sitting next to me and, well, because they know about us…" She shook her head. "They volunteered you to go as my chaperone. Then Elle suggested we pretend to be a couple, a real couple, since I told them that my father would never buy it if I dragged a man who was just a sex-friend along with me." She sighed. "So, that's it. We're heading to the city under the ruse that we believe that he's died, while pretending to be a real couple. Our hope is that I can shake free of my father's hold once and for all. Or at least piss him off enough that he stops trying to play games with me." She shrugged and leaned against the side of the pool.

"What happens when we get there and find out, officially, that he's not dead?"

She sighed. "This is where it gets weird." She moved to sit on the stair. She wrapped her arms around her knees and hugged them to her chest. "In the will his lawyer gave me tonight, it says that my father has left me everything." He watched her frown. "Which is what I've been trying to avoid for years." She shook her head. "Anyway, this is where I'm going to have to do some acting." She glanced at him. "We both will have to."

He moved closer to her and wrapped his arms around her. "I think I can handle whatever you throw at me. I was in a couple plays in high school," he offered with a smile.

CHAPTER 13

This was the dumbest thing she'd ever done. Aubrey frowned down as Aiden loaded her suitcase in the private jet. How had she let her friends talk her into going back to New York, let alone convince her to take Aiden with her?

When Elle had suggested it, she knew it was because of her and Aiden's newly exposed relationship. Her friends were starting to meddle, which is why she'd kept her tryst with Aiden a secret for so long in the first place.

She knew her friends were trying to take it upon themselves to connect the two of them together. Permanently. She should have kept her mouth shut and her secrets to herself.

"Ready?" Aiden asked, offering her help up the ladder.

She straightened her back and climbed up herself. She heard him chuckle as he stood back so she could walk past him. She'd heard all about the Costa's private plane. Dylan had flown Zoey to Vegas and back in it when her and Scar's father had passed away. They'd also taken it on their honeymoon.

Still, her friend's description paled in comparison to the sleek interior of the plane. She'd ridden in first class lots of times, since her father never purchased anything else, but this was something else.

"Nice," Aiden said and then whistled. "Guess I should've asked Owen for a bigger payoff for Hammock Cove," he joked.

She smiled as she sat down on the leather seats.

"We're preparing to leave, if you want to strap in for takeoff," an older man said from the captain's cabin. "Once we reach altitude, there's plenty of food and drinks. Feel free to help yourselves." He motioned to the bar. "There's a bedroom in the back if you wish to sleep."

"Thank you," she said, strapping her seat belt on.

Zoey was the nervous flyer out of the group of them. Still, she was a little anxious since she'd never flown in such a small plane before.

"Nervous?" Aiden asked her.

"No, you?" She glanced over at him and watched him strap his seatbelt on in the seat next to her.

"I meant about seeing your father again."

She sighed and glanced out the window.

"A little," she finally admitted. "It's been years since I've seen him." She closed her eyes and leaned back against the leather. "I thought that he was old the first time I laid eyes on him."

"How old where you?" he asked, watching her closely, his gaze heating her.

God, she'd missed him. Being with him. Being around him. Feeling his touch, knowing he was there to soothe her desires and take away her pain.

But she knew he wanted more from her. More than she could give him. She played with the diamond heart and knew that he had planned on her thinking of him each time she touched it.

He'd told her that he would patiently wait until she was ready for him, but no matter how long he waited, she could never give him what he wanted.

"Eight years old," she answered as the plane started taxing.

"How is it we've known each other for over three years now, and yet we don't know anything beyond the basics about one another?" he asked.

She felt her stomach roll and looked away from him. Just looking into those sexy eyes made her want to drop her guard.

"We had other things to fill our time with rather than talking," she admitted.

"Right," he agreed with a chuckle. "Ever think of trying something else?"

"Like what?" she asked, knowing where he was leading her. She didn't have the energy or the willpower to pull away at the moment. So she decided to hear him out instead.

"Opening yourself up to something deeper?"

She stiffened and said under her breath, "I don't have that luxury."

"It's too bad really," he said as she glanced back at him. "Something tells me you'd learn a lot." He shrugged.

"Like what?" she asked as the plane shoved off, causing her to be pushed back into her seat as they hit the open air.

"Like..." He smiled. "My birthday, my favorite color." He leaned closer to her and lowered his voice. "Not to mention, my favorite song."

She rolled her eyes and tried to hold in a laugh. Deciding to play along, she leaned closer to him as well. "Okay, shoot." She motioned to him.

"No, you don't. It doesn't work like that." He shook his head. "You're either in or you're not."

He leaned back and crossed his arms over his chest as if he were done with the conversation.

Her eyes narrowed as her irritation grew.

God, why did he have to be so good-looking. His dark hair fell across his forehead, and he was doing something new with his facial hair, keeping the stubble so that he looked a little dangerous and even sexier than usual.

"Blue," she said finally and glanced sideways at him.

"Hm?" he asked.

"Your favorite color. Is it blue?" she asked.

He chuckled. "No, that's not how the game is played."

She crossed her arms over her chest and pouted. She hated games.

"Not playing?" he asked when she remained quiet.

"No," she answered.

"Fine." He shrugged. "What if I could guarantee to not cross the line? The same one you set three years ago."

She felt her heart skip as hope filled her. Was he saying they could continue with their physical relationship and he'd back down from trying to get her to fall in love with him?

"What are you saying?" she asked. "Just so we're perfectly clear."

"What I'm proposing"—he leaned closer to her again and smiled—"is a new game. One where you get to keep tight reins on that heart of yours." He glanced down to where the diamond he'd given her lay over her own heart. "While opening yourself up a little and getting to learn more about me."

She thought about it and asked a little breathlessly, "What do I get out of this?"

He chuckled. "I would think that was perfectly clear." He smiled and she felt her heart skip at the thought of his hands roaming over her body once again. How long had it been? God, how had she survived?

She felt her body instantly respond to the possibilities and couldn't stop the smile. "So, it's that way, is it?"

He chuckled. "If you want to play." He was only a breath from her now. "No one is forcing you to go along. After all, it's just…" His eyes locked onto her lips. "A game."

God, she was in trouble. She knew there was no way she was

going to come out of this unscathed. Hell, at this point, she'd already been scorched by him.

"Fine." She threw up her hands. "Let's play. What is your favorite color?"

He shook his head. "Rules first." He held up his fingers. "Two of them."

She'd set her own rules when they'd started playing her game years ago. Still, he'd kept the promise to keep their... relationship away from her friends. He'd also kept what was between them physical. Until recently, when everything had changed all thanks to her breaking things off.

"What are they?" she asked, needing to know before she agreed to anything.

"No more hiding. If we do this..." He motioned between them. "It's out in the open. We're out in the open. One hundred percent."

She held in a groan. "And the other rule?"

"Until I say so, the physical stuff"—he smiled and slowly ran his eyes over her— "is in the background. The game is about getting to know each other in other ways."

Her eyebrows shot up. "What's wrong, Aiden? Don't want to have sex with me anymore?" she teased.

He laughed, the low sound deep in his chest. "God, there's nothing that I want to do more most of the time, especially now, knowing there's a bedroom back there." He nodded behind them. "But let's focus on other things first. Sex comes second. Besides..." He lowered his voice. "We both know we've pretty much conquered that arena."

She smiled as she thought about it. What could she lose? If this was just a game, then the more she played along, the more she knew she'd gain. Besides, she was good at cheating. "Okay." She nodded. "Agreed."

He slowly extended his hand and waited for her to take it. It was warm and callused and so much bigger than her own, reminding her how wonderful it had always felt running over her skin.

"Red," he said finally, reaching up with his free hand and running a strand of her hair through his fingers. "Red is my favorite color."

She felt her entire body flutter with want. She glanced down at his lips. "And your favorite song?"

His lips twitched. "Dark Side of the Moon."

"Floyd." She sighed. "I should've known."

"You?" he asked.

"Blue," she answered, not really focusing on her response.

"And your song?" he asked with a chuckle.

She smiled. "Wind of Change." She knew she was throwing him off but enjoyed seeing his eyebrows rise.

"Scorpions?"

She nodded. "Classic rock was the only thing I knew I could do to really piss my father off. He even destroyed all my records when I was young, so I went digital. If it was loud and I could scream to it, I blasted it." She smiled. "Still do."

He chuckled. "I can totally see that." He glanced down at their joined fingers. "Best place you've visited?" he asked.

She thought about it for a moment. "River Camps," she answered truthfully. When he gave her a look, she shrugged. "It's true. It's the one place that I've dreamed about returning each time I left. There has never been a place I've been as happy."

"No place?" he asked her as he took her hand.

She met his eyes and thought about the past three years.

River Camps was more of a home to her than any other place she'd had before. More than the small apartments she and her mother used to bounce around from or the massive stuffy place her father called home.

Even when the five of them were crowded in the small

three-bedroom two-bathroom apartment, she'd been more at home than anywhere ever before.

She knew it was in part due to her sisters and, as much as she tried to, she couldn't deny in her own heart that part of the reason was due to Aiden being there for her. Always.

"No." She shook her head. "You?" She lifted the diamond around her neck and played with it, noticing that his eyes followed her move. She watched the left side of his mouth twitch and rise as her fingers played over the heart.

"I traveled to Florence, Italy, fresh out of high school. I could get lost in the architecture there. The history." His eyes returned to hers. "Ever been?" he asked.

"No. Italy, yes, Florence, no." She relaxed at the change of subject.

"Favorite food?" He shifted, bringing her closer. "I think I know this one, but hit me with it."

She laughed. "You know it. Burgers and chocolate."

He laughed. "I thought so."

"You?"

"Burgers are right up there, but I'd have to say, instead of chocolate, I have an affinity for strawberries... and cream." He reached up and played with her hair again.

She felt her entire body respond instantly. A small moan escaped her lips as memories of him pleasing her with his lips surfaced.

"Aiden." His name was nothing more than a whisper.

"I never said I wouldn't torture you." His eyes locked with her lips. "Like you've been doing to me over the past seven months." He leaned closer and she sucked in her breath, hoping, dreaming that he'd kiss her. Everywhere.

Instead, he pulled back and stood up suddenly. "Want something to drink?" he asked casually.

"Damn you." She closed her eyes and took several calming breaths.

She heard him chuckle as he made his way behind the bar and started rummaging around. "There's beer, wine, champagne, sodas, juice." He glanced up at her.

"Wine," she answered then added, "white, if they have it."

"They do," he said, pulling out glasses and pouring them each a glass. He handed her a glass and then produced a plate of fruit, cheese, and crackers.

"I'm sure we can have dinner when we land. This should hold us over until then." He sat back down beside her. "So, when we land, what exactly is our plan?" he asked after taking a grape.

"As far as I know, we'll get settled in at the place Owen arranged for us, then…" She shrugged as she thought about it. It was so hard to switch her gears from sex with Aiden one moment to trying to plot out how to deal with her father the next.

"We could always show up at your father's place unexpected. After all, if you believed he was dead, wouldn't you plan on staying there instead?"

She frowned. "Yes and no. The last time I spent a night under that roof was on my eighteenth birthday." She shivered remembering how Harold had coldly turned her away. "I doubt he'd except anything else than me stopping by."

He nodded and took another sip of his wine. "So, we show up after dropping our things off and grabbing some dinner."

"Sounds good." She sighed and closed her eyes. "Not really. What I'd like to do is reroute this plane to somewhere remote and disappear for a week instead."

He set his glass down and picked up her hand. He lifted it to his lips and for a moment she dreamed about how his lips would feel all over her body instead of on the back of her palm.

"But you won't. You can do this. Make a stand once and for all. Show him just how terrible he's made your life. A bully will always bully someone who never stands up for themselves."

"I know you're right." She glanced over at him. "Do you

know, that's initially why I took tai chi and judo. There was this group of girls that picked on me." She chuckled. "It's funny, they chose me because they thought I was too pretty. Too rich." She rolled her eyes. "Too perfect. Judging a book by its cover can leave people so shortsighted."

"What happened?"

"After the first year, I let it slip that I was taking self-defense classes, knowing it would get back to the group. The moment they started picking on me again, I used some of my best moves to disable them without hurting them… permanently." She shrugged. "The Wildflowers gave me the courage to stand up for myself. Without their love and friendship, I probably wouldn't be here."

CHAPTER 14

It was hard listening to Aubrey talk about her tortured childhood. One thing that he'd gathered from listening to her talk was that she'd been all alone outside of the presence of the Wildflowers.

He knew what it was like growing up an only child. Still, after second grade, he'd had Brett Jewel, his best friend. The two of them had gotten in enough trouble as kids that everyone joked that they were brothers. When Brett had chosen a path of law and peacekeeping after school and Aiden had taken business and architecture classes, their friendship hadn't wavered.

Even now, they got together at least once every few weeks for beers or to watch a game. He didn't know what he would have done if he hadn't had a friend throughout his life. He could only imagine what it must have been like for her.

They continued to talk and answer each other's questions until the plane landed. On the taxi drive from the airport to the place Owen had set up for them, they remained silent, and he could tell she was growing more nervous.

He had a fear that the closer they got to her father, the farther she would grow from him.

When the taxi stopped in front of a simple brownstone, he turned to her.

"Who did Owen say owned this?" he asked Aubrey as he helped pull their bags from the trunk.

"He didn't. Only mentioned that we had it for as long as we wanted." She shrugged and took her smaller bag from him as she looked up at the four-story building.

"The entire place?"

"Yes. He said there's a car in the garage out back. The keys are on a hook in the kitchen." She pulled out her phone. "The code for the door." She held up her phone as they stopped in front of the two iron doors.

He punched in the code and motioned her inside a small foyer.

"Let's explore." She set her bag down at the base of the stairs and motioned towards the hallway.

He followed her through a narrow parlor filled with leather sofas, fine art, modern furniture, and absolutely no personal items at all.

"This is set up like a rental," she said as they walked towards the back of the building into a small office. "I think..." She frowned. "Let's find the kitchen." She headed down the stairs.

When they walked into the massive space she laughed. "Isaac's." She motioned to the only personal picture. "This is Isaac's place. I recognized his style." She laughed at the picture of Isaac and his wife. "No wonder we can have it as long as we want. They only come back to the city during the holidays."

"He mentioned something about keeping his place in the city and renting it out," Aiden remembered with a sigh. He chuckled. "So, the mystery is solved."

"Hannah must have arranged this part for us. She's known him for years." She turned around and walked through the kitchen into the dining area. "This place is great. Let's see what else there is to find." She headed down a set of stairs again.

Here, in the basement, there was the laundry room, a small storage room, a bathroom, and a little home gym. They headed back up the stairs, and he grabbed their bags as they climbed up to the top two floors.

The main bedroom was on the top floor. The walls were covered in white and black wallpaper with a massive king-sized bed complete with a very modern canopy bedframe.

"Guess they like black and white?" he said as he set their bags on the bed and then motioned towards a small staircase.

"Want to see what's up there?" he asked.

She smiled as she nodded. They climbed the stairs and stepped out onto a private rooftop garden. Even though they were surrounded by tall buildings, there was enough privacy here to enjoy the outdoors.

"Nice." He did a full circle. "Surrounded by the urban jungle," he joked.

"I miss the country already." Aubrey sighed and wrapped her arms around herself.

Walking over, he pulled her close and her eyes softened.

"We'll only be here for a short time," he promised her.

"You don't know my father." She closed her eyes, and he felt her shiver. "Why put off the inevitable. I'll shower and change."

He frowned down at her. "What's wrong with what you're wearing?"

She laughed. "Like I said, you don't know my father. You know that suit I asked you to pack?"

He nodded. "Yeah,"

"You'll want to wear it for the first act." She leaned up on her toes and placed a soft kiss on his lips. "For what is about to transpire, I'm sorry. And, I'll remind you, you volunteered for this."

He chuckled and leaned in to slowly kiss her back. "So far I have no regrets."

"You will," she added as they made their way back down the stairs. She took her bag and started towards the back room, which he assumed was a bathroom. "So, are you planning on sleeping in here with me?"

He chuckled and picked up his bag. "I'll head down to the next floor and pick a room there. For now," he added as he left.

He knew he was messing with her, but he couldn't chance losing the little control he had over her. If this new plan didn't work, he doubted his heart would recover from the damage she'd done to it.

"Fine," she said before slamming the bathroom door.

He chuckled loudly enough that he knew she'd be even more pissed at him.

Good. If she was mad at him, she wouldn't be thinking of what was to come. The conflict with her father would probably be one of the hardest things she'd ever had to deal with. At least from what she'd told him about the man and from what he'd read about Harold Smith.

He thought about all the possibilities as he showered and changed in the guest bedroom's bathroom.

Harold Smith had been born into wealth, his grandfather having owned one of the more successful iron works companies in New York during the industrial age. Young Harold had attended the finest schools and shortly after graduating Harvard had built several multi-billion-dollar companies before he'd hit fifty.

He'd been in his late fifties when he'd met Nora Murphy, Aubrey's mother. Nora had been nineteen and a stewardess on one of Harold's private jets at the time. However, he'd sold the entire fleet off less than ten years later, shortly after a near fatal crash one winter.

Now, it was rumored that the man hadn't left New York after that day and stuck close to his twenty-thousand-square-foot home just off of Central Park. He was either there or at his main office building less than three blocks away.

He was a shrewd businessman and had made many enemies

and friends in high places, and it was whispered about some of his low friends as well.

It was common knowledge in certain circles that he had a daughter, his only living heir. The man had never been married and tended to not have any affairs. None in the public eye at least.

Pulling on the suit, he glanced at his own reflection and winced. It would be apparent to anyone looking at him that he didn't belong in such fine clothes. He was built for faded jeans with a tool belt hanging off his hips. He was meant to walk in the woods and live off the land, not deal with city dwellers.

Still, he had to admit, the suit he'd purchased with the help of Owen's tailor looked better on him than the old suit he'd had.

"Ready?" Aubrey asked from the doorway. He turned, the silver tie he'd been about to attempt to put on himself held in his hands. Aubrey stood in the doorway dressed in an off-the-shoulder black dress that had a pencil skirt. She looked just as uncomfortable as he felt in her heels and the dress. "Here." She glided across the floor and took the tie from his hands. "Let me help you."

He ran his eyes over her face as she worked on his tie. Her skin was porcelain perfect. Not a blemish on her. She wore only a light dusting of makeup that accented her eyes and lips.

Her long red hair was twisted into an intricate knot at the nape of her neck. She not only looked professional, but she looked like she could be in mourning. Which fit the bill for their first encounter with her father.

"Ready?" she asked when she'd finished with his tie.

"Are you?" he asked, his hands moving up and down her arms. He realized she was chilled and tried to warm her arms by rubbing them.

"I am," she said after a deep breath.

He took her hand as they walked down the stairs together. "Do you have a jacket?" he asked her.

She glanced over at him. "It's not really cold..." He opened the front door and a gust of wind rushed in, making her shiver visibly.

"I'll head up the stairs and get it," she said with a sigh.

"Tell me where it is—"

"No." She shook her head. "You hail a cab. I don't want to show up at his place in Isaac's car. I'll get the coat." She started up the stairs as he glanced out the front door.

He stepped onto the curb, but instead of trying to find a taxi, he pulled out his phone and had an Uber heading their way.

A dark sedan rolled by him slowly, and Aiden felt his spine tense as he watched a man roll down the passenger window and point a camera at him. He took a step closer just as Aubrey stepped out of the front door. The man snapped a picture of her before speeding off.

"Did you get us a car?" she asked easily as she stopped beside him on the sidewalk.

"I did." He frowned as the sedan turned the corner. "It should be here..." He stopped when their ride pulled up in front of them.

"There's a restaurant a few blocks from my father's place. We'll grab some food before we head over."

"How far are we from your father's place?" he asked as they settled in the back seat.

She glanced around and narrowed her eyes at the street signs. "About twenty blocks." She sat back. "Which could mean a five-minute drive or a two-hour drive." She chuckled. "One of the reasons I don't miss the city."

He thought about the dark sedan as they slowly made their way across town. He took in little of the city and instead focused on how someone would have known that they were in town. As far as he knew, their plans had only been shared with a small group.

"Did you tell anyone else we were coming?" he asked her as

they turned towards the park.

"No," she answered with a slight frown. "Why?"

He debated telling her about the sedan, but before he could respond, the car stopped.

"I'm starved," she said as they stepped out onto the curb. "About the only thing I've missed in this city is Mrs. Grimaldi's sandwiches." She motioned to the small shop.

When they stepped in the sandwich shop, she stopped and took a deep breath. "Ah, I've missed that smell. Nothing against Isaac, but Mrs. Grimaldi's soup is the best thing ever."

She motioned to a small table, and he followed her and sat down.

They ordered sandwiches and soup and talked about their plans for dealing with her father.

"I don't know how this is going to go down, but the only thing I can do is warn you that there will be a serious lack of emotion on his part."

"And you?" he asked.

She frowned down into her soup. "I'll play my part." Her eyes moved up to his. "Which will annoy Harold," she added with a slight smile.

He chuckled. "Looking forward to that part?"

She shrugged. "And setting him straight finally."

They finished their meal. He had to admit, the soup was pretty amazing. It surprised him that she knew a couple of the waitstaff by name. They acted like it had been weeks rather than years since they'd seen her last.

"We can walk from here," she suggested as they stepped out onto the sidewalk.

He took her hand and enjoyed the cooler air as they headed away from the shop area.

"Show time," she said, stopping on the sidewalk. She took several deep breaths and closed her eyes for a moment. "Ready?" she asked when she opened them again.

"Are you?" he asked her.

"No, but this has to be done." She straightened her shoulders and glanced over at a massive home.

He followed her gaze and held his breath. He'd seen pictures of the twenty-thousand-square-foot place when he'd researched her father. But pictures didn't properly show how truly massive the home was.

A huge iron gate that surrounded the entire front of the five-story sandstone building had no sign of who lived inside on it. Aubrey stepped up to the security camera and rang the bell.

"Yes?" a man's voice sounded moments later.

"Carl? It's Aubrey," she replied. "And guest." She looked back at him.

The gate buzzed and he easily pushed it open. He held it for her until she passed through it, then stepped in behind her.

"Just... go with it," she said with a slight shake of her head.

"Going," he agreed as the tall iron front door opened for them. A short woman with silver hair waited for them to enter.

"Martha." Aubrey nodded her head and started to remove her jacket.

Aiden rushed to help her and then handed it over to the older woman.

"We weren't expecting you, Miss Smith," Martha replied.

"No, I suppose not." She glanced around. "I would have thought that after everything the estate would be in disarray and the wolves would be knocking down the doors." She motioned around the large marbled entryway.

There were three stairs that led up to another marbled sitting area. Gold iron gates under a massive arch blocked the entryway from the rest of the home. It reminded him of a lobby in a bank instead of the entrance to someone's home.

This is where she'd been raised? No wonder the camp was her favorite place in the world. Anywhere was better than living in a stuffy museum.

"What… has happened?" Martha asked with a shake of her head as her eyes ran over Aubrey's face.

"So," a loud voice boomed through the hallway, "you've finally come back to collect."

He watched Aubrey closely. She was an amazing actress and even paled slightly as her father walked towards them.

"They…" She cleared her throat as she shook her head, all while her hand rose slowly to her throat. "They told me you were dead." She leaned on Aiden as he wrapped an arm around her as if to steady and support her.

Harold Smith was as old as she'd described. His white hair was neatly cut and styled, and he wore a dark grey suit that made him appear as if he was ready to head into work.

He walked like a man still in good health even if he moved slower than most.

The man's silver blue eyes, which matched Aubrey's perfectly, ran over him slowly then dismissed him quickly to respond to his daughter.

"They told you what I wanted you to hear," he said, his voice echoing in the marble room. "Well, come in." He turned and disappeared into the house.

Aubrey looked up at him, and he realized that she'd been shaken at seeing the man again. His arms tightened slightly around her.

"You okay?" he asked softly.

Instead of answering, she nodded.

Walking through the gold gates, they passed by a twisted gold and iron staircase. A two-story gold chandelier hung over the marble stairs. There were even gold-leaf decorations on the ceiling that twisted around the staircase. There was no comfortable furniture. Instead, antique furniture, no doubt more expensive than anything he'd ever own, was neatly placed around the rooms.

There were no warm rugs, no tasteful paintings hanging on

the walls. Actually, the only thing decorating the walls was a massive mirror with a gold leaf frame that hung over a matching table.

When they stepped into a two-story study, he realized that this was the room where Harold Smith spent most of his time.

Here there was warm wood and comfortable leather chairs that faced a massive desk, which sat in front of a fireplace. A fire crackled in its massive hearth, warming the space.

Harold moved over and sat behind the desk before motioning to the two leather chairs. "Sit," he demanded.

Aubrey moved to the other side of the desk, but instead of sitting, placed her hands on the wood and leaned across it.

"You had your lawyers lie to me? Why?" she demanded.

"Did he actually tell you I was dead?" he asked. Aubrey's eyes narrowed. Her father's left eyebrow rose slightly. "How else was I supposed to get you back here? You've made it very apparent that, short of my death, nothing would bring you back to the city."

Aubrey's eyes narrowed. "You've had your fun…" She turned and grabbed his hand and started pulling him towards the door.

"Aubrey," her father's voice boomed. "Enough games."

She stilled and glanced over her shoulder. "I don't play games. I'm not the one who lied to get me back here."

Harold opened his mouth to answer, but just then his gaze moved to a spot beyond them.

Aiden and Aubrey both turned and watched a young blond-haired woman stroll into the room as if she was late for the party.

The fact that the woman was wearing diamonds and an evening gown in the middle of the day had them both stopping.

Then Aubrey stiffened.

"Bridgett?" Aubrey gasped. "What the hell are you doing here?"

CHAPTER 15

*A*ubrey had only seen pictures of the woman before. Wedding pictures of the woman standing in front of them now with Zoey and Scarlett's father, Jean Rowlett.

But Aubrey knew all about Bridgett Rowlett. The woman, who was a mere fifteen years older than she was, had been the cause of her best friends' parents' divorce.

Shortly before Zoey and Scarlett's father's death of cancer two years ago, Bridgett had divorced Jean Rowlett, owner of R&R Enterprises, a company whose power and reach rivaled that of one of her own father's businesses.

When Bridgett found out about her ex-husband's death, she'd tried everything she could to get her hands on the man's remaining money. But their father had changed his will after the divorce and the sisters had spent some of their inheritance on helping out with the camp.

The sisters had decided to use it to build a few more cabins, which had boosted the business greatly.

Bridgett narrowed her eyes. "Do I know you?" It was the slight smile on the woman's lips that had Aubrey's temper growing.

"Don't play games with me," Aubrey hissed. She stormed across the room towards the woman.

How the hell had her father and Bridgett met in the first place? Was she working for her father?

Had Bridgett learned about Aubrey being Zoey and Scarlett's friend and then hunted down her father in hopes of getting her hands on his money like she had Jean Rowlett's?

Zoey had informed her that Bridgett had gotten a lot of their father's money in the divorce, but the last she'd heard, the woman had blown through it. The last the friends had heard of Bridgett, she had been working as a dancer in Vegas.

How long had she been in New York?

Aubrey watched Bridgett lay her hands, which had extremely long manicured fingernails painted in a hot pink, on her father's shoulders, as if they belonged there.

"I'm best friends with Zoey and Scarlett Rowlett," Aubrey answered as she crossed her arms over her chest.

She watched the woman's reaction and noticed the lack of surprise in her eyes.

"Oh, that's wonderful." Bridgett smiled, and Aubrey noticed that her lips matched the color of her nails. She must have known that her father had deemed pink as the only color a woman should ever wear. It was the reason she'd only had the color in her wardrobe growing up. The reason she hated it to this very day. No daughter of Harold Smith was going to be anything less than feminine.

"Harold, dear, those are my stepdaughters I was telling you about." Bridgett turned to Aubrey's father. "I miss them so. They were such wonderful young ladies." Bridgett sighed and rested her hand over her heart. Her eyes returned to Aubrey's and she noticed a glimmer of anger hidden them. Then her eyes turned to Aiden, and Aubrey saw interest flash behind the woman's eyes briefly before she turned back to Harold. "But, sadly, after their father passed, they turned on me. They were hungry for their father's wealth and stole every last dime he gave me." She added with a pout, "They didn't care about anything other than money."

"Yes," her father jumped in, "I know the feeling." Her father's eyes turned to her.

"Me?" she gasped, then laughed. "I don't want a cent from you. I never have. I would have been content living with my mother." Aubrey felt her heart kick in her chest and knew that if she continued there would be no going back. So, she clenched her jaw tight and tempered her anger.

"We shall see." Her father stood up and wrapped his arm around the tall and much younger woman. "Dear, why don't you go and see if everything is ready for the party?"

Bridgett smiled and then leaned in and placed a kiss on her father's lips. Aubrey had to look away in disgust.

"Party?" Aubrey asked, following Bridgett out of the room with her gaze.

"Yes, I did call you and invite you. Remember? We're hosting a party in a few hours." Her father sat back down. "Now, if you don't mind." He motioned to the chairs again.

Aubrey glanced back at Aiden, who shrugged back at her.

Rolling her eyes, she sighed and moved over to sit down. Aiden sat in the chair next to her.

"And you are?" her father asked Aiden.

"Aiden is my boyfriend," she supplied. "He stays," she warned her father.

"Very well." He dismissed Aiden completely. "The will I had Michael Livingston deliver to you is not my latest will," her father said smoothly. "In less than a month, I plan on marrying Bridgett."

"What?" Aubrey gasped and started to stand up. "She's…"

Her father held up his hand to stop her. "I know exactly what she is. She's put her wild days behind her." He leaned slightly towards her and for the first time she could see something else behind his eyes. Was that pain? They were unfocused. In all the years she'd known him, he'd never been less than... well, perfect. Now as she looked at him, she noticed that his tie was slightly askew and one of the buttons on his shirt was twisted and loose. "Tonight is to be our engagement announcement party. I wanted you here."

"And this is how you planned on bringing me here, by lying to me? Letting me think you'd died? Why?" She shook her head. "Have you no heart?"

Her father laughed, which turned into a cough. She watched him struggle to get his breathing back under control. Any other child would have raced to their father in hopes of easing his pain. Her entire body froze in place as she watched the man suffer for the first time in her life.

"I know your games," he said after pouring a sip of bourbon from the small bar area behind his desk. For as long as she'd known him, he'd always drunk several glasses of bourbon each day. "You think you can fool me? You're just like your mother. You've done everything you can in your life to go against me." He slammed the glass down and then walked back over to lean against his desk. "You think I'll give you anything? You demand everything and refuse to abide by my rules. You don't deserve a dime of mine, Nora." His eyes had turn distant and, if she had to be honest with herself, a little scary.

"Father?" She stood slowly and reached out for him.

He shook free of the moment and corrected himself.

"Aubrey." He walked over and downed the entire glass of bourbon. "The party is in three hours. I'll expect you to be changed into something appropriate and on time." He glanced back at her. "Both of you." He lifted his hand and waved as if to shoo them away.

"No." She shook her head and moved closer to him. "I'm no longer yours to command. I rushed here because I was led to believe that you'd died. I didn't give a fuck about your money. I never have." She motioned towards the doorway. "Bridgett does. She'll do anything she can to get every last dime of yours, which she will spend on frivolous things and, within a year, no doubt, go through the majority of it. If that's even possible." She touched her father's shoulder. "You were never really a father to me, but I won't stand by and let that woman ruin another man's life." She dropped her hand. "Whatever happens, I'll do everything in my power to stop her from manipulating you."

"What happens to my money is—"

"As I said," she interrupted again, "I don't give a damn about your money. Give it all to charity, throw it in the ocean, shred it." She threw up her hands. "But I'll be damned if I let you give that bitch one cent more."

"Well!" Bridgett gasped from the door, then rushed over to hold onto Harold. "I told you this was a bad idea, inviting her. She's just jealous." Bridgett wrapped her arms around Harold and almost toppled him over. "You heard her. She's going to try and break us apart." Bridgett turned on her. "I love your father. Nothing and no one can stop us from getting married."

Aubrey laughed. "Care to bet on it?" She turned and stormed from the room.

Aiden caught up with her as Martha held out her jacket for her.

"Are you okay?" he asked her as they stepped out into the cooler air. The clouds had covered the sun, and she could tell that the rest of the evening would be chilly.

"No." She glanced over her shoulder. "I have to..." She stopped when he put his hands on her shoulder. Something close to a cry escaped her, then his strong arms were wrapping around her, holding her as she shook. She didn't know if it was anger or fear, but just knowing Aiden was there for her helped.

"I have to call my sisters," she said into his shoulder.

"We have three hours," he reminded her. "I bet you have a fancy dress that you can wear for the party, but I didn't pack a tux. Not that I have one, but if we're going to play along with this new game..."

She nodded. "You're right. Get us a car. We'll head to the shops while I fill everyone in on what's going on."

She pulled her phone out of her purse and took a deep breath before punching Zoey's number.

"Hey, how was your flight?" Zoey asked cheerfully.

"Good. Can you get everyone else together and put me on speaker phone? I need... to fill you all in."

"Sure," Zoey said. "Is everything okay?"

"I'll let you know all at once."

"Okay, hang on," Zoey said. Aubrey listened as Zoey got on the walkie-talkie and called everyone to meet in Elle's office. Then she heard Zoey making her way to the office herself.

"Did you see your father already?" she asked as she walked.

"Yes," she sighed.

"Was it everything you'd hoped?" Zoey asked.

Aubrey chuckled sarcastically. "More."

"We're here," Elle called out, and the phone was changed to speaker.

"Everyone?" she asked.

"Yes," everyone answered one by one.

She had just climbed into the car and told the driver to head to the local shops she knew her father used for his own suits and tuxes.

"You're shopping?" Hannah asked.

"Yes, apparently my father is holding a party in a few hours." She glanced over at Aiden, who nodded encouragement to her. "The party is his engagement party."

"What?" Several voices rang out.

"What is he? Seventy-eight now?" Elle asked.

"Something like that," Aubrey answered.

"Who the hell would marry him?" Zoey asked.

"A bitch," Aubrey responded, "by the name of Bridgett Rowlett."

The line was completely silent and for a split second she thought she'd lost the connection.

"What the hell!" several people shouted all at once.

"You've got to be kidding me?" Zoey picked up the phone and almost yelled in the speaker. Aubrey had to pull the phone away from her ear.

"No." She rubbed her forehead and closed her eyes. "I'm afraid I'm not."

"How the hell did she and your dad meet?" Elle asked.

"Good question. I was hoping you guys would have some time to do some digging. We're busy buying a tux for Aiden and finding a dress for me." She sighed. The dress she was currently wearing was the fanciest thing she'd packed.

If she knew her father, and from what she'd heard about Bridgett, what she was wearing just wouldn't cut it.

"We're on it," Elle answered. "Keep us posted. We'll let you know what we find."

"Thanks," she said to the group just as the car stopped in front of the tux shop. "Talk to you later."

"Aubrey," Hannah broke in. "Head over to Bella's Boutique. It's near your dad's place. I'll call in a favor and have a dress waiting for you there. I'm afraid you're on your own with the tux."

"Thanks," she said before hanging up.

"It pays to have friends," she added as they stepped out onto the sidewalk again.

"Too bad she couldn't help with the tux." He frowned up at the store.

"Come on." She took his hand. "This won't be so bad."

He laughed as she pulled him through the doors.

A little over two and a half hours later, she frowned down at the limo parked out front of Isaac's place. How had her father known they were staying there?

"I meant to tell you earlier. When we arrived, there was a man taking pictures of us," Aiden said to her as he helped her on with her coat.

A light rain had started and the limo driver, who had rung the door to let them know he was there to take them to her father's party, held up an umbrella for them.

She should have known that the moment she set foot back in the city, her father would find out about it. He probably had known all along that she was coming today.

"It's okay." She sighed and followed the driver to the limo. After climbing in and waiting for Aiden to get in behind her, she sat back as the driver shut them inside.

"Is this normal?" he asked.

"The limo?" she asked. When he nodded, she answered. "Yes, I wasn't allowed to go anywhere without a driver."

"It's very..."

"Controlling?" she offered up.

"Yes." He reached over and took her hand. "You look amazing." He smiled over at her.

"I don't know what Hannah was thinking." She glanced down at the bright teal dress. "It's teal. With red shoes." She held up her heeled feet and frowned down at them.

He chuckled and pulled her closer. "She was thinking that you were going to outshine Bridgett, which will probably piss her off. And the red shoes match your hair perfectly." He kissed her. "Your friend has amazing taste."

The dress was perfectly comfortable and even the shoes fit her like a glove. It was true, Hannah had amazing taste.

She thought about the lapse in her father's mental health. He'd never mistaken her for her mother before. Was he having issues? Was it something Bridgett was doing to him? Is this how she'd swindled her way into her father's life?

The man that had raised her would have never allowed someone like Bridgett in his life. Hell, she doubted the woman would have been allowed to walk past his front door. Why now? Was it a ploy?

So many questions raced through her mind and, before she knew it, they were pulling into her father's driveway.

Every light was on in the place. Cars were stopped out front to let guests out so they could walk through the gates towards the open front doors, where security guards made sure guests were on the invite list. Their limo didn't stop in the street and instead pulled in through the opened gates.

"Red carpet treatment," Aiden said under his breath. "That could be a good sign."

"No." She shook her head and felt her stomach twist. "It means he wants everyone to see me so he can use me." She sighed. "Just like always."

CHAPTER 16

*A*iden had never in his twenty-five years of life felt more uncomfortable. The only thing holding him in place was standing directly beside him.

From the moment they walked through the front doors, they were the center of attention. When Aubrey's name was called out through the rooms, every eye turned towards them. Then the whispers started as her father and Bridgett appeared to greet them.

He'd heard all about the woman from Zoey and Scarlett over the past few years. Zoey had told them how Bridgett had attacked her in the lawyer's office in Vegas at the reading of her father's will, so he was on guard around the woman. Even though he knew that Aubrey could take care of herself, he was determined not to give the woman an opening to harm a hair on Aubrey's head.

There was a glint of something in Bridgett's eye when they were introduced officially. It was funny, even though he'd been present earlier, the woman hadn't paid any attention to him. He was pretty sure that it was because she'd been so focused on hurting Aubrey and making her point that she had her claws in Aubrey's father.

However, this time, when Aubrey introduced him in front of all the watching eyes, Bridgett made a point to hug him and offer him her warmest welcome. He'd held very firm and still.

He noticed the attraction in her gaze as she ran her eyes over his tux, but it was the hint of crazy that he was watching out for.

He saw a flash of it when he helped Aubrey off with her coat. Bridgett ran her eyes over Hannah's dress choice for Aubrey and anger flooded her eyes. Hannah had definitely known what she was doing when she picked the beautiful and expensive outfit for Aubrey. Bridgett obviously couldn't stand competition, even when they weren't competing for the same man, seeing as she was supposed to be in love with Aubrey's father.

Earlier, when they'd been shopping for Aubrey's outfit, Aiden had inwardly balked at the cost of the dress. Then the shop owner had waved away Aubrey's attempt to pay for the outfit and mentioned that she owed Hannah a favor. The dress and shoes were free of charge.

He made a mental note to keep in Hannah's good favor.

Not long after they'd been greeted at the door, a flock of guests surrounded them. Aubrey was asked so many questions that he lost track of some of her answers. It was only after they'd each been given a glass of champagne that he realized she wasn't telling anyone the truth.

Whenever she was asked what she did for a living, she would make something up. Something ridiculous like helping starving children in Bali or working at a plastic surgeon's office in LA.

"What are you doing?" he asked her when they were alone for a moment.

She sipped her drink and shrugged. "These people don't listen or care," she said as she glanced around the room. "If you watch, the moment after I answer their question, if I can't benefit them, they tune me out." She sighed. "I've always messed with them." She chuckled and turned to him. "I've thought of some fun ones. One year at the Christmas party, I told everyone I was a stripper and almost everyone told me how wonderful what I was doing was."

He chuckled. "And here I was telling these people the truth."

She faked a little gasp. "Don't you dare. These people may actually think highly of you." She clicked her glass to his. "Then we'd be stuck here longer."

He sighed. "Is this what your childhood was like?" He motioned to the wealthy people surrounding them. It was true, he'd picked up on the fact that people were only talking to them because Aubrey was Harold's daughter. Most of them began the conversation by exclaiming that they didn't know Harold had a daughter or how much she looked like the old man.

"Some of it, yes. He didn't start inviting me to client dinners until after I hit puberty. My attendance was required. Most of the time he ignored me after he'd rattled off all my achievements. Then again, once I started failing him, he sort of just cut me off. I think it was the reason he kicked me out and dropped me after my eighteenth birthday. I didn't live up to his standards." She shrugged as she sipped her drink. Her eyes moved to where Bridgett was laughing loudly at something someone said to her. "She doesn't fit in," she said to him. "And everyone is making sure to let her know. It's sort of fun watching the wolves surround her."

He glanced across the room and noticed it as well. Her voice rang over everyone else's in the room, and each time she laughed, eyes turned to her in disgust.

Bridgett was dressed in red from head to toe, which caused her to stand out amongst all the black tuxedoes.

Where Aubrey's dress screamed class, Bridgett's dress screamed tainted woman demanding attention.

Bridgett's blond hair was styled so that everyone could admire the massive diamonds on her ears and around her neck.

He turned back to Aubrey and smiled at the small heart-shaped diamond she wore over her own heart.

He ran a fingertip over it. "You can take the girl out of Vegas..."

Aubrey laughed and he lost his breath at seeing her cut loose for the first time in days.

"God, you're beautiful when you do that," he said a little breathlessly.

Her eyebrows shot up. "What? Laugh?"

He nodded and moved a little closer to her. "When your smile reaches your eyes, it's the sexiest thing ever." He wrapped his arms around her. "Just how long do we have to stay here anyway?" he asked, causing her to laugh again.

"What is it you said you do?" They both turned as Bridgett approached them, a flute of champagne in her hand as she practically dragged Harold towards them.

Aiden's eyebrows shot up, then he glanced at Aubrey, who quickly jumped in.

"Aiden owns his own architecture firm," she answered easily.

It was close to the truth, but he would have described his business as a construction firm instead of an architectural firm. He decided to keep his mouth shut all the same.

"Oh?" Bridgett dropped her hold on Harold, who swayed slightly. Aiden frowned down at the older man. His color was off, and he didn't seem focused like he'd been earlier.

He'd seen the man's eyes fog over when he'd confused Aubrey with her mother earlier that day. He wondered how many other episodes the man was having and made a mental note to watch him more carefully.

The entire time Bridgett and Aubrey talked, he watched her father, who looked confused and out of touch. When Bridgett was done trying to belittle Aubrey, she turned around and grabbed Harold's arm and dragged him on to the next group of people to talk.

"Is that normal?" he asked again.

"Hm?" He could see that Aubrey was flushed and slightly annoyed at the conversation she'd had with Bridgett. He hadn't paid too much attention to what had been said because he'd been afraid that Harold was going to fall over at any moment.

"Your father." He motioned to the man, who was standing next to Bridgett, staring off into space as if he was drugged.

Aubrey's eyes followed his and she frowned. "No." She surprised him by pulling out her phone and stepping towards a set of glass doors.

He followed her out onto a balcony filled with potted plants and a large iron bench.

Aubrey sat down and held the phone up to her ear.

"Hi, Dr. Williams, it's Aubrey Smith." She waited as he sat next to her.

Thankfully, the small patio was covered since it was still raining outside.

"Yes, I'm back in town," Aubrey continued. "I was wondering. When was the last time my father came in for a physical?" She glanced towards the doors, and her eyes zoned in on her father. "That long?" She frowned. "Yes, I would appreciate it. Tonight, if possible. I'm here at the house for a party he's holding..." She stopped talking and her eyes narrowed. "Yes, I agree. I'll make sure we wait around to greet you. Thank you," she said before hanging up.

"So?" he asked, guessing most of what had gone on.

"Dr. Williams has been my father's best friend and doctor for most of his life. He's a few months older than my father. The last time he saw my father was a little over a year ago. Shortly after Bridgett appeared in my dad's life." She leaned back in the bench. "He's heading over here now. Whatever happens, we need to stick around until then to ensure that he's gained access to the party." She turned to him. "Dr. Williams said that for as long as he's known my father, he's never thrown a party and that it didn't sound like him. Of course, he'd hosted dinners with potential clients, but parties?" She shook her head. "Never. I didn't have the heart to tell him that this is his engagement party to a woman less than half his age." She sighed and lifted her hand to rub her forehead.

"Headache?" he asked.

"Too much champagne." She sighed. "I need something solid. It should be time for dinner soon." She stood up suddenly.

He stood and stopped her from returning inside. "We'll get to the bottom of this. Even though I had never met the man before today, something is definitely off about his physical appearance. He seems... drugged."

"Do you think..." she started, but then the patio door opened, and a couple came out and lit up cigarettes, forcing them back inside.

When they entered, she motioned towards Bridgett. "Do you think she has anything to do with this?"

"It could be dementia," he suggested. "But from what I've heard about her, I wouldn't put anything past her."

"But to drug someone. How would she get her hands on something that powerful? What would she use to make him act so... out of character?"

He pulled out his phone. "Let's see if I can find out. At least until the doctor gets here."

They stood in the corner, waiting for the guests to be called in for dinner while he searched the internet for possibilities.

When they sat at the massive table, which easily sat all fifty guests, he leaned closer to Aubrey and whispered. "There are lots of things that could cause this. Most likely it's some form of benzodiazepine. Guess we'll have to ask the doc when he gets here. Maybe he can do a blood test?"

Suddenly, a bell rang, which immediately got everyone's attention. Bridgett smiled as every eye turned to her. At this point, Harold looked like he was going to fall out of his chair and slide to the floor. He'd lost most of his coloring, but the odd thing was, he'd heard a few guests joking about how bad he looked. It seemed like no one else cared about Harold Smith.

"Thank you." Bridgett stood up and then nudged Harold, who immediately jumped up and held his glass, which was filled with a dark liquid. "Harold and I wanted to thank each and every one of you for being here to celebrate this important day with us." She nudged Harold again, who jumped in.

"Yes." He cleared his throat and then nodded. "I know it's not customary for me to have people over, but I couldn't contain the joy of sharing this news with my friends and family." Her father's eyes turned towards Aubrey, who sucked in her breath.

Aiden reached under the table and took her hand.

"It's my pleasure to announce that I've asked..." Her father shook his head as if trying to remember Bridgett's name. "Bridgett," he finally said, "to be my wife. She's said yes." He promptly sat back down as he finished off his drink.

There were a few claps in the group, but for the most part the table was silent.

"We'll be married in a week," Bridgett finished with a smile, ignoring the tension around her. She held her glass higher. "To true love," she said and drank quickly before sitting down next to Harold.

The fact that not a single person lifted their glass told Aiden that he wasn't the only one feeling the awkwardness of the situation.

"Is it true?" asked the man sitting on Aubrey's other side.

She shrugged. "It appears so." She glanced at Aiden. He could tell she was growing weary of the game.

Guilt hit him full force about the game he was playing with her. It was no wonder she was afraid of making commitments with her heart. The man that had raised her was void of emotion, even in an altered physical state.

Just as the main course was served, an older man stepped

into the room, glanced around, and then made a beeline towards Harold. Aiden knew immediately what was about to happen next when Bridgett's eyes grow huge at the sight of the other man.

"This should be a fun show," Aubrey said before standing up.

CHAPTER 17

"What are you doing here?" Bridgett almost squealed the question as Dr. Williams stopped beside Aubrey's father. "Harold and I don't want you here."

"I'm here at the request of a family member," Dr. Williams responded, dismissing Bridgett altogether. "Harold, why don't you and I step into your office for a chat?"

"He'll do no such thing." Bridgett stood suddenly, knocking over her chair. Immediately, an employee came and righted it.

"John," Harold said with a slight shake of his head, "I didn't call you." Her father glanced in her direction.

"Dad? Let Dr. Williams take a look at you. Something's not right."

"He's perfectly fine. Probably just a little tired from all the preparations for tonight's party." Bridgett placed a hand on her father's shoulder and held him in place.

"You are...?" Dr. Williams turned back to Bridgett.

Bridgett looked a little put out, now that it was official that they were engaged. She probably expected word to go out to the entire world about their engagement.

"Harold and I have just announced our engagement." She

held up her hand and showed the doctor the massive rock on her finger.

Aubrey smiled when the doctor covered his laughter with a cough. "Then I'm sure you want to make sure your soon-to-be husband makes it to the altar." He nodded to her father, who in the past few minutes had turned even paler and more confused looking.

"Honey?" Bridgett knelt beside him. "How about I help you upstairs to bed?"

"John? I should have called you," her father said again.

"That's it." Dr. Williams motioned to a few employees. "Please help him into his study and have my bag brought in from the trunk of my car. It's parked right out front."

The employees immediately jumped into action.

Dr. Williams turned to Aubrey. "Why don't you join us?" he asked her, then he turned back to Bridgett. "Your presence is required as well," he said in a stern voice. Not giving Bridgett a chance to respond, he turned and walked towards her father's office.

"You did this," Bridgett hissed as she tossed down her napkin. "I will ruin you," she said under her breath.

Before leaving, Aubrey turned to the crowd. "Feel free to finish your dinner. I would request that after you're done, however, you head on out. My father isn't in the best of health right now. Thank you for your understanding."

Bridgett marched back to her and yanked her arm. Then Aiden was there, hovering over her.

"Let her go," he hissed, and Bridgett immediately dropped her hold on Aubrey.

Aubrey could have handled Bridgett herself, but she wanted her father's acquaintances to see Bridgett for who she was. A bully.

"No, please." Bridgett smiled to the group. "Eat, drink. I'll straighten up this mess, and we'll be right back out here to finish enjoying our evening with everyone." She waved the staff over to finish handing out the dinner.

The moment she turned away, her smile dropped, and her eyes narrowed at the pair of them.

"Shall we?" Aubrey asked in a sweet voice and motioned towards her father's office.

"Drop dead," Bridgett mumbled under her breath as she passed by them.

"Nice. Guess it doesn't take much for her to show her true colors, huh?" Aiden said.

Aubrey chuckled. "Thanks to Zoey for cluing me in on that little fact."

Aiden shut the door behind them as they stepped into her father's office once more. Aubrey felt her stomach growl as she stood beside her father's desk and watched. Her father was sitting in his chair with Dr. Williams by his side. He was taking his heart rate while Bridgett hovered over him.

"He's fine. As I mentioned before..." She tried to pull Harold back to his feet, but her father at this point couldn't even stand. "He's just tired."

"Leave Dr. Williams to do his job," Aubrey told Bridgett.

The woman turned on her. "Just who do you think you are? Coming in here, demanding things?"

Aubrey's eyebrows shot up. "Me? First, I'm his daughter." She pointed towards her father. "Second, I haven't demanded anything. Dr. Williams showed up here and made all the demands. No doubt after seeing how sick my father was, he grew worried."

Bridgett opened her mouth to respond, but just then the doctor's bag was delivered.

"I don't like your father's blood pressure," Dr. Williams told Aubrey. The fact that the man wasn't addressing Bridgett just set the woman off even more. "I'm going to call an ambulance." The doctor pulled out his phone.

"No, you won't. Harold doesn't want—" Bridgett started.

"Thank you, Dr. Williams," Aubrey said firmly. "Since I'm his only current relative, I consent to him being taken in." She narrowed her eyes at Bridgett.

"I'm fine, John," her father broke in. His words were slurred, which made her worry even more.

It was strange—her entire life she'd hated the man, but seeing him the way he was now, well, it almost broke her. Maybe because she believed someone had done it to him? Maybe because it was Bridgett? Whatever the reason, she was determined to see that he returned to full health and that Bridgett got what she deserved. Which was absolutely nothing.

"Thanks," Dr. Williams said and touched her arm. "But, seeing as I'm still your dad's official primary physician"—he turned towards Bridgett and added—"it only takes my say so, legally speaking." He stepped away as he called nine-one-one to have an ambulance come get her dad.

"Afraid of what they might find?" Aubrey asked Bridgett quietly.

The woman glanced nervously over at the wet bar that lined the back of her father's office.

"No," she said firmly as she crossed her arms over her chest.

To Aiden's credit, he caught on quickly and strolled slowly over towards the bar and motioned to the bottle her father had drank from earlier that day. "Dr. Williams, can I offer you a drink?" Aiden picked up the bottle.

Aubrey saw Bridgett's eyes grow big.

"No, thank you," Dr. Williams said as he hung up.

"So, doc." Aiden leaned back and slowly poured a glass of her father's favorite bourbon. She knew he wasn't going to really drink it, not if he suspected, as she did, that Bridgett had put something in it. "I'm just wondering, what sort of things could cause these sorts of symptoms in a seemingly healthy man?"

"I'm sorry, young man." Dr. Williams turned to him. "I didn't catch your name."

"Oh." She moved forward. "I'm sorry, this is my boyfriend Aiden Stark. Aiden, Dr. Williams." Aubrey touched Aiden's arm. "He flew out here this morning with me when we heard..."—she shifted—"that my father wasn't feeling well." She decided quickly to keep her father's little game quiet.

Dr. Williams held out his hand. "It's nice to meet you," he said genuinely. "I can't remember the last time I saw Aubrey here, but she looks healthy and happy." He dropped his hand and moved over to once again stare down at her father. He leaned over and looked into her father's eyes. "Well, his eyes are milky and bloodshot; he seems disoriented and confused." He glanced at her. "He can't seem to remember what day it is but knows that there's a party going on in the next room."

"I told you. He's only tired," Bridgett asserted once again.

"And you?" Dr. Williams turned to the woman. "You are?"

Bridgett gasped. "I'm his fiancée." She touched Harold's shoulder again and squeezed it as if to wake the man out of his stupor.

"Which is a funny thing itself. I spoke with Harold just last week; he didn't mention having a fiancée."

"We just announced our engagement tonight," Bridgett said with a smile.

Dr. Williams turned to Aubrey. "Did you know about this?"

"Not a clue. I didn't even know Bridgett, who is the ex-wife of my friends' deceased father, was in New York and not on the stage in Las Vegas. Or that my father was seeing someone."

Dr. Williams was quiet for a moment before turning to Bridgett. "Are you staying here?" he asked the woman.

"I don't see how this is any of your business?" she gasped.

"Medical records." He pulled a notepad from his bag. "Harold has certain medical needs, prescriptions that he has been taking for years. I'm sure the police will need to know who is responsible for ensuring that he takes them daily."

Bridgett visibly paled at this and slid into one of the leather chairs.

"Do you think... that he messed up his prescriptions?" Bridgett asked. "I've warned him to label those things."

"Aubrey," Aiden interrupted holding up the decanter of bourbon. "Do you want a drink?" He poured a new glass for her. Everyone in the room saw Bridgett's eyes narrow as she watched Aiden's movements.

"Sure." She moved over to the bar area, took the offered glass, and then held it up to her lips. Instantly, she frowned down at the amber liquid. "I think this bourbon had gone bad." She jerked the glass away from her face and made a show of giving a disgusted face.

She hadn't smelled anything, but by the way Bridgett was watching her, she knew without a doubt that if the woman had slipped her father something, it was in the bourbon, and if they didn't call it out now, before the ambulance came for her father, that the container would be cleaned.

"Let me." Dr. William walked over and took the glass from her, then stuck his finger into the liquid and tasted it. The doctor immediately spit into the trash can. ". I gave Harold a prescription for it a few months back." He frowned down at the glass. Then he walked over to pick up the Waterford decanter and smelled the remaining liquid. "Enough in here to paralyze an elephant."

Just then there was a knock on the door and Martha rushed in. "There's an ambulance," she said to the room, her eyes going over the entire scene. "Oh, is there something wrong with Mr. Smith?"

"Show them in here," Dr. Williams said, taking the container with him. "I'll have this tested to make sure."

The medics arrived and the doctor stood aside to give them

access. Just then Bridgett jumped up and rushed to Harold's side, knocking the decanter out of the doctor's hands in the process. It hit the carpet with a thud and most of the liquid spilled out of it before the doctor could pick it back up.

"Harold," Bridgett cried as the medics strapped him onto the gurney. At this point, her father was almost completely unresponsive.

When the medics and Bridgett had left the room, Dr. Williams turned to Aubrey. "There's still enough in here to test."

"Take these too." Aiden held up the two glasses he'd poured. "There's probably more in these than what was spilled." He motioned to the floor.

Aiden walked forward and carefully poured the liquid back into the decanter.

The doctor said, "Something tells me you knew there was something in here all along."

Aiden sighed. "I gambled." He shrugged. "Tell me she won't get away with this."

"Will my father be alright?" Aubrey asked, worry filling her.

"Alprazolam can cause drowsiness and problems with vision and memory, but my main concern is that it can cause muscle weakness. I hope Harold's heart can withstand the amount he was given. Any idea how much he drank?"

"Since we got here around three, two glasses then at least one more glass at dinner. But he was acting a little funny then. Who knows how much he'd had beforehand," Aubrey answered.

"Thanks. Can I offer you a ride to the hospital?" Dr. Williams asked them.

"No, we'll head back and change then meet you there." Aubrey stepped forward and touched his arm. "Thank you for coming so quickly and for caring for my father for all these years."

Dr. Williams chuckled. "He may not be my favorite patient, but he is my friend." He tapped her hand before leaving.

"Well," Aiden said suddenly, "that was fun. Kind of reminded me of Clue." He changed his voice slightly. "After following the clues, I determined that it was Bridgett in the study with poison."

She couldn't believe it. At a time like this, with her father's life hanging by a thread, and Aiden still had the ability to make her laugh.

Her laughter turned to tears as his arms wrapped around her. "Come on," he said into her hair. "Let's go back and change then head to the hospital."

"I have to call—"

"You can call your sisters on the way back to our place." He pulled her towards the doors.

As she stepped outside, they were surrounded by some of the guests who hadn't left yet.

"Is Harold alright?" several of them asked.

"Yes, Dr. Williams just wants him to get checked out," Aiden answered for her as he continued towards the door.

"Martha, please make sure all of the guests make it home," she said to the woman as they walked by.

"Please keep us posted about your father's condition," Martha asked her.

"I will," she agreed and let Aiden slip on her coat.

When they stepped outside, the limo driver was waiting for them. "I heard about your father," the older man said. "Do you need a ride to the hospital?"

"If you don't mind, Carl, take us back to our place first so we can change. Then we'll head to the hospital."

"Sure thing, Miss Smith." The man opened the limo door for them.

When the car started moving, she pulled out her phone.

"Hey," Zoey answered. "We're all here," she called out. "Drinking and bitching about men. Well, they are drinking. I'm having milk," Zoey corrected.

"Taking the night off I see. When I'm away you guys play?" She smiled. "What did Dylan do now?" she asked.

"Nothing, it's not my husband that's the issue," Zoey supplied. "He's perfect."

Aubrey heard several of her friends groan or sigh in the background.

"Who then?" Aubrey asked. She needed normal for a moment before she sprung the evening's crazy on her friends.

"Brett," Elle supplied.

"Brett?" Aubrey sat up slightly.

Aiden glanced over at her. "What's wrong with Brett?"

"Our Brett? What did he do to piss you all off?" she asked the group as she turned her phone onto speaker so Aiden could hear.

"He kissed me," someone said loudly.

Aiden looked at her with question.

"Was that..." She frowned down at her phone.

"Dr. Lea Val is filling in for you tonight since you're off in the city dealing with crazy Bridgett," Hannah added with a giggle. "We didn't know that the good doctor would drink us all under the table. I mean, what do you weigh? Eighty pounds?" Her friend's voice was slightly slurred, indicating that the entire group, except for Zoey, were already hammered.

Lea could be heard laughing. "I went to medical school. Where do you think I learned how to drink? I never knew I could have a thing for a man in uniform."

"Speaking of the police..." Aubrey said.

Aubrey heard the phone shift off speaker.

Then Zoey asked, "How are things going up there?"

CHAPTER 18

As they headed back to change clothes, he listened to Aubrey fill Zoey in on what had just happened. The more he listened, the more he realized that it was all extremely bizarre and similar to a horror movie.

"I mean," Zoey said, "did she really expect to get away with poisoning your dad?"

"I don't know. Hey, listen, we're back at our place. We're going to change and then head over to the hospital," Aubrey said.

"Keep us posted," someone shouted. Then the phone was muffled as someone asked a question.

"Val wants to know what Bridgett gave your dad," Zoey said.

Aubrey glanced over at him in question.

"Alprazolam," he supplied.

"How much?" Val's voice came on the line.

"We don't know," Aubrey answered as he opened the front door for them. "Enough to be noticed. He was pretty much passed out when they carted him out of the house."

"Keep me posted," Val said to Aubrey. "He should be okay, if your father's health was good to begin with."

He saw Aubrey wince. "I will. Thanks, Val. Oh, and about Brett." She glanced over at Aiden and smiled. "Did you kiss him back?"

Val laughed. "You know it."

Aubrey laughed again as she hung up.

"Brett and Val." He shook his head. "Now there's a combination. Did you know that Brett hasn't dated since..."? He thought about it as they rushed up the stairs to change clothes. He stopped on the landing and cocked his head to think. "Hell, I guess I can't remember the last time he went out on a date. Then again, we don't gossip like you and your friends do."

She slugged him in the shoulder. "Stereotyping us won't get you far." She rushed up the rest of the stairs.

"It's not stereotyping when it comes to you and your friends. Remember, I've hung out with the five of you over the past three years," he called after her.

He changed out of the rented tux quickly and, while he waited for Aubrey, shot off a text to his friend.

-So, you and Dr. Val?

Brett quickly responded.

-Shit, it was a lapse of judgment.

He sent another quick text after that.

-I do admit that the woman is hot, but she can get under my skin. I only kissed her to get her to stop complaining about my injury.

Aiden punched dial quickly after reading that last bit.

"You were injured?" he asked when Brett answered the phone.

"I got a scratch and a sprain, nothing more."

"How bad?" He knew better. Brett always downplayed everything. Especially when it came to his health and his job.

Brett sighed. "I'll be on desk duty for the next week."

"What'd you do?" he asked.

"It wasn't me. You know how tourists can get when they

party too hard," Brett supplied. "A few big ex-jock types decided they wanted to borrow some golf carts at the country club at one in the morning. One of them ran me over when I informed them that they were all under arrest for a DUI."

"Seriously? Man, they ran over you?" He shook his head.

"It wasn't that bad. Like I said, we were on the greens and it was a golf cart. Top speed of what? Ten miles an hour." Brett chuckled.

"Listen, we're heading to the hospital. Someone tried to poison Aubrey's father. Long story, which I will fill you in on later, but I'll check in with you when we get back from New York."

"Wow, sure thing. Tell her that I hope her old man pulls through," Brett added as Aiden stepped out of his room. Aubrey was coming down the stairs.

"Sure will. Oh, and stay away from drunks on golf carts," Aiden added.

"Will do." Brett chuckled as he hung up.

"Brett?" Aubrey asked.

"Yeah." Aiden sighed. "Okay, so maybe we do gossip as much as you and your Wildflowers." He shrugged. "Sorry I said that." He opened the front door for her.

She turned to respond to him, but suddenly, an explosion of flashing lights caused them both to jump. He pushed in front of her to protect her only to realize that there were more than a dozen photographers standing between them and the limo, all snapping pictures of them standing in the doorway.

"What the..." he said, but Aubrey had tugged his arm and they raced through the growing crowd to jump into the limo.

"Sorry," Carl said as they pulled away from the curb. "They started showing up shortly after you went inside. I suspect that word has gotten out about your father being taken away in an ambulance. They must have followed us from the house."

"It's okay. Just get us to the hospital," Aubrey replied and leaned back. "It's like some bad movie," she said softly once they were on their way.

"Funny, I was thinking the same thing. I mean, what else could go wrong?"

"Don't say that. Remember what Ryan Kinsley did to us?" Aubrey shivered and tugged her coat closer to her.

"Right." He shook his head. "I think Bridgett and Ryan were cut from the same cloth."

Aubrey glanced over at him. "Ryan pulled a gun on Dylan; Bridgett was sneaking around trying to kill. I'm not sure which is worse."

"This changes our plans," he admitted.

She rested her head back as she nodded. "We may end up sticking around the city a little longer. You know, to make sure he gets back on his feet. If he does. Harold's health had never really been... spectacular. Not that he is an invalid. But when I met him for the first time, I remember thinking he was old back then. Now." She shook her head again, then she winced. "You don't think he and Bridgett actually..." She let the rest of her question hang in the air.

"God." He shook his head quickly. "Let's not even go there."

"Too late, it's already seared in my brain." She groaned.

"Hey." He nudged her chin until she looked at him again. "He's going to be okay. I know the two of you don't have the best relationship, and you try to come off tough, but it's obvious you still care for him."

"How can you hate and love someone at the same time?" She glanced out the windows.

He took her hand in his, then tugged her closer and wrapped his arms around her.

When they arrived at the hospital, they were told to wait in a waiting room. They were both slightly surprised that Bridgett wasn't there waiting as well.

"Do you think they let her back there with him?" she asked him.

"Not sure," he answered. "Could she be in police custody already?" he questioned.

"Let me text Dr. Williams and tell him we're here." She pulled out her phone.

Less than five minutes later, the older man walked into the room and glanced around with a frown.

"What is it?" Aubrey went on guard. "My father?"

"He is resting comfortably," he assured her quickly. "We've pumped his stomach and are flushing the drugs from his system, which will take some time. I want to keep him under surveillance for a few days."

"Had he been drugged?" Aubrey asked.

"The lab is confirming his blood and the bourbon now. I'll keep you posted."

"Bridgett?" Aiden asked.

"Didn't get to the hospital, as far as I know," the doctor answered. "The police are already looking for her for questioning. They'll want to talk to the both of you as well. I'll show you to a room where you can wait." He turned to go.

"Can I see him?" Aubrey asked.

Dr. Williams smiled. "Yes, I'll come get you when he's been moved to a private room," he said as they followed him down a hallway. "This is my office." The older man motioned to a large room. "I'll come get you after they move your father. If it's okay, I'll send the police your way as well, so you can both give them your statements."

"That would be fine," Aubrey said with a smile. "Thank you." She touched his arm. "For showing up so quickly. For being there for my father."

Dr. Williams sighed. "I should have checked in on him sooner." He shook his head as he walked out.

They waited for less than fifteen minutes before three police officers knocked on the door and stepped in behind Dr. Williams.

After introductions were made, Aiden was asked by the officers to wait outside while they talked with Aubrey. Dr. Williams disappeared again and told him that when Aubrey was done, she could see her father in room eleven-forty-three.

"She'll have to show ID at the door. The police have put a guard on his room. If Bridgett shows up, they've been instructed to detain her and keep her out of the room."

"So, it was confirmed poison then?" he asked.

Dr. Williams sighed. "Technically, I'm not allowed to say." He glanced towards the door. "Tell Aubrey if she needs anything, I'm heading home for a few hours of sleep. I'll be back around eight." He shook Aiden's hand. "It was smart thinking." He shook his head as he walked down the hallway.

When the office door opened again, he had a fresh cup of coffee in his hands from the vending machine down the hallway and handed it to Aubrey. "Your dad's up in room eleven-forty-three," he said as he stepped past her. "Head on up. I'll meet you there after I'm done here." He nodded to the officer who was watching them.

"Thanks," she said motioning to the coffee. "I'm going to sleep great tonight." She leaned up on her toes and placed a soft kiss on his lips.

When he closed the door behind him, he glanced at the three officers. The woman was sitting behind the desk while the two men were still standing.

Directing his eyes to the woman, he held out his hand for her. "Aiden Stark."

"Detective Rhodes." She shook his hand and motioned to the chair. Her brown eyes assessed him. "I take it you were raised by a woman?"

He chuckled. "What made you suggest that?"

"Most men immediately assume I'm here to take notes." Her

eyes narrowed. He gauged the detective was roughly five years older than he was. Her short brown hair was cut in a style that accented her oval face. If he'd been a single man, he would have probably flirted with her. But the only woman he wanted now and forever had just left the room.

He winced. "First off, I'm not chauvinist. Second, that one"—he pointed towards the closed door that Aubrey had just left out of—"has two black belts. I know better than to underestimate anyone." He sat down.

"Fair enough." The detective smiled at him. "Shall we get started?"

For the next fifteen minutes, he answered all of the detective's questions, no matter how mundane they were. When they had arrived in New York. How they had traveled. Where they were staying. Why he'd suspected the poison was in the bourbon. If he'd met Bridgett before today.

The only question he'd struggled with was when the detective asked what his relationship with Aubrey was.

"We've been… together for over three years," he answered, causing the detective's eyebrows to rise slowly. He chuckled. "It's complicated."

She leaned on the desk and smiled at him.

"Relationships usually are." She ran her eyes over him. "She's one lucky lady," she added standing up. "I think we're done here," she said to the other officers. "We'll keep an officer on Mr. Smith's door until he's released. As I mentioned to Miss Smith, we have an APB out for Bridgett Rowlett. We've sent the local PD out to talk with"—she glanced through her notepad—"Zoey and Scarlett Rowlett to see if they have any further details about Mrs. Rowlett's whereabouts. Per Aubrey's request, I've also requested that a local officer be stationed at the camp for their safety."

"You think she'll go after them?" He tensed. He hadn't thought of that angle.

"No, but your girl seemed to be worried about her friends."

"Yes, me too."

The detective nodded. "That should do it for now. Miss Smith didn't seem to know how long the two of you would be in town..."

"Same. Need us to give you a heads-up when we decide to leave?" he asked.

"If you wouldn't mind." She handed him a business card, then held out her hand.

When he was riding up the elevator to the eleventh floor, he sent a text to Brett.

-Local PD wants someone from your office to watch out at the camp for Bridgett. Think you can get assigned the duty? I know you're on desk duty, but it would help to have someone I trust watching out for my friends.

-On it. Got the call ten minutes ago. Heading out there now. I'll keep you posted.

He knocked on the door to room eleven-forty-three and entered after he heard Aubrey call out for him to come in.

Seeing her sit on the side of the bed with her father's hand in hers and tears rolling down her cheeks tore his heart apart. Seeing the old man's eyes just as wet as Aubrey's had his attitude of the old man shifting.

CHAPTER 19

Aubrey closed her eyes and tried to relax. The taxi ride between Isaac's place and the hospital seemed to take longer than before. It was a quarter past ten and she was beyond tired.

"Are you doing okay?" Aiden asked her. Just the sound of his voice helped her relax even further.

"Yes," she answered with a sigh. "I'm just tired."

"Ditto." He pulled her into his arms, and she relaxed against his chest. "I know I've been trying to stick to the new rules, but I'm willing to bend them, for tonight. I just want to hold you." He placed a kiss on her forehead.

She thought about falling asleep in his arms and nodded. She needed it. She needed him. More now than ever, she just wanted to have him beside her. Holding her.

"I'd like that," she said, stifling a yawn.

"Rest. I'll wake you up when we get there," he told her.

She didn't need any further encouragement and felt herself drifting off, lulled by the hum of the car and the sound of the windshield wipers clearing the rain off the windshield.

She woke when Aiden shifted as the car stopped. "We're home," he said softly.

For a moment, she thought he meant they were back in Florida. At River Camps. Then she blinked and noticed the building they were stopped in front of and scooted out of the back of the cab and let him lead her inside.

She didn't know how she made it up the stairs, but she sat on the edge of the bed as he pulled off her shoes and pants.

She quickly pulled off her coat and then, while keeping her T-shirt on, pulled off her bra and tossed it across the room.

"That was perhaps the sexiest thing I've ever seen you do," Aiden said as he toed off his own shoes.

She'd already crawled under the blankets and was waiting for him to join her.

"I'm too tired to think," she said with a yawn.

"Sleep," he said and when she didn't feel him climb in the bed with her, she opened an eye.

"Are you coming to bed?" she asked him. He was standing at the window, his phone in his hands.

"Soon, I wanted to—"

"Aiden." She sat up and opened the blankets for him. "Shut it off. Come to bed. You can do whatever it is in the morning."

He chuckled, then set his phone on the nightstand, unzipped his jeans and removed his shirt, and crawled in beside her in only his boxer shorts.

He was warm and she relaxed against his chest, enjoying the play of muscles. She'd missed him. Missed feeling him so close to her.

As she drifted off to sleep, memories of Aiden filled her thoughts and dreams.

They both jolted awake to the sound of a phone ringing.

"Mine," she said and noticed Elle's number on her screen. "Morning," she answered the call.

"Bridgett got away?" Elle asked.

Instantly, she knew she was on speaker phone again. Most likely, all of her friends were gathered around the breakfast table in the employee dining hall.

She ran a hand over her hair, pushing the red locks out of her eyes. "Yeah, she never showed up at the hospital. The police are looking for her."

"And you think she'll show up here?" Zoey asked.

"No, I don't think, but I'm not taking any chances," she responded. "Especially since you have a baby on the way." She stood up and walked over to the window and looked out. She was a little shocked to see snow covering the ground.

How long had it been since she'd seen the white powder? Not long enough. She shivered at the thought of heading out in the cold and turned back to the room. Aiden was lying in bed, shirtless, watching her.

She couldn't stop her eyes from running over him. God, how had she not really taken the time to appreciate how perfect he was before? It was as if she'd been given access to a gift and then shunned it. Now she could see what she'd been missing for all these months and desperately wanted to get her hands on it, on him, again.

"Earth to Aubrey." Elle's voice broke into her thoughts.

"I'm here." She shook her head and turned back to the window. "It's snowing here, but we'll be heading to the hospital again soon. I'll let you know how my father is doing then."

"Okay. For now, Brett is staying in the apartment in my old room," Elle added. "You didn't tell us that he was injured."

"He was?" Aubrey turned back to Aiden.

"Sprained wrist, and he looks like someone beat him with a baseball bat," Zoey added.

"Still, he's fit enough to hang out here for a while. It's not like we think Bridgett's going to come here. She hasn't thought of us since the last time she tried and failed to get our dad's money," Scarlett said.

"I doubt she'll come here, but we're on alert," Elle added.

"Good," Aubrey said.

"Now, we didn't mean to wake you up. Get some rest," Zoey added.

"Thanks, I'll keep you posted." She hung up.

"Everything alright?" Aiden asked as he shifted, which had the sheet that covered him falling lower over his hips.

"Yes." She ran her eyes over him. "So, I was thinking." She slowly started to crawl up the bed towards him. "Just how much do we want to change the rules?"

His eyes locked with hers as he reached for her. "I think we could take a few days… reprieve. Seeing the extenuating circumstances." He reached for her and then pulled her up until she was lying over his chest as his hands roamed over her hips.

Instantly, she felt her entire body jump into full speed. She was hot and cold for him at the same time. He was running his hands slowly over her hips. When he nudged his fingers under her underwear, she arched and moaned, trying to get closer to him. She could feel his hardness pressed against her and felt just as affected as he was.

Finally, she laid her lips over his and the rest of her melted.

"I've missed this," he said, his hands firmly on her butt. "Being with you. Holding you. Pleasing you." Suddenly, she was spun around and he was pinning her to the bed.

She laughed up at him. "I let you do that."

He chuckled. "Good, now maybe you'll let me do so much more to you." His hands trailed over her stomach, down to the apex of her legs.

She closed her eyes on a sigh and reached for him, only to have him slip out of her grasp.

"Since we're making an exception, I'm going to make this last," he said.

She watched him slowly lift her shirt, and then she leaned up and he removed it completely. Her skin heated as his eyes ran over her. He leaned down and trailed his mouth over her, causing her skin to vibrate.

"Aiden," she begged as her nails dug into his shoulders.

He'd moved lower, his hands spreading her legs wide until he settled in between her thighs as his mouth covered her silk panties.

She cried out as a finger slipped below to brush against her naked skin.

"Come for me first," Aiden said against her skin as he tugged the material away so he could trail his mouth across her.

She grabbed a fist full of the sheets as she arched and moved under him. God, he was so good at pleasing her.

Maybe that's why she'd allowed their relationship to go on for so long? She couldn't believe how wonderful it felt to have him touch her again.

"Please." She closed her eyes and held her breath. Needing, wanting, the release.

"Come for me," he growled against her thigh. "I want to taste you again. God, how I've missed you."

She felt herself building and knew that she was no longer in control. She would gladly give him anything he asked.

Moments after feeling her release, he moved up and covered her with his own body. She found enough strength to reach up and wrap her arms around him.

"Aiden," she sighed as he slipped into her.

"God, I've missed you," he groaned as he moved above her.

"Please." She dug her nails into his hips, needing him to start moving. Needing all of him.

She wrapped her legs around him, and he laughed as she tried to get him to move.

Since she couldn't get him to start, she decided to try a different tactic and, instead, leaned up and trailed her mouth over his shoulders. When she scraped her teeth over his skin, he groaned, and she smiled when she felt him start to move.

"Witch," he groaned as he trapped her hands in his.

"Tell me you're still under control," she dared him.

"I'm trying to be." He chuckled as his eyes ran over her. When they locked onto her erect nipples, she knew he'd lost the last hold of his control.

He leaned down and covered her mouth with his again. She felt the deepness of the kiss. Knew that whatever happened now, they were in this together.

"I didn't think it was possible to be exhausted and pumped at the same time," he joked as they lay in each other's arms afterward.

"I feel the same." She ran her fingers over his chest. "I've missed this."

"Sex? Or me?" he asked, glancing down at her.

She thought about it a moment and had him shaking her.

"Both," she admitted with a laugh.

"We'd better get to the hospital," he said after a moment. "I know this great little place we can stop and grab some breakfast before we head there."

"Oh?" She glanced down at him. "I didn't think you'd been to New York before."

He shook his head. "Spent a semester here my freshmen year in college," he admitted. "Hated it and transferred down to Georgia instead."

She laughed. "Did I tell you it's snowing out there?" She motioned towards the window.

"I heard." He frowned. "We could be in our swimsuits on the beach right now."

"I know." She let him go and watched him stand up. He walked around the room, comfortable wearing only his skin. Her eyes followed him.

"Well?" he asked from the bathroom door.

She stood and followed him into the other room.

"Damn." He stopped and looked around. "This is a far better bathroom than I have downstairs."

She'd paid little attention to it yesterday, but now she glanced around and appreciated the glass, the marble, and the clean lines.

There was an entire wall for a shower. White tiles and clear glass made the room feel twice the size it was. A modern floating tub sat in front of etched glass windows. Dual porcelain sinks with large mirrors hanging over them filled another wall.

Aiden was right, the bathroom was gorgeous. Better than the one she had back at the camp.

"I guess I didn't get to fully appreciate it yesterday. I was too busy being worried for my father."

"Speaking of which," he said as they stepped into the water together. "I didn't mean to interrupt your conversation last night."

She smiled and wrapped her arms around him. "No, you didn't. He'd just woken up."

"Oh?" he asked, holding onto her.

She sighed and rested her forehead against his chest. It was hard to explain, but she hadn't been crying because she'd been relieved that he was okay. She'd been crying because he'd woken up and once again called her Nora instead of Aubrey.

She had a feeling that her father was slipping away from her. Not that he'd ever been a major part of her life. The entire time she'd lived under his roof, she'd only seen him about a dozen times a year.

He'd controlled so much of her day-to-day life that she knew he'd been watching everything she'd done. It had been almost like living under a microscope. Like she was trapped in prison instead of a home.

She tried to think of one good time she'd had with her father while she got dressed and ready for the day, but the only thing she could come up with was the day he'd ridden with her to drop her off at the airport so she could go to River Camps.

She pulled on the best dress pants she'd packed and double-checked her reflection one last time. Aiden had disappeared downstairs to the room he'd left his luggage in to get dressed.

Her eyes ran over to the bed they'd shared last night, and she felt her body instantly respond to what they'd done to each other earlier.

She couldn't believe the control he had over her body. It was almost as if he snapped his fingers and she jumped to attention.

"Ready?" he called up to her.

"Coming," she replied and then felt her face flush at the memory of him making her come several times that morning in the bed and again in the shower.

Isaac's place was bigger than they needed for the visit, but it was nice to have room to spare and their privacy, which they wouldn't have in a hotel room. She knew that Isaac rented out the empty home when he and his wife weren't living in the beach house that they'd purchased not far from the campgrounds.

They stopped at a little bagel shop a few blocks from the hospital and had breakfast sandwiches. The simple sandwich was one of the best meals she'd had in a while.

They showed their IDs to police positioned outside the room and were approved for entry. A nurse opened the door for them. It was the same nurse that had visited her father last night.

"I just got back on shift and wanted to check in on your father. It looks like he had a good night." She stood back so they could walk into the room. "I was just going to go check and see if Dr. Williams was around." She smiled at them and then left the room.

"Hi, Dad." Aubrey walked over and sat next to her father's

bed. "How are you feeling this morning?" She noticed instantly that his coloring was better.

"Confused." Her father sat up slightly. "No one will tell me where Bridgett is."

She took a deep breath and glanced over to Aiden.

"I'll go..." He glanced towards the door.

"I could use some real coffee," her father threw towards him. "I'm sure you could find a respectable coffee shop somewhere near here. I like it black."

Aiden's eyebrows shot up, and Aubrey shrugged. "Would you mind? I could use another cup myself."

"Sure." He walked over and leaned closer to kiss her, lingering over her lips. She guessed it was so her father would get the hint that he was more than just an errand boy. "I'll be back," he promised her.

"Is that serious?" her father asked when they were alone.

Instead of answering him, she shrugged. "Was what was between you and Bridgett serious?" she countered.

"It is." Her father's eyes narrowed. "What do you mean, was?"

"Dad, Bridgett poisoned you. She's the reason you're in here. You almost died."

Her father shook his head. "No, that can't be true."

"I'm assuming she had you change your will?" She felt her stomach roll at the thought.

"No." He frowned. "She didn't have me change it, but I was going to do so after the wedding." He jerked his hand free from hers, and she felt her heart dip. "She enlightened me about all the things you've done."

"Done?" She frowned down at him. "What have I done?"

"You and your little friends. Just like Nora. She came begging for a handout as well. Of course, she didn't want me to have any say in my own heir. I blame her for ruining you. Had I known that you were a lost cause..." He shook his head. "She spoiled you those first eight years. I believed I could turn you around, but it was obvious that first night when you showed up late for dinner that you were just like her. Wild. Nothing and no amount of money I spent on you would ever tame you."

"Is that what you tried to do? Tame me?" Her stomach was doing small flips as she looked down at him.

"You were my only heir. It's a fortune. I needed to make sure that you understood the responsibility that came with the name Smith." He coughed, then waved her away when she moved to help him sit up a little more. "Over the years all you did was disappoint. First at home, then at school. I thought that forcing you out of the home at eighteen would wake you up." He shook his head. "But you went and started art school. Art school," he added in a distasteful tone. "Then you shacked up with those friends of yours. The only responsible one out of the bunch was the Rodgers girl. Of course, she ended up disappointing her parents as much as you disappointed me. But I was magnanimous and offered you a job anyway." He sighed and rested his head back. "Disappointed me even further."

At this point she felt her temper build.

"You are my father. The only thing I needed from you, you never gave me." She crossed her arms over her chest. "Nor could you ever offer anyone. You are, without a doubt, the most selfish man I've ever known. I was a little girl whose world had been turned upside down, and you were concerned about me being late for dinner?" She realized her voice had risen when he shifted and started to cough.

She wanted to leave him, to watch him suffocate in his own spit, but her kind heart won out and she rushed over and poured him a glass of water and then handed it to him.

He shoved it aside and it spilled onto the ground.

"I'm trying to help you." She was growing even more frustrated.

"You're probably the one who poisoned me," he said firmly just as the door opened and Dr. Williams stepped in.

"Harold." Dr. Williams rushed over to her father and frowned down at his friend. "It's thanks to your daughter and Aiden that you're alive right now. She's the one who called me and asked me to stop by last night. Aiden is the one who found the poison in your bourbon decanter. The police have interviewed your staff and some of the staff have confirmed that Bridgett had been seen sneaking out of your office earlier yesterday morning. No doubt that is when she slipped the alprazolam into the decanter."

The doctor handed her father a glass of water and waited until he took a sip.

"Now, the police wanted me to inform them when you are ready to talk to them. However, if you don't open your eyes to what was really happening, then I'll have to keep them at bay." He walked over to touch Aubrey's arm. "You are indebted to your daughter and Aiden and so am I. Do you know what it would have done to me if I'd lost my favorite patient?"

Her father chuckled then leaned back and closed his eyes. "I'm tired." He turned to the doctor. "Any word on Bridgett?"

"She hasn't been here," he answered. "Aubrey has." He nodded to her. "Now, I'm going to go see about getting the latest blood test results to see if you're clean and clear." He turned towards the door, but glanced back. "I'll order you some breakfast."

He disappeared and she turned back to her father.

CHAPTER 20

When Aiden came back with coffee from the little shop in the lobby of the hospital, he didn't know what else he could do except stand by Aubrey. She was desperately trying to convince her father that she wasn't the monster Bridgett had made her out to be.

Every time her father wanted something, he would glance his way as if he was only around to wait on him. He kept his temper in check for the most part, but when he walked in after getting the man some dinner and overheard him berating Aubrey about how she and her friends had stolen all of Bridgett's ex-husband's money, he had to step in.

"You've got to be kidding." He set the tray of food down with a slight slam. "I'm done playing these games."

"Aiden," Aubrey jumped in.

"No." He shook his head. "I've sat in here all day and listened to you take the word of a woman that you've known for less than a year over the word of your daughter."

Aubrey touched his arm lightly. "Aiden, you don't have to—"

"Aubrey, you've done nothing but give into him your entire life. You dropped everything, your life, your job, to rush up here when you feared he was dead due to a silly game he wanted to play." He turned back to her father. "Something tells me that was Bridgett's idea." The look on her father's face confirmed his suspicions. "That woman has played this game before. I've heard what Zoey and Scarlett and their mother, Kimberly, had to go through all thanks to her." He took a deep breath when he noticed a spark in the older man's eyes. He could've sworn it was pride, but he was too fired up to stop now. "Aubrey and her friends made a successful business out of River Camps long before Jean Rowlett died. They didn't need his money."

"I know," her father surprised him by saying. "I've known everything that's gone on at that little camp of yours since the moment you stepped foot in that place," he told Aubrey. "That doesn't negate the things you've done to get there."

"What are you talking about?" Aubrey asked.

"Bridgett told me everything." He leaned back and closed his eyes.

"Like?" he asked the man. He could tell Harold was tired but knew that Aubrey wanted to get answers.

"How the five of you tricked the camp's owner, Joe Saunders, into giving up the place. How you'd plotted long ago how you were going to take over the camp." He closed his eyes.

"What?" Aubrey laughed. "Oh, that's a great story." She moved over and shook her father lightly. "Don't you fall asleep until you hear the real truth. Elle Saunders, one of my best friends, is Joe's granddaughter. Joe was the only man in my entire life whom I looked up to like a father." Aubrey glared down at her father. "Including present company. We all loved Joe. When he died, we all mourned. By fate, he left the camp to the five of us, and Elle had the idea of turning it into what it is today. We all forked over every dime we'd saved up until then and worked our butts off to turn it into what it is now."

"It's true," Aiden stepped forward. "I own the company that's been in charge of all the remodeling. For the first year, I didn't even take a salary. Hell, I've put more money, blood, and sweat into the camp than most. I know everything that's gone on there since day one." He glanced over at Aubrey. "And I'm Elle Saunders's cousin. Joe was my great-uncle. He'd always intended to leave the camp to the Wildflowers."

"I'm tired. Go away." Harold waved them away.

"No, not until you see the truth," Aubrey insisted.

"Aub." He touched her arm. "Let's let him rest."

Aubrey glanced up at him and shook her head as tears rolled down her cheeks.

"Why?" she said and turned around. "Why do you hate me so much?"

He laughed. "I don't hate you. You're my daughter. My only child."

"Then why?" She shook her head. "Why are you doing this? Why believe her over me?"

"Because I refuse to believe that my only heir would turn her back on me and leave her legacy to run a glorified daycare for adults," he spat out.

His color was improving, almost as if he thrived off the anger and the bitterness. He even looked refreshed as he sat up a little straighter.

"You abandoned me," he finished.

"Me?" She laughed. "You're the one who kicked me onto the street. I worked for years making barely enough to pay rent and eat. Then when I'd been pushed enough, you fired me."

"You quit," he retorted.

"It was either that or be blackmailed and forced to sleep with a coworker so he'd keep quiet as to just whose daughter I was," she spat back at him.

Aiden felt his anger grow. Aubrey had never told him that part before. He noticed her father's face grow red at that news.

"Who?" he asked quietly.

"Does it matter?" she threw back at him. "You're choosing to believe Bridgett over me."

"Why should I believe you? Your mother was nothing more than a drug dealer, a liar, and a cheat. She took you away from me, hid you from me until I tracked her down."

"Did you kill her?" Aubrey moved closer to his bed.

"What?" Harold balked and then looked at him, as if waiting for him to explain what she meant.

"My mother wasn't a drug dealer. She didn't have enough money to buy us dinner, let alone ten pounds of coke. Did you kill her or have her killed?"

Harold was silent for a moment. Long enough that Aiden moved closer to him and Aubrey.

"Answer her," Aiden said firmly.

"No, I never wanted her dead. I just… wanted her out of the way." He waved his hand. "Do you know how long I'd waited for an heir? How long I'd tried?" The old man shook his head. "It seemed impossible. Then… she wanted to keep you away from me after…"

"Did you have someone plant the drugs?" Aiden asked, narrowing his eyes at the man, and anyone could see the truth in her father's eyes. The guilt or hidden knowledge was written clearly on his face.

"She killed herself because of you," Aubrey cried out. "You took the only person who ever loved me away and stuffed me in the attic. You took away any chance I had at being loved or loving someone else. I was raised outside of the presence of kindness with no access to warmth." At this point Aubrey's voice had risen, and a nurse rushed inside and took in the entire scene. Aubrey was hovering over her frail father with Aiden standing just between them.

"Is everything alright in here?" the nurse asked Harold.

"Leave us." The old man waved her away as if she were nothing more than a hired hand.

"I'm sorry." The nurse turned towards Aubrey, ignoring Harold's demands. "I'm going to have to ask you to leave."

"Gladly." Aubrey lowered her voice as she spoke to her father. "If you continue to choose to believe a stranger over your own blood, then I no longer care what happens to you. Let her poison you and steal all your money." She waved her hands. "God knows she's probably spent more of it over the past year than I ever did." She walked towards the door and grabbed her purse and jacket before storming out of the room.

"I don't say this to too many people," Aiden said, turning towards the man, "but you are one of the dumbest people I've ever met." He turned and left the room.

He caught up with Aubrey at the elevator. She was punching the down button so hard, it was a wonder it didn't break.

"Hey," he said when the doors finally slid closed and they were alone in the elevator. Pulling her into his arms, he held onto her and felt her entire body vibrate with either anger or pain.

"What now?" she asked. "How can I get the truth from him? He should pay for what he set in motion." She glanced up at him. He noticed it hadn't been tears but anger she'd battled with while he'd held onto her.

"We'll figure this out. Something tells me that he's not going anywhere at the moment." He sighed. "How about we head out and get some dinner?"

The elevator doors opened, and she took his hand as they walked towards the exit.

"I don't think I could eat." She frowned up at him. "I'm too worked up."

"Want to head back, change, and then go for a run?" he offered.

"Now that sounds more like it. I have all this..."

"Pent-up anger?" he offered.

"What I really want to do is find a dojo and kick someone's butt. Preferably someone bigger than I am."

He chuckled and wrapped his arm around her as they walked out onto the street. "Remind me never to get you angry." He kissed the top of her head. "And never forget that I am thoroughly intimidated and turned on by the way you can move."

She turned into his arms and chuckled softly. "Most men are afraid. So far you're the only one who hasn't run in the opposite direction."

He'd just stepped back from kissing her when he spotted the woman leaning against the brick building opposite the hospital. She's dyed her bright blond hair to a rich jet black, which somehow made her stand out even more. She had a cigarette between her fingers, raised as if she were about to take a puff, when she froze. Instantly, he could tell that she knew that he'd spotted her.

"Call the police," he shouted as he rushed across the street.

He was halfway there when he realized Bridgett had taken off. She'd been wearing jeans and tennis shoes under a long black raincoat.

"I'm faster. You call the cops," Aubrey shouted at him as she darted past him and disappeared around the same corner Bridgett had fled around.

"Shit," he said loudly as he pulled out his phone.

Aubrey was right, she was faster than he was, but he was bigger and... he cursed again. Hadn't he just told her that she intimidated him with her self-defense skills. He knew she could take care of herself, but his fear for her safety kept him a few yards behind her. He was huffing and puffing while he spoke to the nine-one-one operator. He set a mental reminder to start jogging again.

"Aub, I'm behind you," he called out when he gained some ground on her. "Cops are on the phone," he shouted as people separated for them.

"Move!" Aubrey had shouted several times.

He couldn't believe how fast Bridgett was. The taller woman's legs seemed to eat up the pavement, and it was apparent to him now that she knew exactly where she was heading.

Since the snow had made ground slippery, most shops and restaurants had shut down their outside displays.

But when he turned the last corner and almost bumped into the back of Aubrey, he realized she'd led them to probably one of the only outdoor farmers market being held in the big city on that evening.

"Shit." Aubrey glanced around. "Do you see her?"

"No," he said after a moment of looking around. Since he was a deal taller than Aubrey, he could easily see over most of the people's heads.

"There," he said after spotting a dark head in a black raincoat.

They both rushed across the area, only to realize a few feet away that it wasn't Bridgett, but a younger woman with two small children.

"You don't think she'd double-back, do you?" Aubrey asked.

"It's worth a look." He took her hand, and they started walking briskly back the way they'd come.

"Are you okay?" she asked as they walked.

He realized he was still breathing heavy and tried to catch his breath. "I suppose I need to get back into my morning routine of jogging again."

"You could always join one of my classes," she suggested with a nudge.

"How did Bridgett outrun you?" he asked when the hospital was in sight.

"She has almost a full foot on me," Aubrey replied.

He wasn't surprised to see several officers outside her father's room when they stepped out of the elevator. It was the same two officers that had been in the room with Detective Rhodes the evening before.

"Anything?" he asked the two men.

"No. We've checked on Mr. Smith, and he's resting comfortably and alone," the older officer answered. "Did anyone join in your chase?"

"No," Aubrey answered as she peeked her head into her father's room. "I'm going to…" She motioned inside.

He nodded and figured he'd stay outside with the officers to fill them in on how Bridgett had changed her appearance.

When Aubrey stepped outside again, he could tell instantly that she was tired. The chase had burned off all of her anger.

"We're going to head back and get some rest," he said, taking Aubrey's hand.

"We've been assigned here for the night. We'll take shifts sitting with him. From what it sounds like, the doctor is going to release him in the morning," the officer supplied.

"Thanks," Aubrey said with a sigh.

This time when they stepped into the elevator, she rested her head on his shoulder.

"Food first then rest?" he asked.

"Yes." She nodded and held in a yawn. "Why do you think she was watching the hospital?" she asked him when they were in a taxi. Now as the skies grew darker, the snow was starting to fall again.

"I'm not sure," he said after he'd thought about it for a moment. "Maybe to see if the police were after her? I mean, it's being kept out of the news."

"Yeah, Dad's lawyers are all over it. I doubt he'll ever allow the full story to get out. Let alone any of the pictures taken of us last night. After all, he doesn't want to look weak in the public eye." She rolled her eyes.

"At some point," he said when the taxi stopped, and he

helped Aubrey out, "we'll need to talk about your mom and everything."

"Later." She sighed and glanced around. "Where are we?"

"Hannah texted me a few great places to eat earlier. This was number one on her list." He shrugged and glanced up at the Greek restaurant. "She says you like Greek food."

"God"—Aubrey held her stomach—"I love it." She rushed towards the door with him on her heels as more snow fell.

CHAPTER 21

By the following morning, Aubrey was ready to head home. She'd had enough of the city. Enough of the foul weather. She wanted, no needed, her friends and the warmth of Florida.

She'd gotten word from Dr. Williams that her father had already arrived safe and sound at home. So what was really keeping her there? Dr. Williams had informed her that he would be spending a few days checking in on her father personally and had even hired a full-time nurse to watch over him.

"He's not back to his old self quite yet, but he's getting there," Dr. Williams told her over the phone.

"Thank you," she said, glancing out over the wet city. The snow had melted again, leaving everything black and slick. She shivered at the thought of heading outside into the mess.

"He mentioned that the two of you had a misunderstanding," Dr. Williams said.

"Mis..." She held in the chuckle and thought about what her father had basically confessed to them. Shaking her head, she replied. "He's taking Bridgett's side. He actually accused me of poisoning him."

"Aubrey, you can't take that to heart. He was still under the effects of the alprazolam. It wasn't completely out of his system until late last night after you'd left."

Her eyes narrowed as she stiffened. "He has never taken my side on anything, even before he was drugged," she reminded the doctor.

He was silent for a moment, then added, "I remember when you first came to live with Harold. He was so excited to finally have a child. You would've thought that he'd won the lottery."

"Did you know my mother?" she interrupted his memories.

"Well, not really. I'd met her on several occasions. I'm the one who did the paternity tests on you. Naturally, she demanded to be present during the entire process."

"From what you noticed, was my mother doing drugs?" she asked, leaning her head against the cold window glass.

"No, no," he answered. "I said so when I was summoned to court."

She jolted upright. "You testified?"

"When your father sued for full custody, naturally, I was called in to weigh in on the test results and the health of your father. It wasn't easy for a man in his late fifties to take on a child. He'd accused your mother and torn down her lifestyle. He even had a bunch of her past coworkers on the stand saying she had done drugs and left you alone at times."

Her temper grew. Not once could she remember being left alone until Harold had gained full custody of her.

"And you saw her again in court?" she asked.

"Yes," he said softly. "The day before...she died."

"Did she appear suicidal then?" she asked.

"No," he said firmly. "She was angry. Like you were yesterday evening when I walked into your father's room. I've seen that look in your eyes often enough over the years to know it was anger, not sadness."

Aubrey closed her eyes and tried to remember anything

about that day she and her mother had returned home from court. But, as with most of her memories of Nora, they were faded or mixed together.

"Can you get your hands on my mother's autopsy reports?" she asked, feeling her stomach roll at the thought of reading through them herself. But she had to know and, at this point, trusted Dr. Williams completely. He'd never done anything unkind to her, and even though he'd been her father's best friend and physician over the years, she knew he was a just man.

"Aubrey," Dr. Williams started, but then stopped and grew quiet. "I'll see what I can come up with."

"Thanks," she said before hanging up.

Strong arms wrapped around her, and she leaned back against Aiden's chest while they watched the rain soak the pavement outside.

"I want to go home." She sighed. "But I don't think I can until this is finished. If you want—" she started, but Aiden quickly turned her around and wrapped his arms around her.

"I'm not going anywhere," he said into her hair.

"Your work," she started.

"Just like you, I have employees that can easily fill in for me," he answered with a sigh. "Besides, I brought my laptop. I'm working on a few things here. I don't always have to swing a hammer to get work done."

"No." She closed her eyes and enjoyed the smell and feeling of him. They'd just showered together and already her mind was playing over how she could get him naked again.

"How about we order some delivery, crawl back in that bed, and spend the entire day watching movies?" he asked her.

She glanced up at him. "You read my mind, only…" She ran her fingers over his chest. "I wasn't thinking of watching television." Her eyes met his and she saw them heat with desire.

For the past two nights, he'd pleased her, given her exactly what she'd needed, while she'd kept the one thing that he'd wanted from him.

This time, however, when he kissed her, she felt her grip on her heart start to slip and, for the first time, she didn't mind.

"Aub," he moaned against her lips.

"No, don't think. Just show me." Her eyes locked with his. "Please." Her hands were already removing the T-shirt he'd pulled on. His skin was still wet in places from his shower, and she licked the droplets off him as she fisted his shirt in her hands.

"You're killing me," he groaned when she had unsnapped his jeans and lowered them on his hips.

"Good," she sighed as the material fell to the floor. Taking his length in her fingers, she glanced up at him, and his blue eyes searched her own. Then she ran her tongue over his length, and he reached over and wrapped her hair around his fingers, holding her, guiding her.

She knew exactly what it would take to send him over the edge but held off, knowing this time she wanted to take the journey with him. Standing up, she nudged him backwards until the back of his legs hit the side of the bed.

"I'm yours to command," he said with a grin as his eyes ran over her.

"Touch me," she responded. She moaned when his hands gripped her hips and pulled her closer to his naked body.

He tugged her clothes off, dropping them onto the floor as he hoisted her onto his lap and kissed her. Her hips started moving over him, rubbing her body against him as she felt herself growing more determined to enjoy what he was doing to her.

Then she was spinning around as he flung her on the bed. She laughed and wrapped her legs and arms around him.

"Hold onto me," he growled against her neck as he trailed

kisses over her. When he entered her, she arched and cried out his name.

How had she allowed herself to go six months without him? Her mind kept circling back to the fact that she had to protect herself, to stop this from going too far. But as she felt herself sliding over the edge along with him, she realized it was already too late. She'd fallen long ago. Now she just had to admit it to herself and, more importantly, to him.

"Don't move," Aiden said as he rolled out of bed a few moments later. "I'm going to order us some delivery." He smiled down at her. "You stay right here and find us something to watch." He handed her the remote to the flat screen television hanging on the opposite wall.

She lay there, watching him pull his clothes on before he grabbed his phone and disappeared down the stairs.

Lifting her arms above her head, she smiled up at the ceiling and stretched. How could she deny the fact that she was in love any longer? Day and night, she thought about being with Aiden. And it wasn't just physically any longer.

In her entire life, she'd only trusted a handful of people as much as she trusted him, her Wildflowers making up the majority of the list.

Pulling the blankets over her, she found the remote again and flipped on the set. She frowned up at a picture of herself.

Sitting up slightly, she turned up the volume to listen to the news report.

"Daughter of Harold Smith was seen here chasing down Bridgett Rowlett as she tried to visit her fiancé at the hospital. Bridgett is here today with us claiming that Aubrey Smith has accused her of poisoning her fiancé and has convinced the police that she set out to murder him." The camera panned out to focus on Bridgett, who was dressed in a simple blue dress with a dark grey jacket and a set of pearls around her neck. Her newly colored dark hair had been lightened slightly and pulled away from her face so that she looked a little older and very professional.

"Aiden!" she called out. She knelt at the foot of the bed, pulling on her clothes as she watched the set. "She's on the news."

"Who?" He came rushing in, then cursed when he noticed Bridgett. "I'm calling the detective." He dialed his phone while Aubrey listened.

"That's right," Bridgett was saying as she wiped a tear from her eyes. "My fiancé and I signed a prenuptial agreement. In his current will his entire estate is going to his daughter, Aubrey Smith. If I wanted to kill my husband"—she waved her hand in the air—"for his money, like his daughter is claiming, then wouldn't you think I'd make sure I at least get some of the money? It just doesn't add up. Aubrey came into town a few days ago. Until that point, my fiancé was in perfect health. Then, at our engagement party, he takes ill and she starts accusing me of poisoning him." She wiped her eyes again. "I haven't even been able to see him in the hospital. She chased me away."

Aubrey glanced over at Aiden as he spoke on the phone, relaying the news stations' information to the police.

"And you think that it is Miss Smith that is responsible for Harold Smith's poisoning?" the news anchor asked.

"Well, it would stand to reason. I mean, Harold was fine up until she showed up." Bridgett smiled slightly. "You know, we have some history. Aubrey and I do. Her and her little friends,"

"You're talking about Aubrey's friends and business partners, Zoey and Scarlett Rowlett, whose father, Jean Rowlett, you were married to?" the anchor asked.

"Yes." Bridgett smiled as if she was remembering the good times. "Shortly before Jean passed, his daughters convinced him to change his will. Leaving me bankrupt." Her voice pitched slightly.

"When you requested to come on the air, I did some quick research of my own. It appears that shortly before Jean Rowlett's cancer diagnosis, you filed for divorce and received a hefty settlement," the anchor said.

Bridgett waved her hand again. "That was all Jean's idea. He knew he was sick and didn't want the medical bills to drag me down. We both agreed he would leave everything to me in his will. I hadn't counted on his daughters convincing him when he was so sick to change it and leave me out altogether." She sniffled and wiped her nose.

"So, you're saying that this is what Aubrey Smith is doing now?" the anchor asked.

"She tried to kill her father. The woman should be locked up." Bridgett's voice rose. "Harold and I belong together."

"A man easily forty years your senior? It was rumored, shortly after your... relationship was made public that Harold had purchased a new luxury residence for you in Manhattan, along with several vehicles." The anchor shifted some papers and looked directly at Bridgett. "It's rumored that he has spent more than a million on items for you in the past month alone."

"That's preposterous." Bridgett's face heated. "If you want to investigate anything, you should be looking into that little summer camp Aubrey and the Rowletts opened up in Florida. Where did they get the money to open it? I've heard they've sunk a few million into that junk pile."

Aubrey felt her entire body vibrate with anger.

"You are of course talking about River Camps?" the anchor asked.

"Whatever they call it. I've heard its nothing more than a run-down camp filled with swingers and drugs." Bridgett waved her hand again as she smiled. "I can't believe it's not out of business yet."

At this point the news anchor turned towards the camera, which zoomed in and cut Bridgett out completely.

"I can personally give some insight into River Camps. Some of you may know that early last year I got married. Ralph and I had heard from some friends of a wonderful new adult place we could spend our honeymoon." The woman smiled. "We spent a wonderful two weeks at River Camps and not only enjoyed some of their fun activities, such as boating, zip lining, and horseback riding, but also got spoiled with food from the renowned chef Isaac Andrews. We would gladly return to the beautiful resort anytime. The camp, a former elite summer camp for young women, was handed down to Elle Saunders from her grandfather, who had started the camp many years previous. Elle and her five best friends, Zoey and Scarlett Rowlett, Hannah Rodgers, daughter of Andre and Leslie Rodgers, along with Aubrey Smith, pooled their savings together to reopen the camp." The woman turned back to Bridgett, who was staring at her with her mouth opened. "I even enjoyed taking several of Aubrey Smiths' self-defense classes while I was there."

The anchor's eyes narrowed and suddenly Aubrey remembered the woman, Cora, along with her husband, Ralph. Cora Jolett had lightened her hair since her visit, which had thrown Aubrey off.

Just then, there was a commotion off screen. The camera panned out and showed two officers, including the female detective working the case, stepping up behind Bridgett.

"Bridgett Rowlett, you're under arrest," the female officer said as she took Bridgett's arms.

"Oh my..." Aubrey leaned closer.

Then, to everyone's horror, including Cora's, Bridgett shoved the female officer away, jumped over the news desk, and darted past the cameras while screaming at the top of her lungs.

"That was... entertaining," Aiden said when a commercial flashed onto the screen.

"Think they caught her?" Aubrey asked, hitting the mute button.

"They better have." Aiden walked over and wrapped his arms around her. "I know we said we were going to spend the day in bed but..."

"Yeah." She sighed. "I'll change and we can head down to the station." She held onto him for a moment. "Aiden," she said, glancing up at him, "tell me you never thought for a moment that I tried to poison my father. Or that I even give a damn what happens to his money, just as long as that woman doesn't see another dime."

He cupped her face as their eyes met. "Not even for a second," he said softly before kissing her.

CHAPTER 22

It was the very last place he wanted to be at the moment. Sitting in the waiting area down at the local precinct. They'd stopped off and grabbed a couple gyros from a local shop along the way to the police station.

Halfway there, he'd gotten a call from Detective Rhodes informing him that they had Bridgett in custody and were taking her in for questioning. He let the detective know that they were on their way down there. She'd immediately informed them that there was no need, but he let her know that Aubrey had her mind set on knowing what was up after they were done with Bridgett.

So, they sat and waited, much longer than they had planned. More than three hours later, the detective walked into the room and spotted them.

"Well," she said, stopping in front of the pair of them. "Why don't you two come on back to my office. I'll fill you in on what we have."

Aubrey was quiet as they followed her back to a small office through a maze of hallways.

The detective shut the door behind them. She motioned to

the chairs for them to sit. "Normally I wouldn't fill the family members in on an active case, but since we don't have any new information," she said sitting down herself, "I see no harm in talking to you. I was hoping to ask the both of you a couple more questions." She flipped open a file.

"Tell me you still have Bridgett in custody," Aubrey asked.

"Of course. Even if we can't officially charge her with poisoning your father, we have her on evading and resisting arrest," Rhodes replied.

Aubrey visibly relaxed back in the chair.

"Now." Rhodes glanced at him. "You told me that the two of you arrived on a private jet?"

"The Costas arranged it," Aubrey jumped in.

Rhodes eyebrows shot up. "Costas?"

"Owen Costa. I think the jet actually belongs to their father, Leo, or his company, Pelican Investments." He shrugged. "Didn't ask. We were in a hurry to get to the city, since we believed that Harold had passed away." He picked up Aubrey's hand in his.

"Right." Rhodes wrote something down in her file. "And you are staying at Isaac Andrew's residence?"

"He lives at River Camps," Aubrey answered. "He only keeps this place for when he and his wife return for the holidays," she supplied. "We didn't even know…" She stopped and shook her head.

"No, please." Rhodes motioned for her to go on.

Aubrey sighed. "We didn't even stop to ask where we were staying. Hannah arranged everything. She and Isaac are long-time family friends." Aubrey shrugged. "We only realized it was Isaac's place after we arrived." She smiled. "I called him, and he assured me he was happy he could help out during this crazy time."

"But when you found out that your father wasn't dead, why stick around?" Rhodes asked.

"As I said, I was shocked to find out about Bridgett. He said that they were hosting a party that night and..." Aubrey took a deep breath. "When my father says my attendance is required..."

"You jump?" Rhodes asked.

Aubrey's eyes grew sad, and he squeezed her hand. "More like fall in line since I've seen what happens when I don't. He hasn't given me much of a choice over the years."

Rhodes leaned forward, her hands on the desk as her eyes narrowed. "Are you saying your father was abusive to you?"

"God, no." Aubrey frowned. "Not in the physical sense, in any way."

"In any sense, then?" Rhodes asked.

Aubrey bit her bottom lip before answering. "Harold Smith was an absentee father. He threw money at anyone he thought could raise his daughter to be what he wanted."

"And what did he want?" Rhodes asked.

Aubrey's eyes locked with the other woman's eyes. "Obedience."

Rhodes leaned back and crossed her arms over her chest. "Yet, shortly after his seventy-seventh birthday, he meets a woman in her mid-thirties, who for all practical purposes is a hot mess, and decides he wants to marry her. That must have pissed you off?"

Aubrey leaned closer. "Detective, are you asking me if I poisoned my father?"

Rhodes remained perfectly still. "Did you?"

"No." Aubrey sighed. "I won't deny that I've thought of what life would have been like without him, but he's the only blood I have. I didn't want him dead."

"Even if he had something to do with your mother's death?" Rhodes shocked them by asking.

Aiden felt his stomach roll. The way the detective was questioning Aubrey made it seem like she believed Aubrey had something to do with her father's condition.

What had Bridgett told the police to turn the tables?

"Detective," he started only to have Rhodes throw up her hand to stop him.

"I'll get to you in a moment." She turned back to Aubrey. "Well?"

He could see Aubrey choosing her words carefully before she finally spoke.

"If my father had anything to do with my mother's death, I'd want to see the old man rot away in a cell like the one he put me in for most of my childhood. I'd want to see everything he'd worked for, everything he'd lied to get, taken away." Aubrey held up her hands to stop the detective from talking. "No, I wouldn't want a cent of his money. His money has always been tainted to me. Just ask any of my friends. I haven't touched a dime of his since I've been out on my own. Not one cent of Harold Smith's has ever gone into River Camps, nor will it ever. That place is pure, it's the only place I've ever felt accepted or loved." Aubrey's eyes darted over to him for a brief moment. "I would never do anything that would put my business or my friends in jeopardy or in his debt. If you would do some looking into Bridgett's life…"

Rhodes held up her hands to stop Aubrey.

"I have," she said with a smile. "This"—she motioned between them—"was nothing more than a technicality." She moved to write something else in the folder.

"You…" Aubrey glanced at him and then back at the detective. "You don't really think I had anything to do with poisoning my father?"

The woman looked up from her desk. "No," she said with a smile. "Not at all. I do believe that Bridgett is a few cards shy of a full deck. I'm having her evaluated at the moment." Rhodes sighed and wrote something else down.

"You think she's mentally unfit to stand charged?" Aiden asked.

"No, I think she is playing the victim role too well. I think she actually believes she didn't do anything wrong. Just so both of you know where we stand, we found a bottle of alprazolam among your father's medications. There are a few people in the house that had access to the pills, Bridgett being one of them. Her little act this morning set me off in a different direction, and I've been looking into your father's legal standing. I had a nice chat with one of his lawyers just before I came and found you."

"And?" Aubrey asked. Her hand tightened in his.

"Shortly after you arrived two days ago, your father called his lawyer over to the house and drew up a new will. One where you were left out completely. Everything currently goes to Bridgett. We didn't know about it yet because it hadn't been officially filed at the time of the poisoning."

Aubrey made a small noise, and he understood that it was disgust she was feeling.

"Your father's lawyer"—Rhodes glanced down at her notes—"Nicholas Lee claims that your father wasn't his normal self that evening before the party. Several times he had to rehash what he was asking him to do. He's willing to testify that Bridgett was there, pushing your father to change the will and trying to convince him that you were only trying to get your hands on his money."

"I don't want his money. I never have," Aubrey answered. "I'm perfectly happy where I am now."

"So your friends tell me." Rhodes smiled. "Before I talked to your father's lawyer, I called and spoke with your friends, all four of them at the same time." She shook her head with a chuckle. "I've looked into your camp and had a nice chat yesterday with some lawyers who represent you and your friends. I'm very thorough," she said with a smile. "I'm secure in the fact that your business is solid."

"Bridgett just told the world otherwise," Aiden pointed out.

Rhodes chuckled. "Yeah, but even the news anchor contradicted her on that point." Rhodes leaned slightly. "Did Cora Jolett really go to your camp?"

Aubrey smiled for the first time since arriving at the station. "Yes. Her hair was darker, so I didn't recognize her right away. She attended my early morning tai chi classes every day when they were on their honeymoon. Ralph even joked with me during dinner one night that he was going to have to sign her up for classes when they returned to the city."

"I may just have to find an excuse for a vacation soon," the woman said with a shrug. "I've never been one to just sit on my butt in the sand."

Aubrey laughed and he felt her hand relax in his. "That's the exact reason we opened River Camps. We, my friends and I, took a vacation before Joe died and were bored out of our minds."

"That's Elle's grandfather? The man that left you five the camp?" Rhodes asked.

"Yes." Aubrey's smile grew. "He was more of a father figure than... well, than my own father has ever been."

"Well..." Rhodes suddenly stood up. "I won't keep the two of you any longer."

He stood and took Aubrey's arm as they walked towards the door.

"One last question, this one for you, Mr. Stark."

He turned, his eyebrows shooting upward. "Yes?"

"I've heard that you work on the grounds as well?"

"Yes, I'm head of construction and maintenance."

Her eyes ran over him as she turned to Aubrey. "And your reason for tagging along with Miss Smith?"

"I'm her support," he said as his hand moved around Aubrey's waist, causing Rhodes to smile.

"I thought so. Just had to make sure. How long will the two of you be in town?" she asked as she opened the door. He stepped aside, dropping his hold on Aubrey so she could pass by him.

Before either of them could answer the detective's question, he glanced up to see a young officer escorting Bridgett down the hallway. Aubrey's body was turned towards the detective, and he knew there was no way she could see what was coming.

He didn't have time to respond when, after spotting Aubrey, Bridgett screamed loudly as she yanked her arms free from the officer's hold and threw herself at them.

He held his breath as Aubrey and Bridgett landed in a heap on the floor.

Bridgett was screaming profanities at Aubrey, accusing her of ruining her life as she kicked and tried to fight Aubrey.

It took Aubrey all of three seconds to reverse their positions as she held Bridgett's face to the ground while her legs were twisted around her body, holding her arms tight. Bridgett couldn't have moved a muscle in the hold Aubrey had on her.

"Wow," the young officer said as he moved into the room. "I'm sorry, detective, she just sort of slipped out of my hold."

"Carson, would you be so kind as to put this woman in chains? I think she's proven that she can no longer be trusted," Rhodes said as she nudged Aubrey aside and pulled Bridgett up to her feet.

Bridgett was still kicking and jerking her body around as if trying to break free from the detective's hold. Two more officers, having heard all the commotion, rushed into the room and cuffed Bridgett and started pulling her out of the room.

"I'll get you, bitch. You think this is over?" Bridgett screamed. "Everything you have will be mine. Wait and see." She laughed as she was being hauled away.

"Nice moves." Rhodes turned back Aubrey.

His eyes were still locked on Aubrey. He rushed towards her when he spotted a drip of blood slip down her nose.

"You're bleeding," he said softly.

Aubrey lifted her hand and wiped the blood away on her coat sleeve. "I'm fine." She shrugged. "Can you add that little stunt to her list of infractions?" Aubrey asked.

The detective chuckled and slapped Aubrey on the shoulders lightly. "You betcha. You would've made an amazing cop."

Aiden had never been prouder of Aubrey before. He'd witnessed her moves firsthand personally and in class before, but he'd never seen her take someone down who deserved it.

If he had ever questioned if she'd needed him, he had his answer now.

CHAPTER 23

It was decided that they would spend one more day in the city before heading home. Mainly because it took a little time to submit the flight plans out of New York.

She learned there was an actual queue for planes leaving the city. Everything private had to be scheduled ahead of time, around all the public airlines.

After they headed back to Isaac's place, they decided to treat themselves to a nice dinner and picked one of the restaurants Hannah had pointed out for them. After showering and pulling on the soft green dress she'd packed for such an occasion, she took her time curling her long locks into ringlets that fell over her bare shoulders. She was just pulling on the cream heels she'd worn the other day with her black dress when Aiden walked in.

His black pants and light grey button-up shirt had her smiling.

"Wow," she said, motioning for him to spin for her inspection. He laughed and slowly moved in a circle for her.

She gave him a soft growl of appreciation. "Are you sure we

can't just order in?" she asked, slipping on her shoes and standing up.

His eyebrows traveled over her, and he mimicked her request to show him everything. She did a slow circle and laughed when she heard his matching growl of appreciation.

"No way. We look too good to stay in. Besides, Hannah made me promise I'd take you to Mario's tonight." He sighed. "Italian." His smile grew. "I'm so in the mood for pasta."

She felt her own stomach growl and nodded in agreement.

"I worked up an appetite." She frowned slightly remembering she'd had to pile on some extra makeup over her left eye. Her nose hadn't bled that long after Bridgett had jumped her, but Aiden had worried over her like she'd been shot. She'd gotten worse in class and didn't think anything of it, other than she'd been upset at herself for letting Bridgett get the upper hand on her.

Aiden moved closer and softly touched her eye. "Doing okay?" he asked.

"It's a little swollen. The ice pack helped." She shrugged. "That and the wonders of makeup."

He chuckled as his arms snaked around her. "May I say, seeing you in action firsthand was..." He sighed. "Impressive. But let's try to avoid that from now on. Okay?"

She nodded and leaned up to brush her lips across his. "I'm going to miss having you around all the time."

"Oh?" He frowned down at her.

"I mean." She shook her head. "You have your place, I have mine." She shrugged, feeling stupid for bringing it up now.

"We could always..."

She stopped him by placing her fingers over his lips. "Later. I'm starving." She stepped easily out of his arms and gathered her jacket. He helped her slip it on and they headed out.

Why had she brought that up? she asked herself over and over again on the short taxi ride to the restaurant.

Stepping into Mario's was like stepping into a restaurant in Italy again. The smells and sounds reminded her so much of her time in Venice that she found herself stiffening as they were seated near a large gas fireplace. The brick wall in back was covered in white flowers and ivy and as she slid into the leather booth, she took several deep breaths to steady herself.

"Hey." Aiden frowned over at her after the hostess had left them. "Is everything okay?"

She nodded as she swallowed. "Yes, I'm fine," she said automatically.

"Hey." He reached across the small table and took her hand. "It's me. Remember? I can tell that you're about to jump out of your skin. What's going on?"

She closed her eyes and glanced around. "I spent a month in Venice." She supplied. "Shortly after my mother..." She swallowed again. "Harold thought it was best if we escaped the reporters in New York."

"That must have been rough."

"It was. I was eight. I'd never been anywhere and had just lost my mother." She stilled as their waiter came over and introduced himself and asked for their drink selections.

Instead of answering him, Aiden leaned closer. "We could go somewhere else?" he asked her quietly.

"No." She mustered up a smile and asked for a glass of red wine.

"Bring a bottle," Aiden suggested. "Thanks." He turned back to her. "Go on."

She took a deep breath and continued her story. "Up until then, I'd only had fast food. My mother had spent every last dime she had fighting for custody of me. We ate McDonald's more often than not. Harold didn't eat fast food and, as his heir, he demanded I learn all about culture. I was fed escargot, and fish with their heads still on them." She shivered remembering seeing the dead thing looking up at her and knowing that she would be forced to eat it all. "I was eight," she reiterated.

He took her hand again. "I'm sorry you had to go through that."

"It wasn't just that. It was the belief that I would never come back. I think he enjoyed seeing me suffer. He would hint that we weren't ever going to return to the States. Not that I had anything left here, but..." She shrugged. "The feeling of not being in control of anything, it was incapacitating. I guess, walking in here, I just had a little déjà vu." She motioned around the busy restaurant and realized that, after talking it out with Aiden, she no longer felt debilitated. She relaxed almost immediately.

He lifted her hand to his lips and kissed her knuckles just as their wine arrived.

For the rest of the dinner, she thought about why she'd felt so trapped walking into the restaurant and now, after talking with Aiden, she no longer did. Was it the simple act of talking her feelings through or was it because of her feelings for Aiden?

Finally, after enjoying their pasta dinners, Aiden pushed his empty bowl aside. "I know we said we wouldn't talk about it, but I think we need to have that chat." He poured her the rest of the wine.

She had known he was thinking about their arrangement.

She'd told him the truth. She didn't want things to end with them. However, the moment they were back home, she knew he'd return to his demands that she should give him more.

Even after meeting her father and seeing everything she'd gone through, he still wanted to be with her. Didn't that count for something?

"Aiden, I don't know if I can give you what you want. What you deserve." She set her drink down and played with the glass stem.

"You're what I want. What I deserve," he said, his eyes

searching hers. "Since the moment I saw you, you're all I've dreamed of." He took her free hand again.

She swallowed hard and closed her eyes for a moment. "I don't think... I'm not sure I can..."

"Aub, why not give it a try?" he asked softly. "It's not like either of us are going anywhere. We have the camp and our friends. Why don't you let me move in with you into the apartment? We can see where it takes us."

She felt like laughing or screaming. She didn't know which one. But the fact was, the thought of not sleeping in Aiden's arms made her chest hurt.

Instead of answering him, she nodded slightly, since she didn't trust her voice.

His smile was instant. "Great." He held up his wine glass. "To new beginnings." She hesitated for a split second before tapping his glass with her own.

"You'll let me know if you get tired of me?" she asked after taking a drink.

He laughed and nodded. "Right back at you."

After finishing their wine, they stepped out onto the sidewalk and waited for a taxi. Aiden wrapped his arms around her and kissed her in the darkness of the building's overhang.

When they climbed into the taxi, he returned to kissing her. She was so hot and ready for him when they finally arrived back at Isaac's place, she doubted she could make it up the stairs.

"Now." She shoved him back against the closed door. "I can't wait." She pushed his coat off his shoulders.

Her own coat hit the floor as his hands shoved the skirt of her dress higher until he found her wet, ready for him.

"My god," he groaned against her lips.

When he slid his fingers into her, she almost exploded right then. Biting her bottom lip, she tried to focus on him. On his pleasure. Moments later, he circled her wrists with his hands and pinned them above her head as he pushed her against the door.

"I'm in charge," he warned. He slowly ran his mouth lower over her neck. She arched back to give him access and sighed when he nudged the off-the-shoulder dress down until she was exposed fully.

His mouth covered her nipple, sucking and licking her while his fingers worked inside her. She didn't think she'd ever felt anything as wonderful as him pleasing her like this. Him wanting her as much as he did now.

"I can't... Aiden, I can't wait," she said with a slight gasp.

"Don't. Give me what I want." He scraped his teeth over her soft skin and had her jolting in his arms. "Now, Aubrey," he growled, and she felt her entire body respond to him, giving him exactly what he wanted. What he demanded of her.

Then, as her entire body drifted into bliss, she was lifted up into strong arms and carried up the two flights of stairs.

Would it always be like this? Would she always give in to his demands? Was it so bad to?

She was laid on the soft mattress, and he gently removed her dress. When Aiden covered her body with his, she reached up and touched his naked flesh.

Once again, as he rained kisses over her skin, she felt her body responding. She was no longer in control of herself and, as much as she feared it, she realized it was one of the best feeling she'd ever experienced.

***

The following morning, they arrived at the airport after having a quick breakfast of egg, cheese, and bacon croissants at a bakery. They were quiet as they walked through the airport to the private terminal where they would be taken out to the Costa's private jet, which was waiting to take them home.

There was a young woman following behind them and, at first, Aubrey didn't think anything of her. But then the woman bumped into Aiden and started asking questions.

They both noticed at the same time that the woman didn't have any luggage. Aiden's grip tightened on Aubrey's arm as they stepped into the private terminal area where they were to wait for someone to shuttle them out to the plane.

The woman proceeded to ask them where they were traveling to and what flight they were on.

"Are you with security?" Aiden finally asked her.

"Gosh, no," the woman said with a laugh. Then her smile fell away. "I'm from the New York Tribune." She tilted her head slightly and then looked Aubrey in the eyes. "Did you really poison your father?"

"Enough," Aiden said loudly enough that he caught the attention of the security personnel. "You can't follow us in here." He waved the guard over towards them.

"Oh, I have every right to be here," the woman said with a chuckle. "See, I have my press pass." She held it up for security. "Now, why don't you answer my question, Miss Smith?"

"Come on." Aiden grabbed Aubrey's arm and started walking towards the security guard. They spent the next ten minutes explaining to the guards what was going on. The entire time, the woman, Barb Luft, countered with her freedom of speech and freedom to be in the terminal. They were finally shuttled out to the Costa's plane alone, while Barb was escorted off the premises.

"That was..." Aiden said, tossing their bags into the storage closet as she sat down in the leather chairs.

"Fun?" she offered as he sat next to her.

"Tiring. Why do some people believe they deserve..."

"Freedoms?" she said with a chuckle. "Did you hear how many times the woman said that word, as if it was a badge she wore?"

"Even the cops weren't buying it." Aiden took her hand in his. "At least the entire trip wasn't a loss." He smiled over at her then leaned in to kiss her.

"That's right," she said with a chuckle. "I saved my father from poison and was attacked by a crazed woman."

"Two, if you count the reporter back there," Aiden added with a grin.

"Right," she said sarcastically.

"That isn't exactly what I was talking about," he said after the pilot closed the plane door.

"No," she sighed.

"We have this." He held up their joined hands.

"Yes," she said, trying to hide her fears by focusing her eyes on their hands.

"Hey." He lifted his free hand and nudged her face until she was looking at him. "Afraid?" he asked with a slight smile.

Her chin rose slightly, and she shook her head. "No. You?" She arched her brows and waited for his answer.

"Of you?" He laughed. "Most definitely. But not as far as this goes." He leaned in and kissed her. "Never about this," he said softly.

"You're probably going to regret this," she said with a sigh.

"Never," he answered quickly. "I will never regret loving you."

She felt her heart flip in her chest and knew that someday, her own heart would break because of this man. After all, she was destined to never have the love of the people she wanted.

CHAPTER 24

There was nothing like coming home after a trip. Okay, so he could do without the laundry and the work piling up, but just knowing that in a few days Aubrey would be moving in with him had him almost walking on air.

They'd talked it over on the flight home about the logistics of him moving into the apartment with her. After weighing the pros and cons, they'd decided that she should move her things into his place instead.

"It's far more private out there than in the apartment my friends still use occasionally," Aubrey had argued.

He didn't mind, not really. But when she'd brought up the possibility of her friends walking in on them, he'd quickly agreed.

So not only had he spent the first few days back catching up with work and getting his place clean enough for her to move in, but he'd spent his free time hauling Aubrey's things out to the trailer.

Over the past few years, he'd hardly done anything to the place, since he'd deemed it a temporary living arrangement. He'd been thankful Elle and the others had allowed him to continue using the land near the construction entrance to the camp.

"This is going to be fun," Zoey said to him as she sat in his living room. Her friends had helped cart the remainder of Aubrey's things out shortly after the dinner party that evening.

"Fun?" he asked her, noticing that she was running her hands over her growing belly. Since Zoey was expecting, her friends had demanded that she sit out helping with the move.

"Sure, I mean, you and Aub." Zoey smiled. "We kind of always suspected she was hooking up with someone. None of us thought it was you, though."

"Oh?" he asked, watching the rest of her friends cart in boxes of Aubrey's things. Deciding he had a moment, he sat down across from Zoey. "Why not?"

Zoey's eyes ran over him before she shrugged lightly. "You're not the type we expected Aubrey to go for."

"What type did you expect her to go for?" he asked, curious.

"Someone less…" Zoey chuckled. "Manly."

His eyebrows shot up as he leaned closer. "You thought…"

"It had crossed all of our minds several times," she added while glancing over to make sure Aubrey was busy.

He couldn't help it, but he laughed. Loudly enough to get Aubrey's attention.

"Don't," Zoey warned, but it was too late. Aubrey was heading their way, her hands on her hips as she narrowed her eyes at him.

"I'm glad you're having fun," she said sweetly with a smile. "Unless you're currently pregnant, we could still use your help." Her eyebrows shot up, and he stood quickly and wrapped his arms around her.

"Sorry, Zoey was just telling me a funny story." He winked at Zoey behind Aubrey's back.

When everyone finally left, he sat in bed working on his laptop while Aubrey rearranged her things in his closet.

"I haven't had a closet this big in years," she exclaimed as she poked her head out of the massive walk-in closet. She disappeared just as quickly.

"I guess there are a few perks of moving in with me that you never thought of," he joked.

"Like your shower. I hated showering in mine," she called out from the closet. "You didn't really have to move your stuff to the closet in the other room for me. Gosh, I don't think I'll ever come out of here."

He laughed, remembering Zoey's words. He hadn't expected Aubrey to glance out at him again.

"What?" She frowned as she picked up another stack of her clothes from the edge of the bed.

"Nothing." He bit his lip and tried to focus on his screen, but watched out of the corner of his eye as Aubrey set the box down and moved over to stand next to him.

"I know that look," she teased. "You're keeping something from me."

He sighed. She was looking too damn sexy with her hair in a messy bun on top of her head. She was wearing a pair of old sweats and a tank top that showed off some of his favorite parts of her.

"Come here." He snagged her hips after setting his laptop aside.

When she was comfortably tucked under him on the bed, he smiled down at her. "Your sisters believed they knew your type," he said before placing a soft kiss on her lips.

"Oh?" She frowned up at him. "What type would that be?"

"Don't tell anyone I told you, but..." He chuckled again. "They believed I had too much equipment to please you."

Aubrey's eyes grew large, then she laughed. "Seriously?"

He shrugged and leaned in to kiss her again.

She stopped him. "That's why they never suspected you and me." She held him at bay for a moment. Her arms wrapped around him. "So, do you think you have the right equipment to please me?"

He chuckled. "I'm not sure, but I'm up for trying."

He couldn't describe how wonderful it was to know that Aubrey would be spending the rest of her nights with him in the king-sized bed. That he'd be waking up to her scent, to the feeling of her next to him. It's what he'd been hoping for, working towards, over the past few years.

He knew he still had to convince her to take a chance on him long term. Not that he believed she wouldn't, but even after New York, she was still in denial about how deep their relationship went.

The first week they were back at the camp was filled with catching up. He hadn't realized just how much work was on his plate until he'd left it for a few days.

Now that Bridgett was in custody, Brett was back at his place just outside of town. He'd stopped by the night after Aubrey had moved in with him to get the full scoop on what had happened in the city.

After that, it took Aiden a few days to finally catch up and get back in the loop, both at the camp and at Hammock Cove. Work was pretty much completed on the massive club house, gym, sports complex, and swimming pools in the center of the neighborhood. The streets and utilities were almost finished being laid down for each of the roads. All of the home lots had been planned out on the first phase and now that construction trucks could deliver materials, they could start building the home sites.

He'd just taken a break after finishing up roofing one of the new cabins when he made his decision. After all, he knew that the trailer wasn't going to be his permanent place. Having Aubrey there every day proved it. Besides, if he didn't snag one of the good lots at Hammock Cove now, they'd all be gone soon.

He pulled out his phone to call Owen only to glance up and see the man walking down the pathway towards him.

"There you are," Owen called up to him. "I've been looking for you."

"You could've called," he said, tossing down his tools.

"Have been for about an hour." He held the ladder as Aiden climbed off the roof.

"Sorry," he said after getting back on the ground and checking his phone. There were three missed calls from Owen. "Ringer was off I guess." He switched the button, which set his phone to chiming. "Problems?"

Owen shook his head and glanced up at the cabin. "No, just needed to catch you up on some things. Nice place." He motioned to the cabin.

"Elle's titled this one Last Resort since it's the cabin farthest from the main part of the camp." He shook his head. "I was going to call you. Is that offer for a lot in Hammock Cove still open?"

Owen glanced at him and then chuckled. "Yes. Why? Do you need a bigger place now that Aubrey's moved in with you?"

"Yes," he answered with a smile. "And no, not because of her. But because the trailer was a temporary fix. Besides, the rent of the place is as much as I'd be spending on building a home of my own."

"You're renting the trailer?" Owen asked.

"It was my only option at the time. Not a lot of banks wanted to take a chance on an unemployed worker pooling everything he had on a chance to open his cousin's summer camp back up."

"Right." Owen chuckled. "Worked out pretty well in the end."

"Yes, it did." He ran his eyes over the eight-hundred-square-foot cabin he'd almost finished. The cedar shingles set the little building apart from all the green surrounding it. High windows allowed an almost panoramic view from inside. He had plans to have a deck built off the front but needed the basics to be finished first. "So?" He turned back to Owen.

"It's actually why I was coming out to talk to you. Hannah had this idea."

"Oh no," Aiden said with a chuckle. "When she has ideas, it usually means more work for me."

Owen laughed. "True, but I think you'll like this one. There's a patch of land near where you built Dylan and Zoey's place that's up for sale. She convinced me to purchase it and separate it out into four lots."

He knew where Owen was going with this. "How much do you want for a lot?" he asked.

Owen nodded. "The ladies all want to talk about that over dinner, which is why I was sent out here to get you." He motioned behind him. "We can talk on the way back. I assume you were done here for the day?"

Aiden nodded towards his tools. "Help me load up and we can drive back."

Stepping into the employee's lounge, he realized a few things. First, he desperately needed a shower. Second, he'd skipped lunch.

Since food was set out buffet style, he filled a tray full of food before heading back to the large corner booth where Aubrey and her friends normally sat.

He was the last one to take a seat and immediately started eating after kissing Aubrey hello. He made a point to showcase his feelings for her as often as he could in front of her friends. He could tell she was becoming more relaxed and accustomed to the PDA.

"I know it's not supposed to be here for another week. That doesn't mean we shouldn't plan," Hannah was saying to Elle. "The second we stop taking these sorts of things seriously is the moment something bad will happen."

"I'm just saying, this will be, what?" Elle tilted her head as she thought. "The seventh storm we've ridden out?"

He glanced up. "Storm's coming?" he asked. He'd been too busy to pay attention to the news. Besides, most of his evenings had been filled with pleasing Aubrey since they'd returned home.

"Next week. It's just a tropical depression at this point. They don't think it'll turn into anything bigger, but..." Aubrey filled him in quickly while Elle and Hannah continued to talk.

"I'll make sure everything is tied down as far as construction. I just finished the roof on Last Resort," he said to Elle. "I'll move up roofing the other two cabins so they won't get any water damage and see to it that windows and doors are installed before then." He thought about the extra work that would have to be done before the storm hit.

Elle was correct, they'd ridden out half a dozen bigger storms since opening their doors.

"You don't live in Florida without knowing to prepare for a storm," Elle reminded Hannah. "I've ridden out more depressions and hurricanes than I can count. We have plenty of time to prepare," she assured Hannah.

He pulled out his phone and started looking over his storm preparation lists. He shot a quick group text to his team about preparing not only the campgrounds but Hammock Cove and all the work they'd done over there before next week. Even if the storm didn't come their way, he wanted to be ready for anything.

Heavy equipment had to be moved, tools and temporary construction equipment had to be secured.

"Now that that is settled," Owen broke into the conversation, "who wants to buy some land?"

Conversation turned from the coming weather to building homes. Which, of course, included him designing and building everyone's dream homes.

"At this rate, I'm going to be so busy in the coming year that I'm not even sure if I'll have time to think," he joked to the table.

"Well, once these last three cabins are finished up, I think we've all decided to hold off building any more. Not that we couldn't pack them out, but you know, supply and demand," Elle said with a shrug.

He felt his heart skip at the thought of not designing and building more cabins for the camp. "Really?" he asked, trying to hide his disappointment.

"At least for a while," Zoey chimed in. "Until after all the weddings and... baby." She rubbed her belly again.

"Besides, we now have forty cabins. If we want to keep this place in high demand, then we have to cut it off somewhere," Elle added.

Aubrey reached under the table for his hand. "Won't you be busy designing and building homes?"

"Sure." He tried to hide his reluctance about letting go of his daily life at the campgrounds. If he wasn't overseeing and building cabins there, then he didn't really have any excuse to be on the campgrounds daily. Glancing around the table, he realized that he'd grown accustomed to being around the group of friends. They'd become as much his family as they were Aubrey's now. The possibility of losing them had him growing weary.

Scarlett stood up suddenly. "Well, it's my night off, and I'm not going to waste a single moment." She tugged on Levi's hand and had the man following her out.

"We have dinner." Elle stood up and glanced at the rest of the friends.

"I'll see you later." Aubrey leaned down and kissed him. The fact that she had already changed into an evening dress hadn't gone unnoticed by him the moment he'd walked in. It was actually one of the perks of being around in the evenings, seeing her and her friends all glamorized for the dinner parties. Not that he didn't like Aubrey's evenings off now that she spent them snuggled up against him watching television.

Since he had the night to himself, he figured he'd get to work on a few ideas that had been going through his mind. By the time Aubrey walked in a few hours later, he had the entire home designed.

"What's this?" she asked, leaning over his shoulder.

"Ideas," he said, pulling her into his lap. "What are your thoughts about moving?"

Her brows arched as she frowned down at him. "I just did that," she reminded him.

He chuckled. "This would be about a year down the road." He motioned again. "Of course, I'd love your feedback on the closet here." He zoomed into the massive space. "Along with the other rooms."

He felt her stiffen but held her from bolting.

"Easy," he said as he ran his mouth over her neck. "It's just a home. I'm in the business of making them, remember?"

He smiled the moment he felt her relax. "Right," she sighed.

"Let's talk about this later." He felt himself grow hard. "Right now, I want to see what you're wearing under that dress."

He knew he'd hit the mark when her entire body started vibrating. She wrapped her legs around his hips as he carried her into the bedroom.

CHAPTER 25

Aubrey tried over the next few days to avoid talking to Aiden about his home plans. Sure, she wanted him to build his home along with those for all her friends. But every time he tried to bring her into the design process, as if he wanted to design a home for her, she felt herself tensing up.

She had to admit that she was enjoying being out of that apartment. Not only was it great to be staying with Aiden, but having someone around all the time had curbed her loneliness.

It was obvious that her friends no longer had as much time for her as they had before, since they were spending all of their free time with the men they loved. That got her thinking about her own feelings towards Aiden, which she tried to avoid thinking about as much as she could.

She tried to busy herself by adding a few new classes to her already busy schedule. It helped that she'd decided to try a meditation class. There wasn't a lot of call for it, but she did get three people to sign up on her first day. She also added a painting class and more than ten people signed up for that one. She'd held it outside on the beach, which had drawn even more people the following day.

She even volunteered to help out for a few dinners that hadn't been on her schedule, just to avoid the conversation with Aiden.

She was walking to the dining hall to grab some dinner on one of her nights off when her phone rang. She was shocked to see her father's number on her screen and answered it after the third ring.

"Hello, Dad." She moved over to sit on one of the wood benches that Liam had built for around the campgrounds.

"Aubrey." Her father's voice sounded stronger than the last time she'd spoken to him in the hospital. "John has informed me that you've left the state."

So, it had taken Dr. Williams telling her father that she'd left town in order to get her dad to call her.

"Yes, I returned on Tuesday." She relaxed back and watched couples shuffle towards the pool bar or the dining hall for lunch.

"I would have thought we would have talked before you left," her father said.

"I think you said everything you wanted to say to me at the hospital."

The phone was silent and, for a moment, she thought that the call had dropped.

"John has filled me in on my recent behavior."

She was silent, waiting for him to say anything further. The entire time she'd known her father, he had never apologized for anything. As the silence grew, she knew today wouldn't be the day he started.

"And?" she prodded.

"He's changed my prescriptions and removed alprazolam from my regimen. I've also changed a few things around with my security."

Closing her eyes, she shook her head. "So, Bridgett?"

"I'm told she was released."

"She was?" She sat up and stared into the darkness. "Why would they let her go?"

"There was no proof that she's the one who slipped the pills into the decanter," he countered.

"No." She felt her anger boiling again and stood up to start marching down the pathway, this time heading to somewhere less populated. "Of course not. Did you call me to accuse me again?"

"No, John seems to think that the alprazolam was in my system a lot longer than just one day. Which means, it was there before you arrived to town."

"Well, at least that's something," she said dryly.

"I've let Martha go," her father shocked her by adding.

She stopped dead in her tracks. "You believe Martha…" She couldn't fathom the audacity of her father. Martha had worked her him for several years. "You believe someone who's been loyal to you would, what? Suddenly poison you and force you to change your will so that she still received nothing? Father, you're blind as well as stupid." She almost hung up, but her father jumped in.

"I never said that." She waited. "I let her go because she didn't stand up and say anything to me about how Bridgett was acting. She even signed the forced will as a witness."

Aubrey thought about that. "Why?" She shook her head. "Why would she go along?" She would have thought the woman would have at least called Dr. Williams. It hadn't even registered that her father's loyal housekeeper and assistant, someone who had controlled her father's every move for the past few years, had allowed Bridgett to rush in and rule the roost.

"That's why I let her go. John claims she's the one who cancelled my yearly physical with him."

She heard a couple heading her way and ducked down a different pathway. "What happens now?"

"I've returned my will to its previous format."

"I don't want a dime."

"I know you don't, but it's the least I can do. Hell, when I'm gone, do what you want with it. Give it all to charity for all I care."

"Then you do it," she offered.

He was silent for a moment. "That isn't my legacy to leave. I've built up a reputation—"

"Change it," she challenged him.

He was silent again. She knew he was still there because she could hear him breathing.

"You really don't care about the money, do you?" he asked quietly.

"I never have. Tell me if you had anything to do with my mother's death."

"I didn't," he said quickly. "The drugs…" He sighed loudly. "Messed with my mind. Honest, I would have never harmed Nora or you. She'd given me the one thing I had given up hope on long ago."

"The drugs?" she asked. "Mom didn't do or sell drugs."

"No, but the man she'd been seeing…" Her father shocked her.

"Man?" She stilled. "What man?"

He sighed again. "His name was Davis Evans. That's all I know. After Nora's death, the man dropped off the radar."

"Did the police look at him as a suspect in my mother's death?" she asked.

"No, there was no need. The note your mother left you was in her handwriting and the apartment had been locked. The front door deadbolted from the inside. The police ruled it a suicide quickly."

She thought through things and then sat down in the sand. She hadn't even realized she'd walked to the private beach while talking.

"Aubrey, if you ever make it back up to the city…"

"I won't," she countered quickly.

"I understand." He was quiet for a moment, then added, "This isn't how I expected things to be. I know it probably doesn't mean much to you now, but I'm sorry." Before she could respond, he hung up.

Dropping her phone into the sand, she hugged her knees to her chest, dropped her head on them, and cried.

She lost track of time, but when arms wrapped around her, she glanced up through blurry eyes to see Elle.

"I've called the others. Whatever it is, we're here for you," her friend said with a smile.

"My dad," she said.

Elle's arms tightened around her.

"Is he…"

"No," she replied quickly. "We just… He just… He said he was sorry." She shook her head. There was no way she could explain how much those words meant to her. Even more than if he'd told her that he loved her. Those three words were the most powerful in her book, and he'd just said them to her. Finally.

It was like a weight had been lifted off her chest.

"Oh, sweetie," Zoey said as she, Scarlett, and Hannah all rushed to her side. Each of them sat in the sand next to her.

"Is everything okay?" Hannah asked, wrapping her arms around her as much as she could, since Zoey and Scarlett had gathered around her while Elle still held onto her.

"Yes." She smiled up at them. "My father told me he is sorry. I don't know why I'm being stupid about it, but…" She laughed as the five of them almost toppled over.

"He's okay?" Scarlett asked.

Out of the five friends, Scarlett had been the most like-minded when it came to their feelings about their dads. Scarlett hadn't forgiven her father for abandoning his family before he'd died.

Now here she was, crying over the fact that her father had simply said he was sorry. Shaking her head, she sighed deeply.

"How did you find me?" she asked as her friends settled beside her.

"I was heading to dinner when I saw you on the phone. I felt terrible, but I followed you when I noticed you were upset," Elle answered. "I'd thought at first you and Aiden..."

Aubrey laughed. "The only thing we've ever fought over is..." She frowned. "Well, we haven't fought. Not once." She glanced around at her friends as she dried her eyes with the sleeve of her jacket.

"Not once?" Zoey asked. "Even Dylan and I go at it every now and then."

"Ugh, don't talk about your sex life." Scarlett nudged her sister with a chuckle.

Zoey's smile grew. "Okay, make-up sex is the bomb."

Everyone groaned, causing Zoey to shrug. "Fine." She threw up her hands.

"No," Aubrey continued, "we have had a few disagreements." She thought about it and realized the only problems they'd ever had was a direct result of her lack of ability to commit. She took a deep breath and realized that, as much as she hated to admit it, her father had passed his ability to not admit things onto her. "I screwed up," she said out loud.

"How?" Elle asked.

"I told Aiden that I couldn't commit to him," she admitted.

"Couldn't?" Hannah asked. "Or wouldn't? You are in love with him, aren't you? I mean, you moved in together and all."

Aubrey thought about it and swallowed her pride. If her father could admit to his darkest fears, then maybe she could as well. Did she love Aiden?

Scenes of how they'd met to all the great times they'd shared over the last three years played in her head.

He was the only man she trusted, completely.

"You love us, right?" Zoey asked.

"Of course," she answered quickly. "You're my sisters." She held out her hands, and they all shifted into a circle, holding each other's hands.

"Love is easy," Zoey said softly. "When it's with the right people." She smiled and Aubrey watched in horror as a tear slipped down her face.

"Don't cry," Aubrey begged.

"Hormones." Zoey waved her hand, the one that was attached to Hannah's. "I'm allowed to cry. My point is, Aiden is the right person for you. We may not have known it for the past three years…"

"Because you all thought I was into girls," Aubrey added with a chuckle.

Zoey's eyes narrowed as she smiled. "Okay, I take it back, Aiden is all wrong for you. If he can't keep a secret—"

"No," Elle jumped in with a chuckle. "That just means that love was more important to him than the friend code." She squeezed Aubrey's hand. "I'd break the friend code for Liam. It's love."

"Friend code, but not Wildflower code, right?" Zoey asked.

"Of course not." Elle chuckled. "Wildflower codes are unbreakable."

"Agreed," everyone said quickly.

"I want some wine." Aubrey sighed. "Do we really have to work dinner tonight?" She almost groaned it.

"No," Elle jumped in. "That's the joy of being the bosses. What do you say to taking this party up to the apartment? Now that it's empty, we can hide ourselves away up there and have some sister time."

"That sounds like a perfect ending to an otherwise shitty

day." Aubrey stood up and then hugged her friends, her sisters, and knew that just like her father, she had to come clean with Aiden and admit that she was in love. For the first time in her life, she was going to give a man the one thing she'd hidden away and protected all of her life.

CHAPTER 26

Aiden had been so busy over the past week that he hadn't even realized that Aubrey was purposefully avoiding him.

There had to be a better way for preparing for a storm. He and his crew had done it more than half a dozen times since he'd started working at the camp. Most of the storms had passed with only an hour or two of heavy rain, while others had taken out trees or just caused a mess with leaves and branches.

Cleanup usually took a day or two, but preparation took much longer. Small things like a stack of two-by-fours could turn into deadly projectiles and had to be stored properly.

They had small metal storage pods for most of their building supplies, to keep them out of the weather or out of sight. But some of the bigger supplies couldn't fit into the pods. There were only three cabins left under construction, but plenty of supplies and equipment had to be moved and stored.

It was not only keeping him busy, but very tired and sore. By the time he crawled into bed each night, he was too tired to notice if Aubrey had been there for long. Instead, he pulled her close to him and held onto her while he slept. If he couldn't have as much time with her as he wanted during the day, at least he could dream about her.

The following morning, he made a point to carve out time in his morning and drove her up to the main building to enjoy breakfast with her.

"My dad called me last night," she said as he pulled away from their place.

He glanced over at her. "And?" His stomach knotted just thinking of her being left alone after such a call.

She sighed and rested her head back. "For what I suspect is the first time in his entire life, he apologized."

"Really?" He shook his head. "Guess you can teach an old dog... and all that." He reached over and took her hand. "Are you okay?"

"Yes, my sisters helped me." She smiled at him. "It's the reason I got home just before you." She giggled. "And have a slight hangover this morning."

He glanced at her and chuckled. "It looks good on you. Being happy."

Her smile fell instantly, and he wondered what he'd said.

"Is it weird that we never fight?" she asked as he parked.

He flipped off the truck and turned to her. "No, not considering I've seen you in action, remember?"

Her smile was back. "I mean—"

"I know." He pulled her closer. "I guess because we started out with things between us just being physical and let it grow into something more, we focused on pleasing one another instead of the relationship aspect of things." He shrugged. "But if you want... I could always start complaining about how you never carve out time for me or you can nag me about working too late."

She sighed. "What's the point. You're getting things ready around here for the storm. If you spent more time with me, that would mean leaving this place vulnerable." She turned and looked out the front window to the massive three-story main building. "And I'd never do that. This place is my heart."

His eyes were glued to her face, and he could see the love clearly in her eyes. An ache started around his heart as he dreamed of the day that she'd say that to him instead.

"We'd better go inside. I only have half an hour before I have to be across town to help out with Hammock Cove."

"The storm's supposed to hit later tonight," she said as they walked up the pathway. "It's so strange. It's like ninety degrees out and not a cloud in the sky." She glanced around and he stopped to do the same.

"They've moved it up to a category three," he reminded her. "I've been through enough of these in my lifetime to know that if it crosses into a four, we need to evacuate the entire area." He took her hand and started walking.

"It's funny calling a storm Laura. I mean, I knew a couple Lauras in my lifetime. None of them were ever hotheaded."

He chuckled as they stepped into the building. "The only Laura I knew was definitely full of hot air."

"When will we know if it moves up to a category four?" she asked as they moved through the buffet line.

"Could be any minute now or five minutes before it hits." He shrugged. "My thoughts are we should all hunker down in the main building here."

"The last guests are leaving this morning. Every time a storm hits, we have to clear out the cabins," she complained.

"It's for their safety as well as ours," he assured her. "The last thing we want to do is have to rush out to a cabin and try to rescue someone."

"True," she agreed. "Still, it's a pain cutting everyone's trips short. Some of the guests actually complained and tried to stay put. As if they were above being bothered by Mother Nature."

He took her tray from her and motioned to the juice bar. "I'll carry these, you grab us some drinks."

He set the trays down at their standard table, surprised that no one else was there already.

They were halfway through their meals when Zoey and Dylan walked in. A few minutes later the rest of them slowly made their way over to the table.

"I hate you," Scarlett said to Aubrey. "Do you ever have a hangover?"

Aubrey chuckled and shook her head. "Only twice in my life," she answered, and he knew he'd have to make a point to ask her what those two times were. Later.

Talk quickly turned to the storm, and everyone agreed that they would all meet up and camp out in the main building for the night unless the hurricane was changed to a category four or higher. In that case, they would all carpool north.

"Hurricane party," Hannah said cheerfully.

"Dylan and Liam said they'd help you board up the windows on the main building later today," Zoey offered.

"Thanks," he replied. "I should be back here around noon. I have some loose strings to tie up at Hammock Cove this morning." He checked his watch, and his phone chimed with a couple messages. "Well, they need me over at the site." He bent over and kissed Aubrey. "See you later?"

"We'll be here," she replied.

For the next four hours, he hung heavy wood boards over all the brand-new windows he'd helped install at the club house at Hammock Cove while other workers rushed around securing the rest of the equipment.

"There has to be a better way of doing this," Owen complained as they finished with the last board.

"There is, it's called storm shutters," he reminded him. "Which were scheduled to be installed a month from now." He chuckled.

"Damn. Right." Owen shook his head. "The company was booked solid until next month."

"Yup, it's one of the perks of living in the path of storms," he joked. "I'm going to head back over and have lunch before doing this all over again at the camp."

"You know, Hannah has talked me into hanging out at the camp tonight so she can be with all of her friends. I think she mentioned something about a hurricane party."

He groaned. "She mentioned she was going to throw one again this time." He rolled his eyes. "Last time we had about half an hour of rain. The party was good though."

Owen laughed. "I told her it's just an excuse for her to throw a party. She replied that it was an excuse for all of us to come together."

He thought about it. "I guess we haven't all gotten together for a while. I mean, sure, for breakfast and an occasional wedding," he joked, "but nothing like this."

"Just as long as the storm doesn't get too bad, we should be fine," Owen replied.

"Agreed," he added before heading out.

When he arrived at the campgrounds, he radioed and found out that Aubrey was out helping them close the storm shutters on the last cabins. Already, he could see the skies growing darker. Even though the storm wasn't set to hit them full force until ten o'clock, the front was already moving in.

He gauged that they would have rain in the next few hours and he'd have to step up his timeline. He skipped lunch and headed directly to help hang the plywood over the massive deck windows on the pool house.

An hour later, Aubrey found him as he and Liam were finishing sealing up the dining hall with boards.

"Wow, it looks almost the same as it did before we opened the camp back up." She held her rain jacket hood over her head.

He remembered the day he'd met Elle out at the camp to discuss fixing the place up. Joe had sealed the camp years before.

Now it was looking more like a haunted summer camp rather than a functional one.

He wrapped his arms around her and kissed the top of her raincoat just as the first drops of rain fell over them. "We've got another hour or so of work out here," he said with a groan. "Why don't you get in out of the rain and help out inside. I hear we're having a party."

Aubrey chuckled. "It wouldn't be a storm without one." She kissed him back before turning to go. "Oh, Elle wanted me to let you know, in case you were too busy to get the latest update yourself, Laura is still a three at this point." She smiled. "And heading directly towards us."

He frowned. "We could head to Destin?" he offered.

Aubrey stopped and frowned back at him. "And miss all the fun? Besides, they're supposed to get hit too." She shrugged. "I'd rather stay here with the people I love." She turned around and headed down the path.

He'd been so shocked at her casual use of the word love that it had taken him almost five minutes to get back to work. Liam had to nudge him with a board to get him moving again.

The soft rain turned to a torrential downpour a half hour later, causing them to abandon their work and head inside.

"What's done is done." Liam shook his longer hair out, sending rain all over the lobby floor.

He did the same and realized that his hair had gotten longer over the past few months.

"Guess it's party time. Good thing all the guests are gone. I delivered the last of them to the airport shortly after breakfast. They actually tried to convince Elle to let them stay." He shook his head.

"Riding out a storm is exciting and scary at the same time," he admitted.

"I still remember a few crazy ones when I was a kid. The difference between those and the few I've sat through now is shocking. I used to be so afraid," Liam said as they walked into the main dining hall. Then his eyes landed on Elle and he sighed. "Now I'm more concerned about the people I love than my own safety."

He searched the small group of people and frowned when he didn't spot Aubrey immediately. He slapped Liam on the shoulder and headed off towards the group to ask where Aubrey was.

He stopped beside Zoey and asked her.

Zoey frowned up at him. "She was heading out to help the two of you," she answered.

"I sent her back in here half an hour ago." He frowned and glanced around again.

Zoey pulled out her walkie-talkie. "Aub, check in," she asked, and they both waited as static filled the air. "Aubrey, please check in." Zoey's voice rose slightly, catching the attention of a few others around them.

"What's going on?" Elle rushed over to them.

"Has anyone seen Aubrey in the last half hour?" he asked the entire group.

Everyone immediately shook their heads.

"She was heading out to help you and Liam with the last boards," Hannah explained.

"Aiden sent her back inside," Liam answered.

"She could be in the back?" Zoey asked.

"Fan out. First one to find her, call it in." Elle held up her walkie-talkie. "Stay in groups," she called out. "I'll search the third floor. Someone take the second floor." Zoey and Dylan raised their hands.

"Kitchen," Aiden said as he rushed towards the back of the building, not wanting to wait as everyone else organized where they were going to look.

His heart beat quickly as he raced through the dark rooms, flipping on lights and searching every corner. He could hear the wind and rain picking up force outside and cursed himself for not walking Aubrey back inside himself.

When he'd finished searching the massive kitchen area, he met a few others back in the lobby area.

"You don't think something happened to her on her way inside do you?" Elle asked, anxiously.

"I'll take the pathway." He started to head outside.

"We'll go in pairs," Dylan said. "Liam, Levi, you two head to the left, we'll take the right."

The moment they stepped outside, Aiden knew that it wouldn't be long before it would be too bad outside to see anything. Already, it was as dark as midnight outside and they were an hour from sunset.

"Shit, this is going to be a bad one," Dylan called out to him. "If it's already this bad now, what'll it be like in a few hours when the bulk of the storm passes us?"

"Where would she have gone?" he asked. With the wind and rain so loud, he knew there was no way Dylan could have heard him.

They pushed through the heavy rain and wind until they ended up back at the last place that he'd seen her.

"She was right here," he called out to Dylan. They both looked over to see Liam and Levi turn the corner and head their way.

"She wasn't that way," Levi said. "You don't think she got turned around, do you?"

"It had just started raining," Aiden replied.

A small tree cracked and fell a few feet from them.

"Shit, that was close," Liam said. "We'd better regroup. Maybe even call backup for some help? Brett might still be around somewhere," he offered.

Aiden no longer cared about anything other than finding Aubrey and telling her those three words he knew she hated to hear.

CHAPTER 27

She knew it had been a long shot that Aiden would let her help hang the boards. In all fairness, she didn't really want to do the sweaty work. Even though the skies had turned dark and there was rain in the air, it was still in the high eighties. Her shirt was sticking to her and she'd been outside for less than five minutes.

When he'd sent her back inside to help out with the party preparations, she'd gladly complied.

She'd just turned around the building when she noticed a dark figure heading towards the boathouse and the dock area. Since the rain hadn't picked up yet, she decided to make sure that whoever it was didn't need help with something.

She knew that Aiden and the guys had successfully closed up all the other buildings on the grounds, so when she noticed the boathouse's door had been left open, she frowned and stepped inside and called out.

"Hello?" She frowned into the darkness as she reached for the light switch.

Just then, the heaven's opened up outside, and the sound of

rain hitting the metal roof drowned out any noise inside the boat house.

"Hello?" she called out louder. She was just reaching for her walkie-talkie when a dark figure stepped out from behind a kayak.

She had to blink a few times before it registered who was standing in front of her.

"Martha?" she said with a shake of her head. She had to raise her voice to ask, "What are you doing here?"

The woman didn't move. She just stood there as if Aubrey couldn't see her. Aubrey took a step inside and yelled her question again.

Then she felt a sharp pain in her side and gasped.

"There you are," a voice hissed in her ear. "I told you, mother, that she'd fall right into our trap."

The knife Bridgett held against her dug further into her side, and she felt her skin tear open.

"Bridgett?" She tensed, knowing she would be able to take the woman down, even with the knife against her skin. But then Martha moved further out of the shadows, and Aubrey noticed the gun she was pointing directly at Aubrey's chest and froze.

"You've ruined everything we've been working so hard for." Martha started moving towards her, the gun steadily aimed at her chest.

"You worked for my father for almost five years," Aubrey pointed out to Martha. "Why?"

"It's called a long game," Bridgett hissed. "We'd come up with this new angle after it was obvious that we weren't going to get what we needed from Jean. Then he got sick. We knew all about his girls being friends with the daughter of one of the wealthiest men in the world." Bridgett chuckled. "So, I sent dear ol' mother off on a new mission."

"It was easy to fake my references. Bridgett's father used to be so good at it. Before he ended up dead after losing the stash of coke he was supposed to sell." Martha shrugged. "But you know all about that since your mother took the fall for that one."

"My..." Aubrey shook her head. "I don't understand."

"My maiden name was Evans," Bridgett said as if that explained everything.

"I still don't..." Aubrey shook her head.

"My father was Davis Evans," she added.

Aubrey remembered hearing that name and finally pieced it together. Her father had just given her that name earlier, claiming that Aubrey's mother had been seeing a man called Davis Evans.

"Yes." Bridgett smiled when realization dawned about the connection. "When he'd heard about your father and mother's very public legal fight over you, he came up with the idea to shack up with your mom in hopes of getting closer to some of Harold's money," Bridgett added. "He believed that your mother had been getting money from Harold all along. Of course, when he found out that your father hadn't even known about you until a few months prior, he had to come up with a different plan."

"Then your mother went and killed herself and, when the cops swarmed the place, Davis's stash was discovered. Davis always had a few money-making schemes going on in the background. I never approved of his selling drugs, but he'd run into a good deal on the coke and knew how to unload the product quickly enough." Martha shrugged. "He paid the price for it that time though. Shortly after his product was confiscated by the police, we found him outside our place with his throat slit." Aubrey hadn't really given the woman a second thought in the city. After all, she knew that her father had a security firm who vetted all of her father's employees. Now, however, seeing the two women so close, she realized just how alike they were.

Aubrey's head was swimming at the new information. Bridgett's father and her mother?

This family had been trying since Aubrey had been eight to get their hands on her father's money.

That sort of thing didn't happen in real life. Did it? They had to all be crazy. Sure, her father was extremely well known, but what were the odds that something like this could actually happen?

"What about Zoey and Scarlett's father?" she asked. "How did you meet him?" She felt her stomach roll at the possibility that it was her fault that Bridgett had met Jean and ruined the family. Had Martha and Bridgett been watching her and known of her friendship with the Rowlett family?

Bridgett laughed. "That was fate. I ran into him shortly after I'd graduated high school. It was luck really. When I found out how much he was worth, well, I jumped at the chance to get my hands on it. Convincing him to divorce his wife and leave his brats then move to Vegas to be closer to mother was easy."

"I'd been working a scam out there," Martha added with a shrug. "A bar owner was giving me everything I wanted. It was paying off pretty well until he gambled the bar away. Then Bridgett married Jean Rowlett, and we enjoyed spending as much of his money as we could."

"For a while," Bridgett broke in. "Then one day he started complaining about our spending and threatened to cut me off completely. I'd just purchased a new Bentley. It wasn't too much to ask to have nice things. Not after what he made me do with him." She felt Bridgett shiver. "Anyway, we figured that we'd get more money if I divorced him."

"It's all quite the coincidence, don't you think? Everything looped back to you and Harold." Martha moved even closer. Now she was less than ten feet away from Aubrey. "For years we'd been trying to figure out how to get our hands on the great Harold Smith's money. And now we have you."

"My father's cut me out of his will," she said, unsure why she mentioned this at this time.

Bridgett laughed. "Oh, we're not going to wait around any longer for the old man to die."

A shiver raced down Aubrey's spine at the heartlessness of the women's attitude. Could someone really care so little about others? They were so focused on what they wanted that it didn't faze them to hurt others.

Oddly, this reminded her of her relationship with Aiden. For the past three years, he'd only asked her for one thing. And she'd been determined to keep it from him because of her own selfish beliefs. She was no better than Bridgett and her mother. Not really.

"No." Martha shook her head. "We're just going to hold onto you until dear old dad pays the price we want."

She held in a laugh as what they were doing sunk in. "You're going to ransom me? That's your plan?"

"He'll pay it," Bridgett hissed.

"No, he won't," she retorted.

"You forget, I've been around him for the past few years," Martha said as her voice rose. "The man would do anything for you."

"No." She glanced at Martha and could see even more crazy behind the woman's eyes than she'd seen behind Bridgett's. "He wouldn't."

Aubrey knew she was running out of time. She didn't know the women's plan for where they were going to take her or how they were going to leave the grounds. At this point, she could hear the wind and rain increasing outside and doubted they'd get far before the weather would overpower them. If she was going to escape, she had to make her move soon.

"Harold Smith only cares about himself. Until last week, I hadn't seen him since my eighteenth birthday," she told them.

"That's because I convinced Harold to invite you along to the party. I made sure to hint that your presence would make me happy." Bridgett shifted slightly and Aubrey felt the hand she was holding the knife in relax slightly. "After all that your mother took away from us, I just had to see you suffer like we did."

The more the pair talked, the less on guard they were. Aubrey knew that if she was going to have any chance at distracting them long enough to overpower them, she had to keep them talking.

"Why? It wasn't as if I did anything to you." She asked Bridgett.

"Because of you, I lost my father." She practically screamed it. Aubrey felt the knife dig into her side even more. Okay, so it wasn't wise to talk about Bridgett's father.

"My father hates me. He told me that I was nothing but a disappointment to him." She said, trying to change tactics.

"That doesn't mean that he doesn't watch out for you," Martha replied. "Do you know how much he worries about you?" She laughed. "It was almost sickening hearing him constantly talk about you. He kept trying to figure out a way to get you back to the city, back under his control so he could try and change you, mold you into what he wanted his heir to be."

Martha took another few steps towards her, and Aubrey saw her opening. Releasing a breath and relaxing her body so that muscle memory would take over, she prepared for the pain of the knife in her side as she got ready to kick out.

At that exact moment, her walkie-talkie buzzed to life as Zoey's voice rang out.

"Aub, check in."

Martha's eyes darted away as the gun waved away from her chest and zoned in on the walking talkie that hung off Aubrey's hip.

Kicking out and knocking the gun out of Martha's hands was the easy part. Twisting and grabbing hold of Bridgett's wrist and yanking the knife out of her hold proved a little more difficult.

They struggled for a moment, and Zoey called again.

"Aubrey, please check in."

Bridgett yanked the walkie-talkie from her hip and threw it across the boathouse. It landed in the water with a plop, but it gave Aubrey enough time to knock the knife free of Bridgett's hold.

She twisted Bridgett's wrist until she heard a snap and the knife hit the ground. Then she focused on stopping Martha from racing to grab the gun on the ground.

Aubrey had practiced so much in her life that she didn't have to think about what she was going to do beforehand. Her body moved, twisted, and avoided being hit by both Martha and Bridgett as if it had a mind of its own.

She'd practiced with multiple partners over the years, but none of them had actually been trying to kill her. She twisted her legs around Martha's and had the woman facedown on the ground just as Bridgett jumped on her back and wrapped her arms around her windpipe.

For a moment, panic threatened to overtake her, but then she forced herself to relax and think through all the moves she'd perfected. She knew just how long she could go without oxygen and forced herself to think of a way out of the hold. She quickly shoved her fist into Martha's jaw. Blood splattered all over her and Bridgett, and the older woman cried out in pain. When Aubrey felt Martha's body go lax underneath her, she turned her attention to removing the woman who was cutting off her oxygen.

It seemed to take forever for her to twist out of Bridgett's hold, but when she was finally free and had the other woman sprawled on top of Martha, holding her broken wrist and crying out in pain, Aubrey walked over and picked up the gun and pointed it at the pair of them.

"Now," Aubrey said a little winded, "what do you say we take a nice walk in the rain and wait in the lobby for the police to come haul the two of you away?" At that moment, a tree branch landed on top of the metal roof and she winced. "Before we get blown away in this hurricane."

Getting the women to cooperate proved more difficult than she'd anticipated. Since Martha was still unconscious, she tied up Bridgett's wrists first, not really caring as the woman complained about her broken wrist. Then she worked on securing the older woman with thick ropes that had been holding up a small kayak. After Martha woke up, she tied the pair of them together, making sure to wrap the other rope several times around each of their hands just in case.

When they stepped outside, the rain was coming down almost sideways. The mother-daughter duo tried to dart away from her but slipped on the slick pavement of the pathway. She laughed and helped them stand again.

"Shall we try that again?" She shoved them to head down the pathway again.

She had to hold onto them and push them along the pathway the entire trip to the main building. The rain was coming down so hard now that if she hadn't known the route by heart, she would've gotten lost.

She guessed that the power must be out since all the lights along the pathway were dark. It didn't really affect her, since she'd practiced for years walking down the dark pathways, sometimes even with her eyes closed just to see if she could, just like she'd practiced at home and in school. She wanted to know that if it came to it, she could maneuver around River Camps without fear. The only difference was, she'd never imagined she would need to escape the camp and had only practiced it so she could remember every path that she loved. At this point, she was confident that she could maneuver the entire camp blindfolded.

Still, it took the three of them a lot longer than usual to make their way across the grounds. The moment they stepped into the dark lobby, Zoey cried out and rushed forward to greet her. Then she stilled when she noticed Bridgett and Martha and that Aubrey was holding a gun on them.

"What?" Zoey shook her head quickly then moved around and wrapped her arms around Aubrey. "You're safe." She sighed. "We were so worried about you."

"Where is everyone?" Aubrey asked with a frown as she motioned for Bridgett and Martha to take a seat. The three of them were soaking wet and looked like drowned rats with their hair tied in knots from the wind.

"They're out looking for you," Zoey answered with a frown. "Didn't you see them?"

"I could barely see anything out there. If I didn't know this place like the back of my hand, we wouldn't have made it back from the boathouse."

"What are they doing here?" Zoey asked, glancing over at Bridgett and Martha. Bridgett was still crying and complaining about her broken arm while Martha looked stunned and a little in shock.

Aubrey sighed and glanced down at the gun in her hands. "They tried to kidnap me."

Zoey chuckled. "I feel sorry for them." She shook her head. "I can't believe they're still standing. Is Bridgett's arm really broken?"

"Yeah," she answered with a smile. "They weren't fully conscious. I had to wait for Martha to wake up before getting them back here." She motioned to Bridgett's mother.

"Later, you're going to tell us all every detail of what happened," Zoey said and pulled out her walkie-talkie. "She's here. Aubrey's back here with me. She's safe," she said into the walkie-talkie.

Several seconds later, Elle replied, "We're heading back."

"Us too," Scarlett replied.

"We're on our way," Hannah added.

Less than five minutes later, everyone rushed into the lobby, just as soaking wet and windblown as she was, and wrapped their arms around her.

"We were so scared," Elle cried as she held onto her.

"What happened?" Hannah asked as she eyed the two women, who were looking tired and defeated. Martha had closed her eyes at this point, and Aubrey wondered if she'd given the woman a concussion. While they'd waited for everyone to return, Zoey had called Brett, who said that he would get out there as soon as possible to deal with the situation.

"Later," Aubrey said with a smile as she glanced around. "Where's Aiden?"

"He went out with Dylan," Zoey said, picking up the walkie-talkie again. "Dylan, did you copy? Aubrey's back here. Safe."

They all waited, and Aubrey felt her entire body tense as Zoey looked at her with fear in her eyes.

"I'm going…" She turned to go, but someone grabbed her arm.

"You're bleeding," Hannah cried out.

She glanced down at her side where Bridgett had stuck her with the knife and brushed off Hannah's concern.

"I'm fine. It's just a scratch. We need to find Dylan and Aiden." She looked out the front door.

"It's crazy out there," Liam said.

"He's right," Owen added. "Listen, I want to find my brother too, but at this point, if any of us go out there, we might just end up getting lost too."

"I know this place," Aubrey started.

"No, with the power out it's easy to get lost out there," Hannah replied.

"Not for me." She smiled. "Since the first year I came here,

I've practiced walking the pathways with my eyes shut. It's how I found our way back here from the boathouse." She started towards the door. "I like being prepared for anything." She shrugged.

"They were checking the pool house," Zoey called out to her.

"I'll go with you," Owen said.

He and Liam followed her outside. "Hold onto me," she called over the sound of the wind. They all held hands as she led them towards the pool area. The hardest part now was fighting the wind, but since Owen and Liam were bigger and actually helping her instead of dragging their feet, they made better time.

"They're not here," Owen called over the wind.

"There," she cried out when she spotted a dark figure heading towards them.

"It's Dylan," Owen yelled, rushing towards their brother.

"Where's Aiden?" she cried out.

Dylan shook his head and she noticed a stream of blood dripping down into his eyes. "I don't remember. I think a tree fell on us and..." He held his head. "I think he's..."

"Where were you?" Owen asked.

"The boathouse." Dylan motioned behind him.

"Take him back," Owen said to Liam. "Go with them," he said to her.

"No." She shook her head. "I'm going with you. I'm not giving up until I find the man that I love."

CHAPTER 28

*A*iden was fighting to stay alert. He knew exactly where he was and how much trouble he was in. He'd been so determined to do everything he could to search for Aubrey that he'd put his own safety in the background of his mind.

When he'd seen the door to the boathouse wide open, he'd rushed inside, screaming out Aubrey's name. He'd noticed the large oak tree that had been next to the building lying on the roof of the place and knew that any moment it could cause the old building to cave in.

But instead of being cautious, he'd rushed in and called out for Aubrey as he continued looking around for any sign of her.

When part of the roof caved in, Dylan had taken a blow to the head. He'd helped free the man and told him to go back to get help while he continued looking. Moments after Dylan had left, the rest of the roof cracked under the heavy weight of the tree. He had been able to jump out of the way, but had landed in the water.

The waves of the normally calm bay were causing the two row boats that were tied up in the two dock slots in the boathouse to bump into him. His hands kept slipping as he tried to grab hold of the slick ropes holding them in place.

He was pushed under the water several times before he was able to wrap his hand around the rope and hold on. It was like fighting a whirlpool. He couldn't seem to pull himself out of the turning water. His head kept being pulled under and suddenly he realized that he was fighting for his life.

Water filled his lungs as he continued to fight to keep his head above the surface. He'd believed that tangling his hand in the rope was a good idea, but each time his head hit the side of the rowboat, he saw stars. Now he figured there was a possibility that it was going to knock him out and because of all the thrashing around, he was so twisted in the thing, he doubted he could break free.

Was this really how things were going to end? His mind kept returning to Aubrey. Was she fighting for her life now as well? Stuck somewhere trying to break free from the surging storm? Maybe trapped under a tree or worse...

Another wave forced his head under and this time he doubted he'd be able to break free. His mind was already oxygen starved, causing his muscles and limbs to be unresponsive to his commands.

He'd lost track of how long he'd been fighting to break free, to return to the surface, when hands gripped him and pulled him upward. He was waiting to take that first glorious breath of air but came to a jerking halt when the rope tore at the skin on his arm.

Everything was backwards. How could the rowboat be below him now? It was pulling him downwards now. The hands that had been trying to pull him up released him, and he reached out for them in the dark water as he was dragged downward.

Then he spotted a red streak heading towards him along with a glimmer of something sharp. He felt soft hands grip his arm and the sting of a knife nick his skin as it cut the rope. The hands paused for a moment as soft lips covered his. He relaxed into what he assumed would be his last kiss, only to have oxygen shoved into his mouth. He gulped it up, swallowing it and the water that had filled his mouth. The sawing motion on the rope started again and he ignored the pain in his arm as Aubrey worked on cutting the rope holding him and the now sunken rowboat, which lay at the bottom of the bay.

He felt his mind going fuzzy and watched in horror as everything started to gray. Just before he blacked out, he felt his arm jerk free and relaxed as he was carried upward.

"Aiden!" Someone was shouting his name over and over again.

Peeling his eyes open, he reached up to push Aubrey's soaking strawberry hair out of her face.

"He's back," he heard a male voice say from somewhere beyond his sight.

Aubrey threw her arms around him and held onto him while she cried.

"Shh," he said softly, enjoying the feeling of her next to him. "I'm alright," he promised.

His mind was too foggy at the moment to register that she was there. Safe and sound in his arms.

"I thought I'd lost you," she said into his chest.

"We'd better move. I don't think this place is going to hold up much longer. I'll take him, you get out." It was Owen, Aiden thought as he felt the man start to lift him.

"Hell no," he growled. "Put me down. I'm not having you carry me out of here."

Owen chuckled. "I would if I thought you could stand," Owen said, lifting him.

"I can." He shoved the man away and touched his feet to the ground, only to have it rush up towards him.

Aubrey and Owen grabbed him at the same time and the

three of them wobbled out of the building and into the storm together.

He forced his legs to continue moving as they made their way through the rain and wind into the darkness. He shut his eyes at one point and just willed his body to keep moving. He didn't want to be carried anywhere. Maybe it was his pride, but he wanted everyone to know that he was okay. He took deep breaths as he moved and, by the time they stepped out of the rain, his lungs burned and his head was throbbing.

"What happened?" someone cried out.

"He almost drowned. Somehow, he'd gotten tangled in the ropes holding a rowboat. A tree branch broke through the roof of the boathouse and punctured a hole in it, sending them to the bottom of the bay," Owen answered quickly. "Aubrey used a knife to cut him loose."

"He's bleeding," someone said as he was shoved into a chair.

"It was dark, I tried…" Aubrey said with a cry.

"Shh," he reassured her. "I'm okay,"

"I'll get the bandages," someone else said. Since he still had his eyes closed and was fighting to stay awake, he couldn't tell who was talking. But every time he heard Aubrey's voice, he tuned back in.

"Help me get him in my office. We've made up a bed. He can rest there while you bandage him up."

Just as he was helped up, someone mentioned Brett and he stilled.

"What about Brett?" he asked, opening his eyes to look around.

"He just called and said he can't make it to come get those two until after the storm passes," Owen answered.

"What two?" he asked. He looked around the room and spotted Bridgett and Martha. The two women were sitting on the floor with a rope tied around them. Bridgett was holding a very broken arm close to her chest. Both women looked tired and like they'd been beaten, badly.

"What the hell are they doing here?" he asked as Aubrey nudged him towards the hallway.

Owen was helping him walk and answered, "Later. We'll make sure they stay locked up and out of the way until Brett can come get them. For now, you're bleeding all over the place."

"Don't let them near Aubrey," he said as he was shoved onto the sofa in Elle's office.

Owen chuckled. "The way I hear it, we need to keep Aubrey away from them," he said with a shake of his head.

"You're safe." He reached for Aubrey and brought her into his arms. Finally, his head was starting to clear. "I was looking for you."

She held onto him for a moment before pulling back. "I love you," she blurted out. "I didn't mean to take so long to tell—"

He brought her to him and kissed her lips. How long had he waited for her to say those words? Why hadn't he realized that it didn't really matter. What mattered was that she was there, safe, in his arms.

"I love you," she said again when he ended the kiss. "I should have told you years ago." She shook her head. "I was a stubborn fool." Her hands went to cup his face. "You're the only man I've ever said this to. The only one I ever could say it to. You're everything I've ever wanted. Everything I've ever needed, and I was a fool."

He brushed a strand of her wet hair out of her eyes. "Now that we've got that out of the way, I'm going to have to work on getting you to agree to marry me," he said with a smile.

She laughed. "Yes."

"Yes?" he asked. "Yes, I'll have to work on it or—"

She shut him up by kissing him again.

"Yes, you fool. I'll marry you." She laughed as she rested her forehead against his.

He took a deep breath and already felt much stronger than he had before. Maybe it was the oxygen getting to his brain finally or maybe it was the fact that he had everything he could ever want. Either way, Aubrey was his finally and life could only go uphill from there.

"Let me look at your arm," she said, glancing down at it.

He noticed the sting of his torn skin for the first time and ignored the pain while she cleaned him up.

"You won't need stitches," she said with relief. She moved back, and he noticed the blood on her shirt.

"You're hurt." He pulled her up to sit next to him and noticed that she winced when he pulled the blood-soaked material away from her skin.

There, just below her last rib on her right side, was a large nasty gash.

"Bridgett's handiwork. Actually, it's thanks to her that I had the knife to cut you free. I knocked it out of her hands earlier when they jumped me in the boathouse." She shrugged as he bent down and started cleaning the blood from the wound.

"You'll need stitches." He was worried about how deep the cut had gone.

"I'm fine," she said, taking his hands. "Throw some of those butterfly Band-Aids on it and…"

"Let me," he said, looking up at her. "You took care of me, it's my turn to look after you." He nudged her until she was lying down on the sofa. He took his time cleaning the wound and then found a bottle of liquid bandage. He pulled the skin together as tight as he could and doused the area several times. Then he covered it with several butterfly bandages and leaned back to assess his work.

Aubrey was staring up at him. "I love you. You know that."

He bent down and kissed her. "I love you. Just so we're clear, it will never get old hearing those words from you." He grinned down at her just as there was a knock on the door and Zoey and Scarlett walked in.

"How is he?" Scarlett asked.

"Oh good, you patched her up," Zoey said when they noticed Aubrey lying on the sofa.

Aubrey pushed her ruined shirt down and sat up. "I'm fine," she said quickly. "So is Aiden."

"The storm is just officially hitting us, and we thought you two would like to rejoin the party," Zoey said, glancing towards the wall of windows that had been boarded up. "Safety in numbers and all that."

"We'll be right there." He helped Aubrey stand up but pulled her into his arms. "Thank you for saving my life," he said into her hair.

"Thank you," she said, pulling back slightly, "for setting me free from my fears." She leaned up and kissed him.

"Aww," Zoey said as she wiped a tear from her eyes.

"God, are you going to cry for the next six months of your pregnancy?" Scarlett joked as she wrapped her arms around her sister.

He took Aubrey's hand and followed them back into where everyone else was sitting around a circle of candles.

"This looks like a séance instead of a hurricane party," Aubrey said as they walked in.

Food filled the table along the wall, untouched. When they stepped in, Aubrey was pulled aside by her friends as Elle started talking.

"Seeing as this is the last time we'll do this, we decided it had to be a special occasion. And seeing as the pair of you cheated death tonight, we figured it was as good of time as any." Elle chuckled as she pulled a small box from her pocket.

"From us," Elle said, holding the box. Zoey, Scarlett, and Hannah all joined hands with hers as they handed the small box over to Aubrey.

"I never thought I'd ever get this," Aubrey said, wiping her eyes as she looked down at the box. "I never thought I'd deserve it."

Aiden glanced at the guys, who all just smiled at him and shrugged.

He moved over and watched her flip open the small box and looked down at an ugly rainbow unicorn ring nestled in the box.

Aubrey picked the small thing up like it was made of the finest jewels and slipped it on her finger, then held it to her chest.

"I earned this," she said with a laugh as the five friends hugged one another.

Owen walked over and slapped him on the shoulder. "Out of all of us, I'd say you had to work the hardest to win the prize."

"That's a prize?" he asked, motioning to the ring.

Dylan walked over, a fresh white bandage covering the cut on top of his head, a goofy smile on his face. "Hell, yes, it is. The best sort of prize." He shook Aiden's hand and motioned to Aubrey. "One that'll last a lifetime."

He sighed and smiled at Aubrey as she looked at him over her friend's head.

EPILOGUE

When the sun woke Aubrey up the next morning, she at first didn't think anything of it. It had been just after one in the morning when Brett and his partner had come and hauled Bridgett and her mother away.

After that, the hurricane party had turned into more of a slumber party. They'd all gathered their sleeping bags around the candles and camping lanterns and chatted while the rain started to disappear.

"It's morning," she said, sitting up. "Oh god." She glanced around and noticed a few windows had lost the protective plywood.

"What?" Elle sat up and then gasped. "I have to see..." She jumped up at the same time Aubrey did.

The pair of them rushed to the front doors together.

Brett had mentioned that several trees had fallen, which had been the reason it had taken them so long to get to them.

Aubrey helped Elle open the front doors and as they stepped outside, they were joined by Zoey, Scarlett, and Hannah.

"How bad do you think it is?" Elle asked.

"Let's find out together." Aubrey held out her hand for her sisters.

The five of them stepped out into the morning sun together and gasped.

Trees, branches, and other debris lay everywhere. The lush green grass of the fields was littered with shingles from the roofs.

Warm hands rested on Aubrey's shoulders. "I know a guy who can fix all this," Aiden said with a sigh. "He was looking for an excuse to stick around the campgrounds."

"It could be worse," Dylan said, wrapping his arms around Zoey.

"Yes." Aubrey turned in Aiden's arms and smiled up at him. "It could have been," she said before kissing him.

ALSO BY JILL SANDERS

The Pride Series

Finding Pride

Discovering Pride

Returning Pride

Lasting Pride

Serving Pride

Red Hot Christmas

My Sweet Valentine

Return To Me

Rescue Me

A Pride Christmas

The Secret Series

Secret Seduction

Secret Pleasure

Secret Guardian

Secret Passions

Secret Identity

Secret Sauce

The West Series

Loving Lauren

Taming Alex

Holding Haley

Missy's Moment

Breaking Travis

Roping Ryan

Wild Bride

Corey's Catch

Tessa's Turn

Saving Trace

The Grayton Series

Last Resort

Someday Beach

Rip Current

In Too Deep

Swept Away

High Tide

Lucky Series

Unlucky In Love

Sweet Resolve

Best of Luck

A Little Luck

Silver Cove Series

Silver Lining

French Kiss

Happy Accident

Hidden Charm

A Silver Cove Christmas

Sweet Surrender

Entangled Series – Paranormal Romance

The Awakening

The Beckoning

The Ascension

The Presence

Haven, Montana Series

Closer to You

Never Let Go

Holding On

Coming Home

Pride Oregon Series

A Dash of Love

My Kind of Love

Season of Love

Tis the Season

Dare to Love

Where I Belong

Wildflowers Series

Summer Nights

Summer Heat

Summer Secrets

Summer Fling

Summer's End

Distracted Series

Wake Me

Tame Me

Stand Alone Books

Twisted Rock

Hope Harbor

For a complete list of books:

http://JillSanders.com

ABOUT THE AUTHOR

Jill Sanders is a New York Times, USA Today, and international bestselling author of Sweet Contemporary Romance, Romantic Suspense, Western Romance, and Paranormal Romance novels. With over 55 books in eleven series, translations into several different languages, and audiobooks there's plenty to choose from. Look for Jill's bestselling stories wherever romance books are sold or visit her at jillsanders.com

Jill comes from a large family with six siblings, including an identical twin. She was raised in the Pacific Northwest and later relocated to Colorado for college and a successful IT career before discovering her talent for writing sweet and sexy page-turners. After Colorado, she decided to move south, living in Texas and now making her home along the Emerald Coast of Florida. You will find that the settings of several of her series are inspired by her time spent living in these areas. She has two sons and off-set the testosterone in her house by adopting three furry little ladies that provide her company while she's locked in her writing cave. She enjoys heading to the beach, hiking, swimming, wine-tasting, and pickleball with her husband, and of course writing. If you have read any of her books, you may also notice that there is a love of food, especially sweets! She has been blamed for a few added pounds by her assistant, editor, and fans... donuts or pie anyone?

facebook.com/JillSandersBooks
twitter.com/JillMSanders
bookbub.com/authors/jill-sanders

CPSIA information can be obtained
at www.ICGtesting.com
Printed in the USA
LVHW022044210221
679522LV00004B/217

9 781945 100260